P9-BBU-369

# LUCKY STARS

☆

ALSO BY JANE HELLER

*The Secret Ingredient*

*Female Intelligence*

*Name Dropping*

*Sis Boom Bah*

*Crystal Clear*

*Princess Charming*

*Infernal Affairs*

*The Club*

*Cha Cha Cha*

# Jane Heller

☆

# LUCKY STARS

☆

St. Martin's Press

New York

www.stmartins.com

Design by Kathryn Parise

LIBRARY OF CONGRESS CATALOGING-IN-PUBLICATION DATA
Heller, Jane.
    Lucky stars / Jane Heller.–1st ed.
      p.  cm.
    ISBN 0-312-28848-4
    1. Hollywood (Los Angeles, Calif.)–Fiction.   2. Motion picture
industry–Fiction.   3. Mothers and daughters–Fiction.   4. Actresses–
Fiction.   5. Widows–Fiction.   I. Title.

PS3558.E4757 L83 2003
813'.54–dc21

                               2002031898

First Edition: April 2003

10  9  8  7  6  5  4  3  2  1

For my mother

# Acknowledgments

☆

A LOT OF GENEROUS PEOPLE lent their time and expertise to the story that ultimately became *Lucky Stars,* and they all deserve mention along with my very sincere thanks and gratitude:

Jennifer Enderlin, my enthusiastic editor, who pored over several drafts of the book and offered insightful and constructive comments after each reading;

Kimberly Cardascia, Jennifer's capable assistant, who is always such a good sport about wrangling with me over catalog copy;

Ellen Levine, my literary agent, who continues to both guide my career with her customary competence and laugh out loud at my jokes;

Amy Schiffman, who represents my books to the entertainment community, and is so pleasant she even makes bad news sound reassuring;

Ruth Harris, my friend and mentor, who was there for me with this book as she's been there for me with all the others;

The five talented actresses who shared their experiences with me and gave the heroine of this book authenticity and guts–Elisabeth

Blake, Donna Lynn Leavy, Dawn Maxie, Shannon Morris, and Cindy Warden;

Julia Grossman, Howard Papush, Adryan Russ, and Steven Shmerler, who helped me gain access to some of the above women;

Ed Kreins, captain of the Beverly Hills Police Department, and Michael Barrett, former detective of the Westport Police Department, who are wise in the ways of catching criminals;

Laurence Caso, Mort Lowenstein, Tim Mason, and Brad Schreiber, who made suggestions that gave the story credibility and/or just plain made it better;

Helen Gallagher, Patty Bunch, and Maurice Stein, makeup artists extraordinaire, whose contributions were invaluable as I prepared my heroine for her "big scene";

Laurie Burrows Grad, who either knows everything or knows how to find out everything, and is a fabulous cook on top of it;

Kristen Powers, my Web guru, who allows me to communicate with my readers on www.janeheller.com;

Michael Forester, my husband, who, when I whined, "I'll *never* be able to come up with another idea for a book," rolled his eyes and replied, "You always say that."

# LUCKY
# STARS

☆

# Chapter One

✮

I LOVED MY MOTHER, really I did, but there were times when she drove me nuts. And I don't mean nuts, as in: she aggravated me. I mean nuts, as in: she made the tiny vein in my left eyelid twitch. I mean nuts, as in: she gave me hives. I mean nuts, as in: she had the power to cause my period to be irregular.

No, Helen Reiser wasn't a force of nature, just a nagging mother, an overprotective mother, a pain-in-the-butt mother. She meant well, but she just couldn't face the fact that her "baby" had grown up.

She called me a million times a day, offered her advice whether it was solicited or not, had no compunction about saying, "Your hair's too long" and "Don't forget to take an umbrella" and, on those rare occasions when I was actually dating someone, "He's not right for you." She was the opposite of a shrinking violet. She was like a weed that grows and grows and grows until it chokes the entire garden.

She was only five feet two, but she was built like a linebacker—a short but sturdy woman with square shoulders and thick ankles and ramrod-straight posture—and she had this nasal, adenoidal voice that was so unmistakably hers that it got under my skin, haunted me in my sleep, brought me to my knees, especially in combination with the narrowing of the eyes and the arching of the brows.

"Come on, Mom. I'm not a child anymore," I'd pipe up whenever she'd boss me around, "and I don't appreciate your constant interference."

"Oh, so you'd rather I didn't care?" was her typical comeback. "You know, Stacey, there are plenty of mothers who don't care about their children."

"Yes, but caring is a lot different than criticizing," I'd point out.

"Who's criticizing?" she'd say. "You're being too sensitive."

Huh? She would literally stop speaking to people who didn't fall all over her in the supermarket, but *I* was too sensitive?

"I'm just an honest person," she'd add. "And you should thank your lucky stars that I am honest, because not everyone is, dear."

Like that was a news bulletin. I was a thirty-four-year-old actress on a quest for fame and fortune in Hollywood, a place where honesty is hardly ever an option. The minute you get here you start lying spontaneously, as if there's something toxic in the drinking water. You lie about your age (you shave off ten years minimum). You lie about your heritage (you claim to be one-quarter Cherokee, or whatever is the heritage du jour). You lie about needing to supplement your income with a real job (you explain that you're only waiting tables in a biker bar so you can research a character). And then there's the lying that comes at you from the other side (you go to an audition and they tell you you're wonderful and you never, ever hear from them again).

Of course, my mother wasn't thrilled about my choice of a profession, any more than she approved of my boyfriends or the fact that I had yet to get married. When she wasn't hitting me with: "God forbid you should give me a grandchild," she'd hit me with:

"Why can't you do something practical for a living, like Alice Platkin's daughter?" Alice Platkin's daughter was an accountant who, unbeknownst to Mrs. Platkin, was also a psychic with her own 900 number.

But whenever I did land a part, however small, she was right there cheering for me. Cheering for me and then reminding me to drink my milk.

She loved me and I loved her and I understood that one of the reasons she was in my face was because she was lonely. She was a sixty-six-year-old widow living in the same house in Cleveland where she raised me. She didn't have a job. She didn't play bridge. She didn't even belong to a book group. While she did have a few close friends, they were her emotional twins in the sense that they, too, lavished all their attention on their children. Whenever they'd get together, it wasn't a gathering of pals sharing confidences, but a contest between competitors one-upping each other about their offspring. (One competitor: "My Sarah is marrying a proctologist." Another competitor: "So? My Emily *is* a proctologist.") As her only child, I was her focal point, her keenest interest, the center of her universe. In other words, in this era of navel gazing, it was *my* navel she was always gazing at.

Maybe you have a mother like mine–the kind who's there for you but makes you feel like an infant as well as an ingrate. Maybe you've experienced the love/hate, the push/pull, the yearning for approval/the yearning for independence. Maybe you, too, are the good daughter who harbors a secret wish that your mother would leave you the hell alone. But even you couldn't have predicted the bizarre turn my relationship with my mother would take. You see, all I asked was that she get a life. I never dreamed that the life she'd get would be the one I wanted.

But I'm jumping way ahead of myself. Let me go back to the period before the situation with my mother became the stuff of

Greek tragedy (okay, French farce). Let me begin with the day my mother decided that calling me on the phone and leaving messages on my answering machine and reaching me on my pager didn't meet her requirements for mother-daughter closeness, the day that she came up with the brilliant idea of selling the house in Cleveland, moving to L.A., and becoming my neighbor...

I was sitting in the outer office of the casting director, trying to stay calm while I waited for my turn to read. Auditions are a nerve-wracking experience, but it's important to harness your fear, make it work for you. That's what they tell you in acting class–to *use* your emotions. Yeah, well, I used my emotions that day, but not in the way they meant.

This was my second callback for a network television movie (aka movie of the week, or MOW) about a death row inmate, who had twenty-four hours to prove her innocence before meeting her maker. I was there to read yet again for the part of Angie, the strong, brave, utterly unflappable sister of the death row inmate, who was to be played by Melina Kanakaredes. The part wasn't huge, but it was a juicy part, a showy part, the kind of part that gets actresses noticed. I was ecstatic that I had made the first cut and would now be reading for the casting director a second time.

Also sitting in the outer office were seven other hopefuls, six of whom could have been my clones. They were my approximate height and weight (five feet six and 115 pounds) and had my identical look (wavy dark brown hair, fair complexion, pretty face although not breathtaking), and they sported my girl-next-door wardrobe (khakis and a buttoned-down shirt). The seventh hopeful was an actress who bore no resemblance to me or the others–a vixen type whom I'd seen at lots of auditions. How could you miss her? She had boobs that were so high and mighty they could have starred in their own MOW. Plus she was notorious for playing preaudition head games with other actresses, her intent being to sabotage our readings and win herself the parts by default. For instance, she'd say, loud enough for all of us to hear her, "Someone told me they've already cast this thing, which means there's no point in hanging around." Or: "Rumor has it that the director is a prick to work with." Or sometimes she'd just try to rattle us by doing vocal warm-ups, taking deep breaths and, on each exhale, making exaggerated and obnoxious vowel sounds, like *"ahhhh"* and *"eeeee"* and *"ooooo."*

I forced myself to ignore her and instead pumped myself up, remembering that I had as good a shot at getting the part as she did. Better, because I was on a roll at that point in my career, on the verge of genuine success.

I had come to L.A. six years before, full of cockeyed optimism, believing that all my drama teachers back in Cleveland had meant it when they'd said I had talent. During the first few years here, I hadn't gotten anybody's attention and then–bingo!–I'd landed a TV commercial for Irish Spring. The part called for the character to wash in the shower, and I was the only actress at the audition who mimed sticking the bar of soap in her armpit. Big deal, right? Your armpit is one of the places where the soap goes when you're washing yourself in the shower, isn't it? Well, the director thought I made "a really edgy choice" and practically gave me the job on the spot. That commercial led to a commercial for Taco Bell, which led to a stint on *Days of Our Lives,* which led to guest-starring roles on *Boston Public* and *Ally McBeal.* Before I knew it, I was shooting a pilot here, a pilot there. Before I knew it, I was no longer waiting tables at the biker bar. Before I knew it, I was moving out of the Burbank fleabag I was sharing with three other women and moving into my own apartment in Studio City. Before I knew it, I had a part in a feature film. It was a comedy called *Pet Peeve,* in which Jim

Carrey played a veterinarian and I played his receptionist. I was only in two scenes with Carrey and I didn't have a lot of lines, but hey, it was a feature film, for God's sake! It was going to make a fortune on opening weekend! I was on the brink of being considered hot, which is, hands down, the best thing that a person in Hollywood can be considered!

But in the meantime, while I waited for the release of *Pet Peeve*, I continued to go on auditions, like the one that day for the MOW about the death row inmate. I was sitting there in that outer office, contemplating the motivation of the character, trying to channel the strong, brave, utterly unflappable Angie, when my cell phone rang. I glanced at the number of the caller, hoping it was my agent's. That's why you take your cell phone everywhere, even to auditions—in case it's your agent. But, no, it was just my mother checking in.

I'll let my voice mail talk to her, I thought, stuffing the phone back into my purse. No way she's going to distract me before I go into this reading.

A few minutes later the phone rang again. As before, the caller's number was my mother's.

I'm busy, I growled silently. May I *please* just get this job and then call you back, Mom?

A few minutes later, the phone rang again. Guess who.

I waited, tried to put myself back in the mind-set of Angie, the sister of the death row inmate, but my mother's voice kept creeping into my head. Maybe it's urgent, I allowed myself to think. Maybe she's sick or in trouble or needs me. Maybe I shouldn't blow her off this time, because if I do and something is really wrong, I'll never forgive myself. God, the guilt.

Against my better judgment, I played back the messages.

The first one said, "Stacey, it's your mother. I have news."

The second one said, "Hi, Stacey. I'm not sure if the first message got through. There was terrible static on the line. You should switch wireless carriers, dear. Verizon is a lot better than AT&T, in my opinion, so listen to your mother."

The third one said, "So where *is* my little Meryl Streep today? And did she remember to take a sweater with her? The Weather Channel said it was chilly there. Not as chilly as Cleveland, naturally, but you won't have to worry about me freezing to death anymore. That's what I'm calling about, Stacey. I have a big surprise for you. I've sold the house and I'm coming to live in L.A. with you. No, not *with* you. I would never impose like that. I meant I'll be living nearby, in my own place but close enough to stop by and see you every day. I'll be able to make sure you're eating enough and taking care of yourself and keeping your apartment clean. And I'll be able to see who your friends are—including your men friends—and you'll be able to tell me everything that's on your mind, face to face. It'll be just the way it should be between a mother and daughter. No more of this long-distance nonsense. Whenever you turn around, there I'll be. Now, don't thank me. I'm sure you're very grateful that I'm uprooting myself for your health and well-being, but that's the way I want it and I won't hear a word of protest. So listen to your mother and don't try to talk me out of this. Understood? Fine. Speak to you later."

I was stunned, a big, hard knot forming in the pit of my stomach. Stunned! My mother was coming? For good?

It'll never work, I thought. We'll kill each other first.

I had a tough enough time when she'd visit me for a week. At the end of her trip, I'd put her on the plane and immediately head for the nearest bar. It would usually take two, maybe even three, margaritas before my pulse returned to normal. So if a week with her made me looney tunes, what would *forever* do to me? How would I survive?

So much for the part of Angie in the MOW. I began to dwell on the notion, the specter, of my mother taking up residence in L.A.

and invading my space. I began to picture her dropping by my apartment, toting casseroles consisting of food groups I hadn't eaten in years, rearranging the contents of my kitchen cabinets, stripping my bed in order to make better hospital corners. I began to imagine a typical conversation between us, during which she would criticize some aspect of my life and I would ask her not to and she would say why not and I would explain that it was upsetting and she would tell me I was overreacting and I would argue that she was the one who needed to change and she would act hurt and disappointed and I would end up apologizing.

"Stacey Reiser?"

I heard someone calling my name, way back in the outer reaches of my consciousness, but I was still obsessing about my mother's news and couldn't quite focus.

*"Stacey Reiser? Hello!"*

I snapped back to reality. It was the assistant to the casting director who was calling my name. Apparently, it was my turn to read for the part of the strong, brave, utterly unflappable Angie.

I went into the casting director's office and took my place opposite her and, after the obligatory pleasantries and a moment to collect myself, I launched into the part of Angie.

"Of course I believe in my sister's innocence," I began. "I've always believed in her, even during the trial, even with the awful things people have said about her, even after the guilty verdict. It's all been a mistake and I hope and pray she'll be granted a stay of execution." I paused, waited for the casting director to feed me the next line. "You bet I'm standing by her. And yeah, I'm strong. In our family we don't knuckle under when times get rough. We learned that from our mother."

On the word "mother" I felt a catch in my throat. Well, a sort of a gulp. A bubble. A glob of phlegm. I coughed, said, "Excuse me."

"Would you like some water, Stacey?" asked the casting director.

"No, thanks. I'm fine," I said, the lump growing, taking on a life of its own.

"Why don't you pick up with 'we learned that from our mother,' " she instructed me.

"Oh. Sure." I took a second, tried to ignore the jumble of emotions that were exploding inside of me, not to mention the tears that were pricking at my eyes. "We learned that from our mother," I proceeded. "Mom taught us to believe in ourselves. She wasn't, uh, like one of those mothers who tells her daughter what to do or cross-examines her about what she ate and who she went to the movies with and whether it was chilly when she got out of the movie theater and if she brought a jacket that was warm enough and if the neighborhood where she parked the car was safe or should she have stayed home and rented a movie and–"

"Stacey?"

"Yes?"

"None of that stuff about the movies and the weather and the neighborhood is in the script. And we're not doing any improvising today. That's not what the callback is about. It's about reading the script as written."

"Oh. Right. Sorry."

"Not only that, Angie is supposed to be unflappable and you're playing her as if she's on the verge of a breakdown. Want to try it again? Make an adjustment?"

I tried it again. I made an adjustment. But in the end I blew it. I couldn't get Helen Reiser out of my mind during that audition, couldn't get over that she was moving to town–my town.

By the time I left the casting director's office, I was a basket case. On my way out, I walked over to the actress with the big attitude and the even bigger rack and said, "Do you have a mother?" She looked at me as if I'd lost it, which, of course, I had. "Because if you don't," I said, "I've got one I could lend you."

The sad thing is, I wasn't kidding. At that moment, I wanted to lend Mom to somebody, to drop her off on somebody's doorstep, to sell her to somebody on eBay–anything to avoid having to deal with her. But she was mine, all mine, and, like it or not, my ability to function as an adult was about to be severely tested.

# Chapter Two

★

MY MOTHER MOVED to L.A. two months later, having flown out to look at rentals the week after she'd sold her house and then finding one literally two blocks from mine. She had wanted to be close to me; now she was on top of me. I fortified myself by asking my internist for a prescription for Valium.

Her spacious, fully furnished, three-bedroom townhouse, in contrast to my cramped, sparsely furnished, one-bedroom apartment, felt like a home, particularly after she unpacked her knickknacks and displayed them everywhere–photos of me, photos of my father, photos of her friends in Cleveland, as well as her books and porcelain figurines and needlepoint pillows with little sayings on them like "A Girl's Best Friend Is Her Mother." While my place looked as if no one lived there, mostly because I regarded it as just another pit stop on my journey to stardom, her place looked as if she'd lived there for years. It smelled like it, too; immediately after I'd helped her settle in, I'd taken her to the nearest supermarket, where she'd loaded up her shopping cart and come back and cooked, storing her creations in plastic containers, labeling them "entrée," "vegetable," and "starch," and popping them into the freezer. Conversely, there was nothing in my freezer except ice cubes–oh, and two packages of Lean Cuisine, in case I had somebody over for dinner. (I was not remotely domestic, in a subconscious stab, I suppose, at distancing myself from Mom.)

I tried to be supportive of her after her move, really I did. I familiarized her with the neighborhood, drove her to Loehmann's, even went with her to the DMV so she could get her California driver's license. I also invited her along whenever I'd have dinner with my closest friend Maura, a makeup artist for *Days of Our Lives*, whom I'd met when I'd worked on the show. Maura thought my mother was funny as opposed to scary, and couldn't understand why I was so tormented by her.

"Please. You weren't raised by her," I said one night while the three of us were at a restaurant and my mother was in the ladies' room. "When I was in elementary school, she wouldn't let me have sleepover dates at my friends' houses unless she interrogated the other mothers first."

"Interrogated the other mothers about what?" asked Maura.

"Oh, let's see. She'd ask them if the batteries in their smoke detectors were working. She'd ask them if their basement had been checked for radon. She'd ask them if their children had recently come down with head lice. It was as if I were the president of the United States and she were my Secret Service agent, my advance person. Only I wasn't the president. I was a little girl with a mother who couldn't let go. And her tendency to overscrutinize things and people only got worse. When I was in junior high, she actually made random visits to the cafeteria to sample the food and ensure that it wasn't 'too greasy for my Stacey.' But the best was when I was in high school; she accompanied me on my shopping excursions so she could render an opinion about which clothes made me look fat and which clothes made me look thin and which clothes made me look like Marilyn Olander's daughter, who had a 'reputation.'"

"Okay, so I'm glad she's not my mother," Maura conceded, "but I still think she's funny."

"You can afford to think she's funny," I said. "She doesn't call you at seven o'clock every morning with the weather report."

"I know, but I love how she opens fire and gives it to people. Did you see the way she told the waiter how drafty it is in here? Most people would just say, 'Could you bump up the thermostat on the air conditioning?' Your mother goes, 'A person could *freeze* to death in this meat locker!' She's a hoot, Stacey. A real pistol."

A pistol. Maybe that was the answer: get a gun and–

"Here I am, girls," said Helen Reiser, returning to the table.

I regarded my mother as she sat back down, rested her napkin across her lap, and launched into a monologue about how two of the three toilets in the ladies' room were out of service and how the faucets in the sinks were the kind where you have to hold them down in order for the water to come out and how she couldn't tolerate–absolutely could not abide–those automatic hand dryers, not when good, old-fashioned paper towels did the job just fine.

Who is this person who yammers on and on about nothing? I thought, appraising my mother's appearance as she continued to find fault with the rest room and other aspects of modern life. She was wearing a yellow dress with a floral pattern–she wore skirts and dresses religiously, never slacks, even when she was at home by herself–and sturdy, practical, low-heeled pumps, and her chin-length brown hair, with its strands of gray, was in its customary pageboy. She was hardly the essence of chic, but she was a pleasant-looking woman with solid, midwestern values and more energy than people half her age, and I often wondered why she hadn't remarried in all the years since my father died, especially since she'd seemed

to enjoy being a wife. She and Dad had been a perfect fit, probably
because they were such opposites in temperament. She nattered
constantly; he listened patiently. She was quick to become agitated;
he hardly ever got angry. She was too stubborn to say she was sorry;
he didn't equate apologizing with weakness. He was quiet and gentle
and accepting—the type that's mistaken for a doormat but was anything but. He appreciated Mom's feistiness, got a kick out of her,
the way Maura did. Yes, he was the ideal husband for her: he earned
a comfortable living as a banker, was well-spoken and well-groomed,
and didn't flinch when, every single night of their marriage, she
reminded him to floss before bed.

As for me, I never could warm to the notion of my mother marrying somebody else. Who needed a new guy barging in and trying
to take my father's place? I didn't. I was happy with the memory of
the decent, fair, easygoing man who'd raised me—the man who was
a calming presence in my life. Whenever Mom would nag me, he'd
soothe me, whispering, "Don't worry. I'll have a talk with her." His
talks with her never changed anything, but his willingness to run
interference for me made him a hero in my book.

"You're too much the way you notice everything, Mrs. Reiser,"
Maura was telling my mother while I was tripping down memory
lane. "You totally crack me up."

I had to agree with Maura there. My mother was cracking me
up, too, only not in a good way.


The following week I had a date, a rare occurrence. It wasn't that I
didn't want to meet a guy, fall in love, and get married. It was that
I wanted to meet a guy, fall in love, and get married to someone
whose expectations in a mate didn't involve Julia Roberts. What I'm
saying is that finding Mr. Right is tough everywhere, but finding
him in L.A. is a near impossibility. If he has anything at all going

for him–physical attractiveness, power job, engaging personality (not necessarily in that order)–he's got a city full of bona fide movie stars to choose from, so why choose me? Not that I was a bowwow, as I've said. I just wasn't glamorous, voluptuous, or any of those other adjectives that end in "ous." Of course, the other reason I didn't date very often was that I was focused on my career. When I wasn't auditioning, I was spending time on my personal grooming, a must for an actress in Hollywood. You've got to show up at every meeting looking like a million bucks, which means facials and manicures and stints at the gym. I mean, there are only so many hours in a day.

Still, when Maura called to say she had a friend she wanted to fix me up with, I was delighted and made room in my busy schedule.

"His name is Ethan," she said, "and he's a hairdresser. A straight hairdresser. Oh, and he's Welsh."

"How old is he?"

I asked this because while I had mother issues, Maura had father issues. She was always dating men who were old enough to have sired her. Her last boyfriend, a real estate developer, was a good thirty years older than she was, and they had nothing in common except his interest in her body and her interest in his money.

"He's forty-four," she said. "And he's not only a genius with scissors, he's fabulous with color. He's been doing my hair for months now and I've never been happier." Maura's hair was cranberry, which is an okay color for a car but not for a person's head. She wore it just below her ears in a style I'd call virtual cowlick. It was layered and spiky–a cranberry crossed with a cactus. Hopefully Ethan had other skills.

He and I made plans to do dinner and a movie. Except for the fact that he had seven studs in his right earlobe, he was very appealing, regaling me with tales of all the divas whose hair he'd cut and/or colored. I sort of liked him and he seemed to like me, so we decided to skip the movie and scoot back to my apartment for coffee.

Coffee led to conversation, which led to kissing on my sofa. As I said, I didn't date often, so when I did–and was actually attracted to the guy–I tried to make the most of it.

Ethan and I were going at it–nothing serious, just lip action– when my doorbell rang.

"Let's ignore it," he said, as I nibbled on his earlobe, the one that wasn't pierced in seven places.

I murmured my assent and caressed Ethan's neck.

When the doorbell rang a second time, he broke away to check his watch. "It's bloody ten o'clock," he said. "Who'd be coming around at this hour?"

Well, there was only one person I could think of, and it was late, even for her. Something must have happened, I decided, disentangling myself from Ethan's arms and jumping up to open the door. Something that couldn't wait until morning.

"Mom? What is it?" I said, worried but relieved to see she was in one piece. She looked fine, in fact. More than fine. She was wearing a very fetching navy blue dress with the sales tag still hanging from the sleeve.

"Like it?" she said, hands on hips.

"Like what?"

"My new dress. I bought it at Loehmann's this afternoon. It was marked down by fifty percent so I couldn't resist."

"You came here at ten o'clock at night to model your new dress?" I said, itching to blast her but reigning myself in. She was living down the street now, not staying in a hotel for a week. We were in this for the long haul, she and I. If I provoked a confrontation, she'd get all huffy and it would be uncomfortable and I couldn't deal with that. Call me a wuss if you must, but I was overwhelmed with conflict. I was raised to be respectful to my mother, but I also needed to set limits with her, boundaries. If only she'd get a life, I kept telling myself over and over. Then I'd be off the hook.

"If I can't share a terrific bargain with my daughter, who can I share it with?" she said, walking right past me into the living room, where she came upon Ethan, who was still stretched out on the sofa. "Oh, my. I had no idea you had company, Stacey."

No idea I had company? I had told her I had a date only that morning! But she just had to see Ethan for herself, didn't she? I was dying to remind her that I was entitled to my privacy. Instead, I said, "Mom, this is Ethan. Ethan, this is my mother."

"Helen Reiser," she volunteered, planting herself on the sofa next to Ethan and pumping his hand.

"Pleasure," said Ethan, who was polite but clearly put out. He had visions of us doing more than kissing, I guessed.

"So tell me, Ethan," she said, peering up at him as if he were an exhibit in a museum. "What's with all the earrings?"

"My mother's a very direct person," I explained to Ethan.

"As if that's a bad thing," she said with a shrug.

"Maybe Ethan doesn't feel like discussing his personal life with someone he's just met," I said.

"What personal life?" she scoffed. "I was asking about his jewelry."

"I had my ear pierced," Ethan said tightly. "It's no big deal."

"It must have been a big deal because you did it seven times," said my mother. "Stacey wanted to pierce her ears when she was in high school, but I put my foot down. She went and did it anyway, when she was away at college, and wouldn't you know that she developed an infection. In her right ear, I think it was. Apparently, whoever did the piercing didn't use a sterilized needle. The ear became inflamed and started oozing, and if it weren't for the antibiotics they gave her in that infirmary, she would have been in real trouble. And speaking of antibiotics, there are strains of bacteria now that are resistant to the drugs, were you aware of that, Ethan?"

He shook his head helplessly.

"That's right," she went on. "And I don't mind telling you that it infuriates me. The fact that the geniuses in this country can't cure a common case of diarrhea *absolutely* infuriates me. A child eats a bad hamburger and the next thing you know that child is clinging to life in a hospital bed. It's a national disgrace! We can send a man to the moon. We can clone sheep. We can invent computers that show every kind of X-rated trash known to man. So why in the world can't we save a child who eats a bad hamburger? Why?"

Look, I'm as sympathetic as the next person when it comes to children or anyone else who contracts E. coli, but I was totally humiliated by my mother's latest performance. There wasn't a chance that Ethan would call me again. He sat there with this odd expression on his face. It was not one of bemusement or impatience or even hostility. It was one of fear—as if he were trapped in a train wreck.

"You must be tired," I said to my mother, in an effort to tell her to beat it without actually having to. "It's late and you did all that shopping today. Want me to walk you home?"

"Thanks, dear, but I'm fine. Being out in the night air gave me a second wind. So, Ethan, what do you do for a living?"

"Hair," he said in a snippy monotone he hadn't used with me.

"What, exactly, do you do with hair?" she said, boring in on him. "Do you wash it? Cut it? Remove it? What?"

Remove it. Yeah, he does waxing, Ma. "Ethan is a very successful hairdresser in Beverly Hills," I said.

"How nice," she said, nodding at him, "although I've read that those dyes you people use can cause cancer of the scalp."

"That hasn't been proven," he said. "It's perfectly safe to use color, Mrs. Reiser."

"Call me Helen. Please. And tell me something else: Do people often assume you're gay?"

"Mom!"

"I only ask because so many men in your profession are gay, just as so many anesthesiologists are Indian. It's an interesting phenomenon, the way certain groups seem to gravitate toward certain careers, isn't it?"

Let me say, in my mother's defense, that she was not bigoted in any way. She despised injustice and, as an example, lobbied her congressman to pass the hate crimes law in the state of Ohio. She was just incredibly blunt, had a tin ear when it came to conversational blunders, didn't have a clue how to edit herself.

"I've got to be going," said Ethan, who rose from the sofa, shook my mother's hand and my hand, and then told me he'd be in touch. Right.

The minute he was out the door, she said, "My, he was a quiet one. He's not the right man for you, Stacey, so listen to your mother."

"There's nothing wrong with being quiet," I said, wishing she would be.

"No, I suppose not. Do you think he's just shy or was he upset about something?"

"I think he was upset about some*one*," I said, too softly for her to hear me.

# Chapter
# Three

☆

M Y MOVIE WITH JIM CARREY, *Pet Peeve*, was finally coming out, which meant that I was scheduled to attend my very first premiere. I didn't have a date for either the premiere or the party afterward, so I planned to take Maura. My mother was profoundly insulted.

"My daughter is going to a movie premiere and she invites her friend instead of her mother?" she said, pressing her hand against her heart, as if she were bracing for cardiac arrest.

"Maura's doing my makeup that day," I said. "She's done my makeup for a million important occasions, just as a favor to me, so I think it's the least I can do to repay–"

"Oh, and I suppose *I* haven't done you any favors?" she cut me off, her whine becoming sort of an Edith Bunker screech. "What about all those hours I spent rehearsing your lines with you when you were in high school? Do you think I did that because I'm wild about *Our Town* and *Hedda Gabbler* and *Flower Drum Song*? Well, let me tell you, Stacey, I did it because I love you. I did it because I would sacrifice anything for you. And this is how you thank me?

This is how you treat me? By forcing me to watch you from the sidelines, like a perfect stranger? And in your hour of glory yet?"

"Oh, Mom." I tried to hug her but she turned away. She was a big baby when you got right down to it. "Please try to understand. I would take both of you if I could, but the studio only lets us bring one person. And I promised Maura, before you even moved here, that she could come with me if I didn't have a date."

"But I did move here," she said. "Why can't Maura be the understanding one?"

There were a few more back-and-forths, but in the end I caved. And Maura did understand. "Maybe your mother's starstruck," she said. "Maybe it's not so much that she wants to be with you as she wants to brush up against Jim Carrey."

I laughed. "My mother doesn't even know who Jim Carrey is. She has virtually no interest in the entertainment business. She has virtually no interest in anything except insinuating herself into every conceivable aspect of my life."

"Well, look on the bright side," said Maura, who was much better at looking at the bright side than I was. Her last boyfriend, the one before the rich real estate developer, was a rich department store heir and when she found him in bed with another man and he begged her not to tell anyone, she asked for and got a lifetime discount on all merchandise in his stores.

"Okay. What's the bright side?" I said.

"If you take your mother to the premiere," said Maura, "she won't call you the next morning and make you give her a blow-by-blow description of the event. That'll save you a headache, right?"

I had butterflies the day of the premiere, was as excited as I'd been the first time I'd stepped on a stage at age eight. For me, the premiere was confirmation of my having "made it," albeit in a minor way. The fact that I had scored a speaking part in an actual movie and that the movie was sure to be a hit and that I would be mingling with Hollywood's elite along that red carpet gave me hope that I really was on the brink of bigger things, that my stint at the biker bar would soon be a distant memory, that from here on I'd never have to do a Taco Bell commercial again, never have to be told I wasn't skinny enough or young enough or tall enough or that my lips weren't the size of Angelina Jolie's.

People often ask me why I became an actress, why I subjected myself to the rejection, the rudeness, the assault on my self-esteem, and the answer is: I couldn't picture myself doing anything else. The rush you get when you stand up there in front of an audience and manage to elicit a response—whether it's laughter or dead silence—is so intoxicating that you can't wait to feel it again. It's like the effect of a drug, that rush of approval. Actors are basically pleasers—if we can't please our parents, we might as well please somebody—so we're addicted to being applauded. Sally Field was lambasted for her "you like me" unraveling, but every actor who made fun of her knew exactly what she was talking about. So I became an actress to win approval, to cause a reaction, to make an impression. But I also went into the business to become someone else. Imagine being a good girl in real life and playing a total bitch in a movie. Imagine playing any role to which you have to bring emotions and actions and words that are foreign to you in the everyday. Imagine getting to experiment with personalities that are the polar opposite of your own. Imagine leaving your insecurities and conflicts and inhibitions in the dressing room and emerging as someone else. It's like a thrill ride, that's what it is. And it's that thrill ride that keeps actors in the game, not the fame or the money or the chance to hang out with Jim Carrey. I played his receptionist in *Pet Peeve*, not his leading lady, but I played her with everything I had and I loved the experience. It could only get better from here, right? That's what I thought. That's what I really, truly believed.

On the night of the premiere, my mother and I did the red carpet number. The cameras were out in force, the reporters clamoring for a whiff of anyone famous. It was such a glittering event that I didn't even take it personally when a jerk from *Extra!* stuck a microphone in my face, then pulled it away, muttering, "Damn. I thought you were someone."

Undaunted, I smiled and waved at the crowd, was determined to enjoy myself. Who cared that my mother kept reminding me to stand up straight and get the hair out of my eyes? Who cared that she complained bitterly about the flashbulbs that were blinding her or the TV cables that were tripping her or the smog that was inflaming her sinuses? What mattered was that, once inside the theater, everyone seemed to love *Pet Peeve,* my mother included. She hugged me when the movie was over and the credits rolled, told me she was proud of me, called me her little Meryl Streep. Even Jim Carrey gave me a reassuring thumbs-up.

I was off and running.

And then came the movie's opening day, three days later. At eight o'clock that Friday morning, my mother showed up at my door carrying every newspaper she could find and proceeded to spread them out on the floor of my living room and read the *Pet Peeve* reviews aloud.

The *Los Angeles Times* mentioned me briefly but glowingly: "As Lola, the receptionist, the energetic Stacey Reiser is a scene stealer." *The New York Times* mentioned me briefly but less glowingly: "In a small role as Carrey's eager-beaver receptionist, Stacey Reiser is grating." *USA Today* didn't mention me, and part of me was grateful.

"I'd like to give that *New York Times* guy a kick in the pants," said my mother, my fiercest defender as well as my toughest critic.

"How dare he call my daughter 'grating.' I'll give him 'grating.' I'll write him one of my complaint letters."

I smiled. My mother was renowned for the letters she regularly fired off to people, corporations, any unlucky soul who needed to be reprimanded, in her opinion. For instance, when she bought a box of All-Bran that turned out to be only three-quarters full, she wrote to Kellogg's, declaring that she would never buy their products again unless they apologized. They not only apologized but sent her coupons for twelve boxes of All-Bran.

"Thanks, Mom, but I'd rather you didn't write to him," I said. "He might hold it against me the next time I'm in a movie. Besides, he only gave me an adjective's worth of ink. Hardly a real review."

"All right, dear," my mother agreed grudgingly. "If you're sure. Now, it's almost nine o'clock. I'll turn on *Good Morning, Hollywood* and we'll see what that rascal Jack Rawlins has to say about you."

I cringed at the mere thought. *Good Morning, Hollywood* was a weekly half-hour television show devoted to show business goings-on, sort of a highbrow *Entertainment Tonight*. Its host, Jack Rawlins, was a total gasbag—a know-it-all whose reviews always created a buzz within the industry, I suspect, because he was a Harvard grad and spoke in multisyllables and looked, not like those blow-dried studly types you see on the other entertainment shows, but like some tweedy young college professor who has all his female students in heat. He was handsome, in other words, with blue eyes framed by tortoiseshell glasses and reddish-blond hair that curled around his ears and a long, straight nose that tilted up at the end and a very generous mouth, out of which spewed some very ungenerous words on occasion. Personally, I thought he was an effete snob whose sole purpose in life was to impress people with his wicked wit. What particularly galled me was how tough he could be on up-and-coming actors and how his comments could literally torpedo a budding career. Don't get me wrong, he could be hard on the big stars, too, but they weren't as vulnerable to his criticism, given their established fan bases, and they managed to stay on top whether he damned them or praised them. No, it was the strugglers like me who were really defenseless against him. For instance, he once said about my former roommate, after she'd given only her second performance in a film, "Watching Belinda Hanson is like swallowing an Ambien. In fact, she induces sleep better than any pill *I've* ever taken." Poor Belinda didn't work again for a year. At least, not as an actress. Everywhere she went, people made snoring sounds.

"Here he is, dear," said my mother, turning up the volume on the television set.

I leaned in, prepared myself for Rawlins's review of *Pet Peeve*. I was sure he would loathe the movie, given his preference for serious art-house films as opposed to broad comedy intended for the multiplex crowd. The question was, would he loathe me or even mention me?

"Opening today in wide release is the new Jim Carrey vehicle *Pet Peeve*," he began. Then he chuckled, which was not a good sign. Not the way that guy chuckled. "Of course, I use the term 'vehicle' loosely. *Webster's Dictionary* defines 'vehicle' as a conveyance–something that transports. Well, *Pet Peeve* doesn't do much transporting, unless you enjoy being carried off into a world where a toilet overflows, a hamster receives CPR, and a plate full of spaghetti lands in the lap of the Queen of England."

"*I* found the movie very amusing," sniffed my mother.

"Pay no attention to him," I said. "He has zero sense of humor."

We listened as Rawlins proceeded to rip the movie, its director, and its stars, especially Carrey, whom he referred to as "a mediocre clown masquerading as an even more mediocre actor." And then, as I was turning away from the TV, figuring he was about to move on to another review, he said, "As Carrey's receptionist, Stacey

Reiser uses her precious few moments of screen time to pound us over the head with her lines. She has the subtlety of a sledgehammer and should consider applying for a job in construction."

I couldn't speak at first, couldn't process what Jack Rawlins had just said about me. If my mother hadn't been there, I might have remained on the sofa for hours in a state of shock, hoping the floor would open up and swallow me whole. I mean, the guy didn't just dis me; he annihilated me in front of a live television audience–an audience that included every important producer and director and casting agent in town. He absolutely drove a stake through my heart with that review, and I didn't want to deal with it, didn't want to deal with the fact that I could be the next Belinda Hanson, but my mother *was* there and she was as mortified as I was. Before I knew it, I was the one consoling her.

"Don't take it so hard, Mom. He didn't trash me. He trashed my performance," I managed, trying to pull myself together and cleave to the mantra I'd learned in acting class: in order to deal with a negative review, you must distance yourself from it, tell yourself that reviews are subjective and not necessarily the Truth and that one person's harsh opinion of your work doesn't make you a talentless fool.

"Well, he should be ashamed of himself," she said hotly. "It's one thing to be a movie critic. It's another to be a horse's ass."

This was strong stuff from my mother. She was a pistol, as Maura called her, but she rarely cursed.

"If you ask me, I think he should be fired for incompetence as well as impudence," she went on. "In the meantime, I will never watch his show again. I bet no one will. I bet *Pet Peeve* will be a big success and your career will reach new heights, dear."

By the following week, it was clear that my mother was no prognosticator. The movie was a box office disaster, despite Jim Carrey's popularity, and my career, unlike his, didn't rebound. Jack Rawlins's review—"Stacey Reiser has the subtlety of a sledgehammer"—clung to me like a poisonous snake, just wrapped itself around me wherever I went. Thanks to Rawlins, I was now officially tainted in the business. Sledgehammer Stacey. That was my adorable new nickname. My agent tried to do damage control, mailing the positive reviews I'd received to all the major players in town, but he couldn't convince people—any movie or television people, that is—to take another look at me.

"We're gonna have to wait this out a while, let the dust settle," advised Mickey Offerman, who'd been my agent through thick and thin. (Well, through thin and less thin.) Despite an inauspicious first meeting during which Mickey had said, "If you get your hair bleached, your teeth capped, and your tits inflated, I'll sign you" and I had said, "I'm an actress, not a beauty pageant contestant, and if you're not interested in representing me I'll find someone who is," our partnership had gone very well up to that point. But Jack Rawlins had handcuffed Mickey. "We could go back to sending you out for commercials," he offered. "So you can keep the money flowing in."

Back to commercials. Swell.

When I discussed this with Maura, she came through yet again with a glass that was half-full instead of half-empty.

"Look on the bright side," she said in her customarily upbeat tone. "Before Jack Rawlins, you were hating your mother. She probably looks good to you now, compared to him, right?"

# Chapter
# Four

★

I WAS DETERMINED to claw my way back into the movies. I was determined to show everyone I was not Sledgehammer Stacey. I was determined to prove that Jack Rawlins's negative assessment of me was merely an example of his snotty, mean-spirited personality, with no basis in reality whatsoever, and that I was, in fact, an actress with range and nuance and, damn it, subtlety.

But just in case he was a teensy-weensy bit accurate in that I did have a slight tendency to go for too much in front of the camera (*The New York Times had* called me "grating"), I decided to take a few brush-up acting classes. Why not, I figured, given that I had time on my hands while I waited for Mickey to send me out on auditions. It wouldn't hurt to perfect my craft, would it?

I enrolled in a class given by a rather well-known teacher named Gerald Clarke. I'd heard about him for years, heard how actors swore by his supposedly radical approach to teaching.

Well, I found out just *how* radical on my very first night in his Santa Monica studio.

"Let me begin by stating right at the top that this class is not going to be about nurturing you or making you feel safe or reassuring you that you have talent," Gerald said to the twenty of us who had gathered precisely to be nurtured and made to feel safe and reassured that we had talent. He was standing up on a small stage and he was wearing a pair of jeans and a black turtleneck. He was in his early fifties, I guessed, with a receding hairline, a protruding gut, and a complexion that bespoke teenage acne. "This is a class for actors who want to be better actors, actors who understand that in order to be better actors they must be stripped down, forced to confront their vulnerabilities, forced to confront the personal conflicts in their lives that prevent them from losing themselves in a character. In this class you'll learn that you don't *play* a character, you *become* the character, which necessitates–no, *demands*–that you be stripped down to nothing. *Nothing!* Does everyone *hear* me?"

"Is this guy a drill sergeant or an acting teacher?" I whispered to the woman next to me, who, I realized with some dismay, was the vixen I'd been running into at auditions, the one who annoyed everyone with her bullshit gamesmanship and gigantic hooters. We had to stop meeting like this.

"He just wants us to get in touch with our issues," she whispered back. "If you don't think you can handle it, honey, maybe you should sneak out the side door."

"I can handle it fine," I said. "If anyone should sneak out–"

"You. The one who refuses to keep her mouth shut while I'm talking." It was Gerald Clarke and he was pointing at me, shooting daggers at me, making me the focus of every eye in the room. "Step on up here and let's see what you've got."

"Me?" Nothing came out but a croak. "You want me?" I tried again.

"Why not?" he said. "Since you seem to be the chatty type, let's have you chat us all up. What's your name?"

Sledgehammer Stacey. "Stacey Reiser," I said with false bravado.

"All right, Stacey Reiser," he said, "let's have you come up here and blow us away. I'd like you to do an improv of approximately three minutes. Here's the premise: You're a customer in a department store, browsing at the perfume counter, and an attractive man sidles up to you, asking for your help. He claims he's there to buy some perfume for his wife, but the more he talks the more it's clear that he's there to score with you. Go."

Go. Yeah. Well, it wasn't as if I hadn't done improvs before. They were a staple of acting classes. I just hadn't done one after being decimated by Jack Rawlins, so my confidence level wasn't particularly high.

I inhaled, exhaled, took a moment to collect myself, then arranged my body as if I were standing beside a department store perfume counter.

"Oh," I said, spinning around to indicate that I'd just been tapped on the shoulder by the phantom man. "So it's your wife's birthday? Well, I'm not sure I'm the one to ask about the right fragrance. I've just been standing here trying different ones, spraying on a little of this, a little of that, to see what smells good on me. No, I guess I don't mind." I held up my wrist so he could sniff it. "You think your wife will like–"

"Stop stop stop," barked Gerald, waving his arms in the air. "I can't listen to another word of that crap."

I froze, my arms at my sides.

"You're much too frightened to connect with the primitive sexuality needed here," he went on. "Too inhibited. Have you ever actually had a man come on to you, Susan?"

"It's Stacey," I said, trying not to dissolve into tears and/or vomit. "And the answer's yes." Just not in a long time, unless you counted Ethan, the hairdresser, and we had come on to each other.

"I don't believe you. You move as if you've been in a nunnery all your life."

"But that's not true. I studied movement when I was–"

"Excuse me. Are you the acting coach or am I?"

"You are, but I don't understand why you're–"

"Why I'm what? Trying to put you in touch with your issues? Trying to strip you down to your basic shell? Trying to undo all the bad habits you've picked up during your stab at acting?"

My *stab* at acting. I'd done more than stab at it. I'd thrown myself at it. And my efforts had paid off. I'd gotten a part in a feature film, and if it weren't for Jack Rawlins I'd be getting parts in other feature films.

"Here's my guess, Sally," said Gerald.

"It's Stacey," I said.

"Someone down the line told you not to overact, so you've pulled inward, crawled inside yourself. Am I right?"

Yikes. Had he seen Rawlins's review, too? "I suppose that could have happened," I acknowledged. "Down the line, I mean."

"Okay. So here's your way out of the problem. You're going to put yourself in contact with your body."

"Oh, you mean I should stand differently when I talk to the man at the perfume counter?"

"No. I mean you should start moving your hips in a circle."

"Move my hips?"

"Yeah, and lead with your pelvis. Now! Do it!"

I took a huge gulp of air and, in front of a roomful of strangers, I began rotating my hips in a circle. I felt like a kid playing with a Hula-Hoop.

"Now touch your breasts and your ass," he commanded. "Really connect with your sexuality."

Touch my breasts and my ass? How about connecting with *this*, I wanted to tell the twisted jerk. I decided then and there that I was not interested in starring in Gerald Clarke's peep show. Maybe I *was* uptight. Maybe I *was* self-conscious. Maybe I *was* out of touch with my sexuality, but I had my standards of conduct and they didn't include prostituting myself for my art.

While I stood there not touching myself, Gerald looked at the group and said with an exasperated sigh, "Obviously, Samantha doesn't want to work on her issues. Anyone else want to try the exercise? Volunteers, please?"

Naturally, the vixen raised her hand.

"Ah, good," said Gerald. "Your name?"

"Brittany Madison," she said as she sashayed onto the stage, planting herself next to me. She was a very big girl. It was like standing next to Mt. Rushmore.

"Okay, Brittany. Now why don't you show us how it looks to connect with your sexuality. Rotate your hips in a circle, leading with the pelvis."

Brittany complied willingly.

"Now touch your breasts and your buttocks and let all your inhibitions go. Do what feels good to you, what feels fun to you."

I continued to stand there, dripping with flop sweat. It was a toss-up which made me more uncomfortable: failing Gerald's test or having to witness someone else pass it.

"This is wonderful," cooed Brittany, who was now sliding her hands down her body, swaying from side to side, licking her lips.

"You see this, class?" Gerald exclaimed. "Brittany is connecting with her sexuality, getting in touch with it, breaking down the destructive barriers in her psyche. Brittany, ladies and gentlemen, is what *I* call an actor."

Brittany, ladies and gentlemen, was what *I* called an exhibitionist.


I quit Gerald Clarke's class—he wouldn't refund my money, the bastard—and told myself to go back to my roots, stick with what I knew, rely on the skills that had served me well in the past, before

Jack Rawlins (or, as I had come to refer to it in this dismal period, "pre-JR").

I also told myself that I didn't mind dropping down a rung on the acting ladder by auditioning for commercials again. As Mickey said, I'd be keeping the cash flowing in while we waited for the movie and television people to come to their senses. Commercials were a sure thing, we agreed—a needed boost to my fragile ego.

The first commercial I went out for was a national spot for Tide. I was supposed to play a young mom who does the laundry, dresses her kids for school, hands her husband his neatly folded shirts, and then says, with a big smile, "We're a Tide family. Shouldn't yours be, too?" It was dopey in that way that a lot of commercials for household products are dopey (why would a young mom be excited about her stupid laundry detergent?), but I was just the hired help, so it wasn't my place to judge. The main thing was that I was a shoo-in for the job. The entire creative team led me to believe I was. But when they showed my tape to the client, he nixed me for the part. Turns out I reminded him of his dreaded ex-wife. No Tide commercial.

The second commercial I went out for was another national spot, this one for Midol. I was supposed to play a hip young woman who's sitting in a restaurant with her friends, doubled over because she's been stricken with horrendous menstrual cramps. As the camera comes in for a close-up of her face, she winces in pain, turns to one of the friends, and says, "If only I'd brought my Midol." As I'm pretty good at wincing in pain, I got the job. Unfortunately, on the day of the shoot I was in a nasty fender bender en route to the studio and ended up wincing in pain for real. Not only did I arrive at the shoot over two hours late, but I arrived with a neck that was so whiplashed I couldn't make it turn the way it was supposed to. What's more, the two Percocet I popped wreaked havoc with my speech and instead of saying, "If only I'd brought my Midol," I said what sounded like, "If only I'd brought *my doll.*" Yup, I lost the job. And to add insult to my pathetic injury, the person they replaced me with was none other than Brittany Madison.

The third commercial I went out for was a national spot for Tic Tacs. I really wanted this one, because it was a cute spot, a funny spot, a spot that would showcase my comedic flair. I was up for the part of a bride who's standing at the altar during her wedding, about to be kissed by the groom in front of a church full of family and friends, when she stops, stares into the camera, and says, panicked, "Does *anybody* have a Tic Tac?" The minister reaches into his robe, pulls out his Tic Tacs, and hands her one. She swallows it, smiles gratefully. The minister says to the groom, "You may now kiss the bride," at which point the bride and groom suck face.

The ad agency had already cast the actor who was playing the groom, so they brought all the actresses in to read with him—and to kiss him—to determine which couple had chemistry. He was a great-looking guy—sort of a young Mel Gibson—and I had no trouble getting in touch with my sexuality where he was concerned. Consequently, I won the job. The Saturday before the shoot, I went to the beach with Maura to celebrate. It was a relaxing day, during which we read, talked, napped, people watched. Big mistake. Two mornings later I woke up with a huge and thoroughly unsightly cold sore on my upper lip. Was I pissed! I had applied and reapplied the sunscreen. I had worn a hat with a wide brim. I had done everything I was supposed to do in order to *not* get a cold sore and, yet, there it was—a blister the size of a nickel and still growing. Maura did her best to camouflage it with makeup on the day of the shoot, but it was pretty damn ugly. Still, I wanted the job so much that I showed up and tried to pretend it wasn't there. I ducked into wardrobe, donned my bridal gown, and kept my hand over my mouth until the cameras rolled. No one mentioned the Thing—not until the groom stepped closer in anticipation of our kiss and took a good look at me. Mel Gibson Junior lowered his head and was about to pucker up when he recoiled in horror and announced, "There's no way I'm kissing *that*." So much for the Tic Tacs commercial.

"Maybe I should write Jack Rawlins one of my complaint letters," said my mother, after I arrived home from yet another tough day and moaned that he was responsible for my career woes. She had used her key and let herself into my apartment and was busily alphabetizing the cookbooks in my kitchen. "Or maybe I should give you a nice haircut, dear. Those split ends aren't very flattering."

"Maybe you should stay out of this, Mom," I said, losing my patience with her. I knew she was only trying to help, but what I needed was for her to leave me alone. "Maybe you should find something constructive to do with your time."

She reacted as if I'd slapped her. "What did you say?"

"I said that you need to involve yourself in an activity, a project, anything besides me."

"Oh, I see. So I suppose you're not a worthy project? I should go and volunteer someplace, spend my days with strangers, while my only daughter is struggling?"

"I'm not struggling," I said, sinking onto the sofa. "I'm plateauing. I was on the rise and now I've leveled off. The business goes in cycles. I'll be up again. I know I will."

I didn't know anything of the kind. I just wanted my mother off my back.

"Fine. I won't cut your hair for you," she said huffily. "And don't bother thanking me for organizing your cookbooks. Cookbooks. Ha! God forbid you should fix a decent meal once in a while, Stacey. If you ask me, you got that cold sore because you don't take care of yourself."

"I do take care of myself," I said. "I'm a grown woman, as I keep reminding you."

"A grown woman? Then where's the ring on your finger? Or am I supposed to keep quiet about that, too?"

"Oh, please, Mom. Not the marriage routine again."

"Yes, the marriage routine again. Grown women not only have lovely houses instead of apartments that look like a girl's dormitory–" she gave my living room the once-over–"they have husbands, Stacey, nice husbands with nice jobs and nice manners. Some grown women even have children. But then I should be so lucky to be a grandmother. Of all my friends in Cleveland, I'm the only one whose daughter isn't–"

I grabbed the two throw pillows from each end of the sofa and covered my ears with them, stopping her latest harangue in its tracks. Not very mature of me, I admit. Not very *grown woman-ish*. But it worked. It shut her up and was, therefore, the best course of action under the circumstances.

# Chapter

# Five

★

I WENT OVER TO MAURA'S the following Saturday, hoping she would cheer me up as she always did. From the first day we'd met, when I was playing the part of a nurse on *Days,* she'd been my rock, my champion, the person who told me the truth but never criticized, never judged. That's what a best friend is, isn't it? Someone who talks you off the ledge when times are tough; who celebrates your success when others are envious of it; who can joke with you as easily as share intimate confidences with you; who urges you to keep going, keep pushing, keep remembering that life is full of possibilities and that even a bad review from a pompous movie critic isn't the end of the world.

It was an "up" just to watch Maura bustling around in her new house. Thanks to her steady work on *Days* and her occasional freelance gigs on movie sets, she earned a decent living as a makeup artist and was able to buy a house–the kind of security struggling actresses would kill for. Her place, a Spanish-style three-bedroom in Burbank, needed a little TLC, but she was committed to fixing it up and had already replaced the avocado shag carpet in the living room.

"The kitchen cabinets are next," she said as she handed me an iced tea. "I'm not wild about the orange Formica."

"I admit I won't be sorry to see them go," I said. That was another thing about Maura: she was a doer. She made the most of everything—whether it was a house or a guy. Yes, she had a father complex and dated men who were certified geezers, but she saw the good in all of them, even the ones who couldn't get it up without the Viagra. "So. How's life at the show?"

"Crazy as ever," she said. "We're doing sort of a science fiction story line where Deirdre Hall, Kristian Alfonso, and some of the other cast members have to age forty years. It's tougher than the usual stuff, but I love it. It makes me feel like a magician."

"You are a magician." Maura was wonderfully talented. Never mind how she transformed me with her makeup brush now and then; she could render actors unrecognizable, because, unlike most people in her field, she knew how to work with prosthetics and wigs and wardrobes, having gotten her start on one of the *Planet of the Apes* films. When Maura Lasky gave you a makeover, you got a makeover!

"How's everything with your mother?" she asked after we'd moved outside, onto her patio, and sat down.

"Same answer as yours: crazy as ever," I said. "She needs to get a life, Maura. She really, really needs to get a life. She's smart and energetic and she should be doing something meaningful instead of nagging me twenty-four/seven. I wish I could make her see that."

"Sounds like she should apply for a job."

"Exactly. She's a college graduate, with a degree in education. She's well-spoken, if you don't count the fingernails-on-the-blackboard voice. She's domineering, as we know, but she's not a bad caretaker. And she's amazingly organized. She'd make a terrific office manager, for example."

"Hey, that's a thought, Stacey. Why don't I ask my producer if there's an opening in the production department at *Days?* Maybe your mother would enjoy working in the wacky world of television."

"My mother?" I shook my head. "She despises show business. She's made that clear to me over and over. No, she has to find something practical, like a position in a marketing research firm. Or maybe a doctor's office."

"I've got just the spot for her." Maura laughed. "How about getting her a job at a prison? She'd be the perfect warden, wouldn't she?"

I laughed, too. "She'd be totally in her element as a warden, bossing all the inmates around, sticking them in solitary confinement if they messed up, forcing them to listen to her consumer complaint rants, like all the reasons why she prefers Quilted Northern toilet paper over Cottonelle."

"Speaking of jobs," said Maura, her tone turning serious, "have you gotten any lately?"

I reported on my flameouts with the Tide commercial, the Midol commercial, and the Tic Tac commercial. "I'm supposed to go out for a Maidenform commercial next week, but the way things are going, I doubt I'll get it."

"Hey, that's not the Stacey Reiser I know. You've got to stay positive."

"I usually do stay positive, but the bras they're advertising are their soft cup line. I think you need actual breasts to wear them."

She smiled. "There'll be other commercials then. There always are."

Dear Maura. As I said, she was my rock.


Unfortunately, there weren't other commercials. At least not within the next few weeks. I'd go on auditions and fail to get the jobs every time. The casting directors dismissed me with either "You're not the look we're going for" or "We need someone less ethnic" or just plain "Thanks anyway."

Hoping for some sage career advice, I went to see Mickey Offerman, my agent. Mickey was not one of the trendy young men in black that you see everywhere in L.A.–the ones that are always shouting into their cell phones and hustling deals over drinks at the Four Seasons and getting written up in *Variety*. No, Mickey was a throwback agent–a cheesy-looking guy with a bad toupee and an equally bad nose job. He was in his late sixties, when nose jobs tended to be about nostrils–i.e., you could see right up them. The other thing you could see when you trudged up the stairs to his seedy little office in West Hollywood were black-and-white photographs of people he used to represent ("used to" being the operative words). Sally Struthers. Gabe Kaplan. Joan Van Ark. Actors of a certain era who were no longer in the spotlight, to put it diplomatically.

So what was I doing with Mickey and why didn't I dump him for one of the trendy young men in black, particularly since my career had stalled? A couple of reasons. First, I was loyal. When I'd come to L.A. in my twenties and pounded the pavement with my head shots and résumé and couldn't get anybody to take me seriously, Mickey was the only one who would. Sure, he'd turned me off with his tacky, Rat Pack-y style. For example, I think he actually said to me at our initial meeting, "I just love to find gals, bring 'em in off the street, and make 'em stars." He even called me "little lady," as if that's what men call women in this century. But while the other agents in town wouldn't take my calls, wouldn't see me, wouldn't lift a finger to help me, Mickey did. And because he was a one-man operation, he handled movies and television as well as commercials– a plus, as far as I was concerned.

The other reason I stayed with Mickey was less altruistic: he was the only one who still wanted me. When you've plateaued in the business and can't get work no matter how hard you try, it's not the best time to go looking for a big-time agent. So it was Mickey I clung to, Mickey I listened to.

"Like I told you, we're gonna have to let the dust settle a little," he said the day I went to see him. He was wearing tight blue jeans, a purple shirt unbuttoned mid-sternum, and a pair of sunglasses on top of his toupee, as if to hold it down. "*Pet Peeve* tanked and Jack Rawlins trashed you. We're gonna have to deal with that."

"How?" I said. "Unless I get some commercials soon, I'll start panicking about my finances."

"Take a part-time job until things pick up again, kid." By now, he had dispensed with the "little lady" and referred to me as "kid," probably because he had no desire to sleep with me. As he had a desire to sleep with every woman he saw, I felt somewhat insulted.

"No more biker bars for me, Mickey. Been there, done that."

"So do something else. There are plenty of jobs in this town. Why don't you take one until you're hot again?"

"When do you think that'll be?"

Mickey patted my hand. I braced myself for him to say, "When hell freezes over," but he said instead, "When your time is right. This business is all about timing, Stacey. You know that. You were the fresh face when you first came here. Now there are a million new fresh faces. You're in your—what—mid-thirties?"

"Early thirties." Thirty-four *was* early, compared to thirty-five.

"Tough age bracket," said Mickey. "They all want twenty-year-olds now."

"But I can play twenties, Mickey," I said, hearing the desperation in my voice. "I'll redo my head shots, dress edgier, walk the walk." Whatever that meant.

"Look, kid. Let's get real about this, okay? I'll keep doing my best to send you out for stuff whenever I can, but you gotta face facts. It's possible that you won't make a comeback tomorrow. You might have to wait until you're old to get parts again."

"Old?"

"Yeah. Once you're in your forties, you can play mothers, aunts, teachers, judges. The meaty character roles."

I just sat there, feeling like a tire that had blown out. Mickey must have felt sorry for me, because he patted my hand a second time. "This is a tough, tough business," he said. "At some point you may decide it's not for you, not anymore."

"Acting is all I've ever wanted to do," I protested, fighting off tears. "It's all I've ever imagined myself doing. And I'm good at it, Mickey. I know I am. Okay, maybe I'm not Oscar caliber, but I'm not Sledgehammer Stacey, either. I mean, am I really supposed to quit a profession I love because Jack Rawlins didn't like my performance in a movie that sank at the box office? Jim Carrey's doing okay. *Pet Peeve* didn't hurt his career one bit. That doesn't seem fair."

"Nobody said this business was fair. Take Jack Rawlins, since you brought him up. Is he a major talent? No. He's a good-looking guy with a better-than-average vocabulary. And now he's getting rewarded for trashing movies. It's not fair, but it's the business."

"He's getting rewarded? How?"

"You haven't heard? They're expanding his show to an hour and going wider with it. He's not just gonna review movies now; he's gonna interview guests. Sort of a Charlie Rose meets Roger Ebert."

"But that's–"

"Not fair, right. Jack Rawlins is gonna be a big star and that's how the cookie crumbles and you gotta concentrate on you, on what you're gonna do."

"I'll tell you what I'm not gonna do," I said resolutely. "I'm not giving up. I'm an actress—even if I have to get a part-time job to pay the bills. If a lightweight like Jack Rawlins can make it in this business, so can I."

Talk about a stirring performance. Mickey was so moved he let out a long belch.

"It's the cholesterol medicine they've got me on," he explained. "Gives me gas."

I trudged out of his office, more determined than ever to hang in, hang on, hope that my big break was just around the corner.

# Chapter

# Six

☆

ICKEY SENT ME OUT on yet another commercial audition, this one for a local fast-food chain. I was supposed to play a woman in her twenties (I'd told Mickey I could play twenties, remember, and he'd agreed it was worth a shot) who stands behind the counter in her cute little uniform and says cheerfully to the next customer, "How may I serve you today?" After three callbacks, I lost the job, not because I was too old but because I was too chaste. The actress who won the part spun the line into a sexy double entendre, as in: "How may I *service* you today?"

Dejected but not suicidal, I decided to look for a part-time job, just as a precautionary measure while I waited for my luck to change. Maura suggested that, since I had no interest in waiting tables again, I should consider retailing. So I scanned the *L.A. Times'* classified section and found an ad for a part-time salesperson at a fancy-shmancy shop in Brentwood called Cornucopia! (the exclamation point is theirs, not mine). I assumed it was a fancy-shmancy shop, not only because they were paying more than the other stores with ads in the paper, but because they were in Brentwood, the poshest of the posh in West L.A., or, let me rephrase, the self-annointed poshest of the posh. While the old money lives more quietly in Pasadena, the newly minted—many of them movie and television producers and their trophy families—hunker down in their faux chateaux in Brentwood, where a two-bedroom fixer-upper on a decent piece of property goes for a cool three million dollars. This is just a guess, but I'll bet there are more nannies in Brentwood than anyplace on earth. More SUVs, too (the Mercedes ones). It's a place where the wives are blonder, the husbands are tanner, and the kids—well, when you're six and your parents have already run out of ways to spoil you, it's a problem.

I called the shop and spoke to the manager, a woman who introduced herself as Cameron Slade and asked me to come in for an interview, which I did the very next morning.

"Nice to meet you," said Cameron, who clearly didn't think it was nice to meet me, just a dreary necessity. She was as cold as an ice sculpture and just as chiseled. Her dark brown hair fell smoothly around a face that had been whittled and carved and planed so as to render her one of those women with virtually no lines or spots, no imperfections, no character. She was in her early forties, I figured, but seemed older, despite the cosmetic surgery, probably because she looked so joyless.

"It's nice to meet you, too," I said. We sat in her office in the back of the store, which, by the way, reminded me of a stage set, because it felt so manufactured. Cornucopia! specialized in imported accessories for the home—from furniture, linens, and tableware to custom stationery and an entire children's department—and every piece of merchandise was romanced, displayed beautifully, displayed artfully. The store symbolized wretched excess at its most subversive—not the kind you see on Rodeo Drive in Beverly Hills but the kind you see in upscale suburbia. It had an aura of preciousness, of We-know-what's-best-for-you, of Shop-here-if-you're-the-third-wife-of-a-movie-mogul-and-you-don't-have-a-clue-which-fork-to-use-for-which-course.

"Do you have any sales experience?" asked Cameron.

"I worked in the hosiery department at Macy's when I lived in Cleveland," I said. "But that was years ago. I've been working as an actress since I moved to L.A."

"Interesting. I've always wanted to be an actress."

I tried not to roll my eyes. The woman who cleaned my teeth always wanted to be an actress. So did the woman who taught my yoga class and the woman who owned the apartment I rented and the woman who sold me my health insurance policy. Los Angeles has almost as many aspiring actresses as it does cars.

"Would I have seen you in anything?" she asked.

"Probably. I've done a lot of television. And I was in *Pet Peeve,* the last Jim Carrey movie."

Cameron nodded in recognition. But not because she'd seen me. "Jim Carrey has been a customer of ours," she said. "Which prompts me to tell you about Rule Number One here at Cornucopia!: No member of the sales staff must ever be a gushing fan around a celebrity. In other words, there will be no discussion of their films or television programs, no attempts to make a connection for personal gain, no pestering them for autographs."

"Understood." I assumed that if there was a Rule Number One, there must be other rules. I braced myself.

"So you'd like to work part-time, between auditions. Is that it?"

"Yes. I could give you all day on Saturday and Sunday, plus I could fill in on weekdays if my agent doesn't have anything for me."

"You'd be paid a commission on any item you sell."

"I'm all for that."

"Good. Are you a careful person?"

"Careful?" No, I'm a bull in a china shop. "Sure. I'd treat the merchandise as if it were my own."

"That's Rule Number Two: If a member of the sales staff breaks, scratches, or soils an item, he or she must repair or replace it out of his or her paycheck."

"As he or she should."

"Now, are you familiar with the type of merchandise we stock? Our inventory embodies the best of France, Italy, and England. We have exquisite table settings, for example, decorated with French faience such as Quimper or the more subtle colors of Vietri's *cucina fresca*. We carry the distinctive D. Porthault line of French linens as well as the silken luxury of Cocoon. In our children's collection, we have whimsical bedding from Banana Fish and Freddie's Daisy and imported layettes from Petit Bateau. And for the bath, we carry fragrances and candles from Palais Royale and Dipytich. You *have* heard of Dipytich, I presume."

I'd heard of dipshit, which is what this chick was making me feel like. As far as I was concerned, she was speaking in foreign tongues. "Of course I've heard of it," I said with a straight face. "No wonder Cornucopia! has the classy reputation it does, as well as legions of loyal shoppers."

"Yes, well, I think both our custom stationery and our bridal registry contribute to our success, too," said Cameron. "Which brings me to Rule Number Three: Since gift wrapping is our specialty, every member of the sales staff must be competent with a glue gun."

"Hey, just call me Annie Got My Glue Gun," I said jauntily, slipping in a joke that would incorporate my background as an entertainer as well as my team spirit and, hopefully, nudge Cameron toward hiring me.

"Oh, there's one other thing," she said. "Do you know how to iron?"

"Iron?"

"Yes. Sometimes the linens need to be ironed if we're changing a table setting or a bedding display or if the fabrics have been picked over by the customers."

"I can do that," I said, my ironing skill on a par with my ability to pilot an airplane.

"And, of course, there's the vacuuming. We usually have the sales staff vacuum right after we close at night."

"That's a given." Just hire me already, baby, before I turn around and head back to the biker bar.

After a few more questions, Cameron did hire me, and the victory was bittersweet, obviously. It was tough to face the fact that I wasn't cutting it as an actress, but so was watching my bank account dwindle to nothing.

When I got home, my mother was vacuuming the carpet in my bedroom.

"Gee, maybe you should take the job I just applied for," I said.

"What job is that?" she asked.

"A job at a snooty retail shop in Brentwood. One of my tasks will be vacuuming."

"Speaking of that," said my mother after shutting off my Hoover, "they don't make vacuum cleaners like they used to. The suction isn't there. You have to keep going over the same spot until you finally catch all the dirt, which is terrible for your posture and a major strain on your back. I–"

"Isn't it lunch time?" I said, finding this latest speech excruciatingly numbing and, therefore, eager to silence it, silence her. "Maybe you'd like to run home and fix yourself something. You know how you hate to skip meals."

"Why don't I fix us both something," she said, thwarting my plan. I had hoped to crack open a jar of peanut butter, stick my finger in it, and curl up in front of *Days* so I could watch Maura's expertise in action—alone. "How does tuna on whole wheat sound? Remember how you used to love my tuna fish sandwiches, Stacey?"

Yeah, when I was four. "That would be great, Mom. Thanks."

I set the table while she puttered around in the kitchen. She had just started scooping the tuna out of the can, into a bowl, when she shrieked. Totally went berserk. Figuring she must have cut herself using the opener, I hustled over, prepared to wrap her finger in a napkin or hold her hand under cold water or call 911 if I couldn't stop the bleeding, when I saw that she was perfectly intact.

"What's the matter?" I said.

"This!" She pointed downward, into the bowl, as if there were a giant tarantula crawling around in it.

"What?" I said again, not seeing anything but chunks of Fin's premium solid white albacore in water.

"There's a bone!"

I peered into the bowl and sure enough there *was* a bone—a long skinny fish bone that had no business being in anyone's tuna sandwich. "Wow. I'm glad neither of us choked on that."

She gathered herself up to her full height and waved her fist in the air. "We will never have a bone in our tuna fish again, not if it's up to *me*." She said this as if she were a political candidate giving a stump speech promising reforms in education, taxes, and gun control. "I am appalled—absolutely incensed—that a reputable company like Fin's Premium Tuna could be so lax in their quality control that they'd allow *this* to happen. Get me some Scotch tape, Stacey."

Okay, I wasn't exactly pleased to find a bone in the food I was about to eat, but Scotch tape wasn't the first thing I thought of as a solution. "Why do you want the tape?"

"Just get it, dear."

I found the tape and brought it to her. By this time, she had separated the bone from the tuna fish, rinsed it off in the sink, and dried it with a paper towel. "What are you planning to do with it?" I said. "Have it made into a necklace?"

"No, Miss Fresh Mouth. I'm going to tape it to my stationery–as evidence–and then I'm going to write Fin's one of my complaint letters, demanding an apology for nearly killing us. They'll be sorry they ever dealt with Helen Reiser, I guarantee you."

My mother picked through the rest of the tuna, to make sure it was safe for us, then added some mayo and a little seasoning to the bowl, and threw a couple of sandwiches together. While we ate, she continued to rant about our near-fatal accident.

"In the blink of an eye, our lives could have been taken from us," she stewed.

What neither of us realized–how could we?–was that in the blink of an eye, our lives *would* be taken from us. Our lives as we knew them, that is.

# Chapter Seven

★

"Miss! Uh, *miss!*"

It was my third week of employment at Cornucopia!, and it was a wonder I was still showing up at the joint, given how insistent—okay, obnoxious—the customers were.

"Miss! Hel-*lo!*"

As an example, why was this person yelling at me when I was clearly working at the computer, ringing up a sale for my previous customer—a customer who had just bought a four-hundred-dollar picture frame, imported from Scotland and handpainted with colorful golf balls on it? The frame, by the way, was a gift for her husband's fifty-first birthday. Oh, and she was, at most, twenty-five. Not that there's anything wrong with that.

"Miss! What are you, deaf?"

I wheeled around to face the woman who was banging on the counter, seemingly oblivious to the fact that I was busy. She was a blonde wearing a black leather bomber jacket and carrying a canvas tote that read "Breathe deeply and let it go."

"I'll be with you in a minute," I told her. "I'm finishing up with another customer."

"But I'm in a *major* hurry," she said. "I'm double-parked and my kids are in the car and I have to buy a birthday present for my daughter's friend Lily. I need an outfit for the girl. And I need it, like, *right away.*"

Wow. A fashion emergency, I thought, wondering why it doesn't track with some people that they're not the center of the universe. "Just give me a few seconds and I'll be glad to help you," I said.

The woman huffed but stayed put until I finished my transaction.

"Now," I said as I walked her over to Cornucopia!'s children's department. "How old is your daughter's friend Lily?"

"Six."

"Okay. What about this dress?" I took a pretty silk frock off the display. "It's from France and it's adorable, don't you think?" It should be. It cost more than any of my dresses.

"No. Too girly."

"Isn't Lily a girl?"

"Yeah, but I'm looking for something hot, something hip, something that says to me 'trendy designer.' How about the one over there?"

She pointed to an outfit that was more of a costume than an appropriate article of clothing for a child. It was a leopard-skin jumpsuit with a black leather belt, and what it said to me was "JonBenet Ramsey."

"Do you like it?" I asked, wondering how anyone could.

"It's great. Fine. Wrap it as a gift."

She shoved her American Express platinum card into my hand and took off for the glass cabinet in which the store's china and silver pill boxes were displayed. I speculated about what sort of pills she might be taking and whether she'd forgotten to take them that day.

*   *   *

On the home front, my mother had composed her complaint letter to Fin's Premium Tuna and mailed it to their corporate headquarters in San Pedro, about a half hour south of L.A., depending on traffic. Apparently, Fin's was the only big tuna company with its office and canning plant still in the southern California harbor, the others—Star-Kist, Bumble Bee, and Chicken of the Sea—having defected to foreign ports.

"I'm telling you right now, Stacey, I'd better get a response from those people," said my mother. "I don't intend to be dismissed as just another cranky consumer."

"You're hard to dismiss, Mom. At the very least, they'll write you back to apologize."

I was right about the "at the very least." A mere two weeks after my mother sent her missive to Fin's, she received a letter from the company's public relations director, not only apologizing for the bone and assuring her it was not the norm to find anything other than pure premium tuna inside a can of Fin's, but inviting her to stop by the cannery, observe the canning process for herself, and see firsthand how deeply committed Fin's is to providing consumers with the best quality control in the industry.

"Well, that was nice of them," I remarked after my mother read me the letter. "Do you feel vindicated?"

"Not yet," she said. "Not until I get a look at that cannery and find out what goes on there."

I laughed. I honestly thought she was joking. "You're not really going to San Pedro, Mom. Tell me you're not."

"Of course, I'm going. I was invited."

"Mom." I sighed. "They didn't mean for you to make a special trip down there. They were just blowing you off in a very smart way from a PR standpoint. They want you to keep buying their product and quit badmouthing them to other people, so they said, 'Sure, come on by when you're in the neighborhood.' You can't take any of that stuff seriously."

"And since when did you become such a cynic? Is this what show business has done to my little girl? Turned her into a person who scoffs at everything?"

Did I scoff at everything? Had show business turned me into a cynic? Had all the posturing and pretending and jockeying for position taken away my ability to trust? To believe that there really were people who cared if you almost choked on their tuna fish bone?

Nah.

"I'm not a cynic," I said. "I just think you should be glad you got your letter from Fin's and leave it at that. Buy Star-Kist from now on, if it'll make you feel better."

"I'm going down to their plant and getting a look at their operation," said my mother, sounding like a five-star general. "If they're just 'blowing me off' as you suggest, a visit from me will catch their attention."

I couldn't talk her out of it. In a way, I didn't want to. The more involved she became with Fin's and their quality control, the less involved she'd be with me, I figured. And wasn't that what I'd been praying for? That she would get a life of her own?

"Of course, since I'm new to southern California," she went on, "I don't even know where San Pedro is. Would it be too much to ask that you go there with me, Stacey? You could drive and I could read the directions out loud, and we could stop for lunch somewhere, just the two of us. It might be fun, don't you think?"

No, I don't think. "I'd like to, Mom, but I've got to work."

"You couldn't skip a day at that store when your own mother needs you?"

"Well, it's not only the store. I've got my auditions."

"You could miss one of those, couldn't you? Just this once? Just for your old mom?" She said this not in her five-star-general voice but in her five-year-old-child voice, the voice that made the guilt kick in. "Besides, a day away from all those show business types would be good for you, a nice change. So listen to your mother and come with me."

"All right, I'll come with you," I said, because I knew she'd wear me down eventually, so why not knuckle under early.

She smiled. "You won't regret it, dear. You'll see."

She was incorrect. As *you'll* see.

On a bright and sunny Monday morning, we waited out the rush hour traffic on the 405 and headed down to San Pedro at about 10:00 A.M. It was actually a more scenic drive than I'd anticipated, sailing over the Vincent Thomas Bridge to Terminal Island, the Port of Los Angeles and the hundreds of ships docked there in full view from the car. If it weren't for my mother's endless rants about her sunglasses that kept sliding down the bridge of her nose and the garbage truck that woke her up at five o'clock that morning and the call she'd gotten from Cleveland from her friend Rosalyn, inviting her to her daughter's wedding ("God forbid my own daughter should be having a wedding."), it wouldn't have been a torturous trip.

"This is kind of cool," I remarked as we wound our way from Ferry Street to Terminal Way to streets with names like Tuna and Albacore and Barracuda—all home at one time to the various tuna companies. When we arrived at Fin's on Cannery Street, we parked in their lot and walked to the front of what was an enormous, cavernous building.

"What's the plan here?" I said. "You don't have an appointment, right? You're just planning to breeze in and announce yourself and hope they'll remember your letter to them?"

She tapped her handbag. "I brought their letter with me. I'll show it to the receptionist and she'll see to it that we get the tour I was promised. If she doesn't, I'll have to go over her head."

I nodded, pitying the poor receptionist.

"Hello," my mother said to her. She was about my age and had a hairlip. "I've been summoned by your director of public relations, a gentleman named Mr. Corbin Beasley, to come here and inspect your plant."

The receptionist gave my mother a quizzical look. "Summoned?"

"That's correct. It's all in this letter." She reached into her handbag and handed the letter over to the receptionist, who read it without enthusiasm, as if she'd seen such letters before. They were probably boilerplate responses to consumers with complaints. Just as probably, my mother was the first recipient to ever follow up on one.

"So you don't have an appointment with Mr. Beasley." This was more of a statement of fact than a question.

"No, but I assume he'll make time for me. I'm one of the Fin's consumers about whom he's supposed to care so deeply."

"It's not that he doesn't care, Mrs.–"

"Reiser. Helen Reiser. My daughter and I have driven almost forty-five minutes to come here this morning. We have no intention of leaving until we're given a tour of your operation. Understood?"

Again, I felt sorry for the receptionist. She was no match for my mother, who, although not as rude as the customers as Cornucopia!, was just as pushy.

"The thing is, he's in the conference room with the advertising agency this morning," she explained. "It's an important meeting and all the executives are in there."

"So? They have phones in conference rooms, don't they?" said my mother. "Call him and tell him that Helen Reiser has arrived for her tour. Oh, and be sure to add that I'm the one who nearly choked to death on the bone I found in my can of Fin's premium solid white albacore a few weeks ago and that if he doesn't give me the tour and prove to me that the quality control here really is up to snuff, I intend to take my case to the Better Business Bureau, not to mention *Dateline*."

The receptionist turned pale–green, to be really accurate–and picked up the phone and dialed. She had discovered what I had known since I was a child: my mother wasn't to be messed with.

"There's a woman here to see Mr. Beasley," she said to the person who picked up the phone. An underling, no doubt. "She claims she found a bone in one of our products and nearly died from it."

"Not 'claims,'" said my mother, leaning across the receptionist's desk so she could make her point clear. "'Did.' I *did* find a bone in my tuna fish and Mr. Beasley did tell me it was an aberration; that the quality control at Fin's is top-notch. I'm here to see if he was being truthful and if not, I'll have to inform the public."

We waited a few seconds, during which I considered slipping off to their ladies' room and disappearing down the sink. Eventually, the receptionist said, "Mr. Beasley will be right with you."

My mother beamed as she nudged me with her elbow. "You see that, Stacey?" she whispered as we sat in the nearby visitors' chairs. "You speak up, you get somewhere."

She was about to get somewhere, all right. Just not where she expected.

# Chapter
# Eight

★

AFTER A TEN-MINUTE WAIT, during which my mother and I
sat in the small lobby leafing through uninvolving trade jour-
nals having to do with the canned goods industry, Corbin Beasley,
public relations director of Fin's, emerged.

"Welcome, Mrs. Reiser," he said, extending his hand toward my
mother's. The extension, by the way, was no small matter, as Corbin, a thirtysomething with a geeky grin, was easily six foot six to
my mother's five foot two. "Great to meet you. It's always a delight
to relate to our customers on a face-to-face, one-to-one basis."

"Thank you," she said briskly, indicating she had come for the
inspection, not for the pleasantries. "This is my daughter, Stacey. It
was her can of Fin's that contained the bone, as a matter of fact. If
I hadn't been at her apartment that day, she could have been the
one to choke and die."

Corbin smiled inappropriately, exposing jack-o-lantern teeth. "I'm
terribly sorry you were alarmed," he said to both of us. "But I'm
here to assure you that, while bones do find their way inside the

cans on occasion, your experience is not the usual course of events here at Fin's. Not by any means."

"Then what is?" said my mother.

"What's what?" said Corbin.

"The usual course of events here at Fin's. That's what I came here to investigate. I'm not one for frivolity so why don't we get started?"

"With?"

"The tour. The inspection. The step-by-step look-see. In your letter you invited me to pay you a visit and check out your quality control. Since you're such a busy man, let's get on with it already."

Clearly, Corbin had been under the illusion that he could pop out of his meeting with the advertising people, shake my mother's hand, do a little bowing and scraping, and send her on her merry way. Wrong.

"I expect the grand tour—start to finish, stem to stern, A to Z," she said, running out of clichés, mercifully. "I want to observe the entire process."

Corbin checked his watch. "I do have to get back to my meeting," he said, "but I'd be privileged to give you a quick tour of the facilities. Follow me."

We followed Corbin through the lobby door, down a carpeted hall, and into his cushy office where he handed us two construction worker-type hard hats and asked us to put them on. "Everybody touring the cannery has to wear one," he said. "It's a safety regulation."

"I approve wholeheartedly," said my mother, donning her hard hat. "Safety first."

I was less enthusiastic. I was anticipating a bad case of helmet hair.

Our field trip took us outside the executive offices, across a parking lot, and out to a marina, where several large boats were being unloaded in the water.

"These just came in," said Corbin, pointing to the recently docked boats. "They come in every day, all day, filled with catches from local waters as well as elsewhere in the Pacific. The fish are frozen at twenty-seven degrees Fahrenheit as soon as they're caught, then they're brought to us in storage containers."

"How does Fin's know the fish on these ships is any good?" asked my mother. "You hear stories. My friend Esther ate at one of the best seafood restaurants in Cleveland–she had grilled swordfish, if memory serves. Anyhow, she got so sick she couldn't look at fish ever again. She won't even touch scrod now, poor soul."

Corbin tried to seem empathetic. "At Fin's we're very mindful of possible spoilage, and we take great pains to prevent it."

"Name one great pain that you take," challenged my mother.

"Well, we cut samples from eight fish out of every load, and these eight samples go straight to our lab, which I'll show you later if you like. Our technicians test the samples for the histamine levels in the fish, which tell us if there's been spoilage from high temperature. Then they do another test to determine the acid content in the fish, in case there's been spoilage from low temperature. And finally they test the percentage of salt in the fish, which should be in the one-point-five to one-point-seven range. If any of the test results look the least bit suspicious, we throw the entire shipment of fish out."

"Good riddance," I said. I was bored silly, but thought I should interject a remark now and then, so they'd know I was breathing. My mother, on the other hand, was fascinated by every morsel of trivia Corbin threw at her.

"All right, ladies, let's move ahead to the thawing facility," he said, leading us over to an area where rows and rows of containers held tuna–big tuna, medium tuna, small tuna, blue fin tuna, yellow fin tuna, More tuna than you'd ever want to deal with. They were stiff–dead-body stiff–and were waiting to be thawed. "See how that one's eyes are clear, not cloudy?" Corbin had selected a rather colorful fish for his show-and-tell and was running his fingers all over it. "And see how the skin is shiny and firm, not mushy to the touch?"

My mother leaned over and fondled the fish herself. "I do see," she acknowledged.

I should add here that the smell of fish was as omnipresent as it was vile. There was no question that I would have to burn the clothes I was wearing, especially the shoes, which were covered in *jus de* fish guts.

"The fish will be thawed over here," said Corbin, moving into an area with giant hoses everywhere, along with more containers of frozen tuna. "They'll be soaked in water for five hours until the backbone temperature is thirty-five degrees. Then, our people will remove the entrails and cut the fish into chunks and cook them at two hundred and fifty degrees for forty-five minutes to four hours, depending on the size of the fish."

While I attempted to keep my breakfast down, Corbin walked us into yet another area. "I call this the London Fog room," he said, gesturing into the air, which was fetid with steam haze and foul with fish fumes. "It's sixty degrees in here and a hundred percent humidity, so the fish can cool down enough for the skin to be cut off easily."

"And then what happens?" asked my mother. "Because I have a feeling we're getting to the crucial stages of the process."

Corbin concurred. "I'm about to take you into what is essentially our mission control." He laughed. Even he knew how stupid this exercise was.

He escorted us into a warehouse-type space where there were hundreds of women with plastic caps on their heads and plastic aprons over their clothes and small instruments that looked like carrot peelers in their fast-moving hands. They stood shoulder to shoulder—as close together as sardines in a can (sorry, but I've got smelly fish on the brain)—at a conveyor belt that ran the length of the room.

"Look how hard they work," my mother marveled as we passed by the women, who were chattering amongst themselves in Spanish. As I had studied the language in both high school and college and become even more proficient in it after moving to Latino-populated L.A., I understood what they were saying. ("My back is sore." "My car needs new tires." "My husband sings in the shower, like he thinks he's Ricky Martin." Nothing of consequence, in other words.)

"They do work hard," said Corbin. "They're the core of our operation, the heart and soul. They skin and bone the fish—by hand, hour after hour, day after day—and place the cleaned product onto the conveyor, which carries the fish down to the canning area. Then the fish is put into the cans, either with our vegetable broth or in oil, and steam heated in an oven to kill any possible bacteria."

"Very responsible," my mother mused. "About killing the bacteria, I mean." She leaned over and spoke to one of the women, who was, at that moment, cutting the bones out of a tuna. "How do you know you've gotten them all?"

"Excuse?" said the woman.

"I'm talking about the *bones*," yelled my mother, as if the woman were hard of hearing, not foreign in extraction. "How do you know if you've taken them all out?"

"Ah, bones," said the woman. "I know because I do for thirty years. When you do for long time, you know how."

"I suppose that's very true," said my mother, thinking, no doubt, of how she had been nagging me for thirty years and that, therefore, she knew how. She and the fish-bone cutter-outer were kindred spirits, that's what they were, and who could have predicted it. "But occasionally, you make mistakes, right? Not on purpose, of course, but a bone *can* slip through, isn't that so?"

"Could get hit by bus, too," said the woman in an utterance of wisdom that provoked a vigorous nod from my mother.

"After the canned fish is steamed, it's cooled," said Corbin, hurrying us along on the tour. "Then the cans are lidded, labeled, and shipped. And that, ladies, is that. End of story."

"Very impressive, I must say," my mother declared. "I don't know what I expected, but it looks as though Fin's has its act together."

Corbin seemed greatly relieved. Perhaps he'd taken my mother's *Dateline* threat seriously.

"What would completely restore my confidence in Fin's, however," she went on, "would be to get a sense of the chief executive here, the man or woman in charge of the company, the person who sets the tone when it comes to quality control. I'd like to meet with him or her while I'm here, Mr. Beasley. Just for a few minutes."

"I'm sorry, but he's with our advertising agency this morning," he said. "He's in the same meeting that I should be getting back to. So I'm afraid—"

"But *you* were able to take time out from the meeting," she interrupted. "I'm only asking for a moment or two with the president of Fin's, to ask him a few questions. My daughter and I did nearly die, Mr. Beasley. And it was your company that would certainly have been liable."

God, she was a battle-ax. Why wasn't I even more screwed up than I was, I wondered, growing up with a mother who demanded audiences with presidents of tuna fish companies?

Corbin sighed. "Let me see what I can do." He left us back in the lobby with the receptionist while he went off to either find the president or pretend to. We waited.

"Why don't we just go?" I suggested at one point. "They were nice enough to show us around. Isn't that enough?"

"Stacey, there's something you don't understand, dear."

There was a lot I didn't understand. Like why I was in a tuna cannery in San Pedro instead of on the set of my own TV series in Hollywood.

"I'm not doing this for myself," my mother continued. "I'm here to represent all the little people, the people who are too frightened or sick or busy to rise up and complain about their consumer goods. I'm staying for them. I want to make sure that they don't get bones in their tuna fish. I want them to feel safe when they go to their pantries to make lunch."

"A noble, noble cause," I said, wishing there were a video of this. I could have sent it to one of those funniest bloopers shows and given my mother's "little people" a very big laugh.

Just then, Corbin reappeared, breathless with news. "Mr. Terwilliger, the president of Fin's, will see you, ladies. But his time really is limited today, so I'll have to insist that your visit be a short one—about five minutes, tops."

"Five minutes is all I'll need with him," she told Corbin, squaring her shoulders and winking at me. "I'll state my case and you can all get back to business."

"Then follow me," said Corbin, taking us to his leader.

# Chapter
# Nine

★

WE HAD EXPECTED to be shown into Mr. Terwilliger's office for our brief meeting, but we were ushered, instead, into the executive conference room.

"Wait. Isn't there some big powwow going on in here with your advertising agency?" I asked nervously as Corbin was about to open the heavy paneled door. "My mother only wanted to–"

"She wanted to speak to Mr. Terwilliger," he said. "For that to happen, she's going to have to speak to him in front of the little group we've assembled today. He doesn't have time for a private meeting, as I explained."

We walked into the room, where at least a dozen people were gathered around a long rectangular table. I figured that the man at the head of the table, the one with the gray hair and gray suit and gray complexion, was Terwilliger. He was also the one without a pen and legal pad in front of him, which tipped me off that he was the boss, the guy who didn't have to take notes.

"Ladies and gentlemen," said Corbin, getting everyone's attention. "Say hello to Mrs. Helen Reiser and her daughter, uh–"

"Stacey Reiser," I volunteered and gave them my best actress-y smile. I wondered if any of them recognized me, either from the commercials or the TV guest spots or even from *Pet Peeve*. Yup, I decided. That cute guy in the corner knows I'm an actress. I can tell by the way he's looking at me, trying to figure out what he's seen me in and which part I played and whether I'll give him my autograph when the meeting is over. Fame was fun, I had to admit. Even at my level.

"Mrs. Reiser wrote to Fin's a few weeks ago with a complaint about our product," Corbin went on, directing his remarks toward Mr. Terwilliger. "In response, I invited her to tour our cannery and see for herself that we care very much about quality control and that we'd like her to remain a loyal Fin's customer." He turned to my mother. "Mrs. Reiser, why don't you tell Mr. Terwilliger what's on your mind as succinctly as you can, and then we'll let you drive back to Los Angeles with your daughter, all right?"

"All right," said my mother, who, I suddenly realized, had not the slightest trace of performance anxiety, despite the fact that she was about to speak in front of a roomful of strangers. Actors are trained to deal with such anxiety–I had taken several courses in overcoming stage fright–but she neither shook nor sweated nor blinked an inordinate number of times. She was as self-possessed as if she were about to lecture me on the subject of my messy kitchen. "But before I speak, I'd prefer to know to whom I'm speaking. Would those around the table please state their name and position with the company?"

Boy, she had a set of balls, didn't she?

Without missing a beat, each person identified himself, humoring her, I assumed. Among the star attendees of the meeting were Frank Terwilliger, president and CEO of Fin's Premium Tuna; Gregg Hillman, vice president of marketing for Fin's; Louise Cardoza, vice president of product development for Fin's; Peter Sacklin, vice president of Wylie & Wohlers Advertising; Julie Denton, creative supervisor of W&W; Susan Hardaway, W&W's art director; and Larry Franzen, a copywriter at W&W. All professionals in their field. My mother wasn't intimidated by that fact, either.

"Thank you," she said, stepping further into the room and planting herself next to an easel. It held a poster depicting a large can of tuna that appeared to be swimming in a body of water by virtue of its cute little *fins.* "First of all, I want to thank Mr. Beasley for responding so quickly to my letter of complaint." She nodded at Corbin. "But most of all, I want to thank Mr. Terwilliger for allowing me to get a few things off my chest." She nodded at him, too, but she accompanied the nod with actual finger pointing in his direction. He flinched slightly but let her keep talking. "I was visiting my daughter Stacey one afternoon and suggested I prepare us both lunch. I rummaged around in her pantry and found a can of Fin's premium solid white albacore tuna packed in water, the brand our family has always preferred. As I was emptying the tuna into a bowl, prior to adding mayonnaise and other seasonings, I spotted a large bone. That's right, Mr. Terwilliger, a bone. The kind of bone you don't always spot because it blends in with the tuna, color wise. The kind of bone you can swallow accidentally. The kind of bone that can become lodged in your throat and cause you to choke. The kind of bone that can kill you, Mr. Terwilliger." She let her words sink in, for effect, the way she always did with me. "Now, I don't mind telling you I was furious at Fin's, because I trusted your brand, was a loyal customer, stayed with you even though you were the last tuna company to come out with single-serving-size cans. In other words, I *believed* in Fin's and yet *this* is how you reward me? By nearly *killing* me?" I glanced around the table to see if there was eye rolling, snickering, squelching of laughter, but everyone was riveted, apparently. Either that or they were asleep with their eyes open. "However," she went on, "after my tour of the cannery today, after inspecting your operation, after observing the safety and health features you have in place, after watching the women slaving away on that assembly line—those good, decent, hardworking women—I have reached the conclusion that your quality control is what it should be and that the bone I found was an honest mistake and that I can probably make a tuna sandwich for my daughter without fear." She paused again, this time to press her hand to her heart and heave a deep sigh. "Surely, you can understand how mothers strive to protect their children," she said, regrouping, gaining momentum. "It's our God-given impulse. Our biological need. We can't live with the thought that the contents of a can of tuna fish might harm our loved ones. We must have a sense of security when it comes to our food. We must have a sense of confidence in all our consumer products. We must and we should and we will, if *I* have anything to say about it!" She stopped to raise her fist in the air, a Jewish Erin Brockovich. "But the person with the power to fully restore my confidence in Fin's is Mr. Terwilliger. So, I'm going to shut up now and let him have the floor."

There was silence, nothing but dead air for about a second or two. And then, before Mr. Terwilliger could utter a single syllable, the executives at the table applauded loudly, wildly, as if my mother had just delivered the State of the Union Address. One of them—I think it was the ad agency's creative supervisor—even gave her a standing ovation. I was astonished by their reaction, amazed that they would respond positively to her browbeating when I had always responded negatively to it. What in the world was going on here?

"Mrs. Reiser," said Mr. Terwilliger after the applause had died down. He was a thin-lipped man with sunken cheekbones and a dour expression. I had a hunch he wasn't a picnic to work for. "I'm sorry that you were put through such anguish over our product, but

I'm a man who appreciates bluntness and you were blunt here today. I won't promise that there will never be another bone in a can of Fin's premium tuna, but I will promise you that we'll continue to do our best to cut down on the problem. It's customers like you who remind us that we're not just catching fish and canning it and shipping it out to faceless individuals, but that we're providing healthy, nutritious meals to real human beings with real concerns. As a matter of fact, you're exactly the kind of person we're trying to reach with our television advertising. That's what we've been doing here all morning, you know—talking about our advertising. Our agency seems to think our customers are morons, as evidenced by the crap they wanted us to go with today." He glowered at the easel with the poster of the tuna can doing the backstroke. "It's an embarrassment, isn't it? So now that I've rejected it, they've got exactly two weeks to come up with something we won't be ashamed to put on the air." He glowered again, this time at the W&W folks. "Well, this isn't your concern, Mrs. Reiser. *Helen.*" He rose from his chair and shook my mother's hand. Mine, too, although he didn't call me Stacey; he didn't call me anything. "Thanks for stopping by and reading us the riot act. We could all use a little cold water thrown at us from time to time." He turned to Corbin. "See that we send Helen a complimentary case of tuna, would you, Beasley?"

Corbin said he would, then hustled over and escorted us out the door of the conference room. "Wow. You were a big hit," he told my mother during our stroll back toward the lobby of the building. "Mr. Terwilliger doesn't usually dole out parting gifts. He's on the frugal side, just between us."

"We won't tell a soul," I said, dying to get away from this bizarro tuna company and wondering why I consented to be dragged along in the first place.

We were chitchatting with Corbin and giving him my mother's mailing address and inching toward freedom when one of the men from the ad agency sprinted down the hall and rushed over to us.

"Don't go, Mrs. Reiser," he said breathlessly, grabbing her hand and pumping it. "I'm Peter Sacklin, a vice president of Wylie and Wohlers. I'm the W and W executive in charge of the Fin's account and I wonder if you'd mind coming back into the conference room for a few minutes."

My mother's eyes narrowed. "What for?"

"We'd like to talk to you about the television advertising we're doing for Fin's."

"Talk to me? What do I know about that kind of thing? It's my daughter who knows about commercials. Personally, I never watch them—except the ones she's in, of course."

Peter Sacklin gave me a puzzled look, as if trying to figure out what she could have meant. Obviously, he'd missed me as the Irish Spring Lady, the Taco Bell Lady, etc.

"If you'd just give us a few more minutes of your time, Mrs. Reiser," he said, "we'll explain everything."

My mother shrugged in resignation. "Sure. Why not? I've got nothing else to do today."

Peter Sacklin smiled, took her arm in what I thought was a rather courtly gesture, and walked her back toward the conference room. I, meanwhile, was left standing there with Corbin Beasley, feeling like I'd been turned down for parole.

"Are we supposed to go with them?" I asked.

"We could," he said. "I'm curious about what they plan to talk to your mother about, aren't you?"

Was I curious? A little. I just figured that since Terwilliger appreciated my mother's bluntness, he wanted her blunt opinion of the agency's ideas. Mostly, I was just glad *I* wasn't the recipient of her bluntness for a change.

\* \* \*

Corbin and I followed them back into the conference room, pulled up a couple of chairs, and listened.

"Sorry this is so impromptu," Peter Sacklin was saying to my mother, who had been given a prominent position at the head of the table, to Mr. Terwilliger's right. "Obviously, we haven't had time to prepare a storyboard, let alone a script. But as you heard before, Mrs. Reiser, our client has rejected our latest TV ad campaign and our backs are against the wall here. We need to go on the air with something dynamite and soon–something that will gain market share for Fin's, something that will really grab the public. Star-Kist has Charlie the Tuna. Chicken of the Sea has the mermaid. And Bumble Bee has the bumblebee. What we want–what we need–is for Fin's to have you, Mrs. Reiser. Just you, talking to the camera in the same tough, no-nonsense manner that you used with us."

I bolted up in my chair, felt my stomach tighten, felt my eyes bug out of my head. They wanted my mother to star in their commercial? My mother, who didn't have a nanosecond of experience as an actress? My mother, who was, well, my mother?

Ridiculous, I scoffed. She'll never do it. She hates show business and everything remotely related to it. They'll have to hire some other complaining consumer as their pitchwoman.

"I'm very flattered," my mother responded, "but I can't imagine why you'd put me, an ordinary woman in her sixties with the crow's feet to prove it, on TV. Not when you could get a young one like Heather Locklear."

Everyone laughed. Everyone except me. Why didn't she say, *Not when you could get a young one like my daughter Stacey?* Did she suddenly develop a brain cramp and forget that I did commercials for a living? Did it slip her mind that I was in a goddamn Jim Carrey movie? Did she go nutso during the tour of the cannery–someplace between the fog room with the 100 percent humidity and the thawing room with the smelly fish fumes?

"The reason we want you, Mrs. Reiser," W&W's creative supervisor piped up, "is because you're so credible, so *real.* When you tell the public about Fin's, they'll listen. They'll listen and they'll buy."

"Exactly right," said Terwilliger, the big cheese. "You have that bluntness we discussed earlier, Helen—a directness that translates into trustworthiness. If you say Fin's is the best tuna, everyone will believe you."

My mother tapped his arm. "But I found a bone in my can of Fin's," she reminded him. "That's why I came here in the first place—to complain about your tuna. Now that I've seen your operation and met your employees, I understand that mistakes happen every now and then, but it doesn't mean I would I go on television and endorse your product. I have no intention of lying to the viewers. A bone is still a bone."

"We don't want you to lie," said W&W's copywriter. "Just the opposite. What we're playing with at the moment is a problem-solution type of ad. You state the problem, which is that you found a bone in your Fin's tuna, and then you explain the solution, which is that you visited the cannery and were so impressed with what you saw that you agreed to work for Fin's, to be the public's eyes and ears within the company, to make sure that those mothers you talked to us about—the mothers who need to feel secure about the foods they feed their loved ones—will never have to worry when they open a can of Fin's premium tuna." He leaned back in his chair and grinned. "I don't know about everybody else in this room, but I think we've got an award-winning commercial on the drawing board. I think we're looking at making Helen Reiser the next Clara 'Where's the Beef?' Peller."

There was nodding all around. I, however, was incapable of nodding. My neck was rigid with tension as I flashed back on Clara

Peller, the woman in the old Wendy's hamburger commercials, the one who became an overnight sensation simply by acting crabby. I was stunned by the possibility that my own mother might become an overnight sensation, too, absolutely undone by this odd turn of events.

"But you see," she said to her new best friends, "I don't care for show business, never have. I can't imagine myself standing in front of a camera with a puss full of makeup."

"Try to focus on the numbers of consumers you'd be reaching," said the account executive. "We're talking millions of people here, Mrs. Reiser. How empowering would that be for you to be able to speak directly *to* them and *for* them? You'd be a consumer watchdog for an entire population of mothers just like yourself."

That seemed to clinch it, that reference to empowerment. I could tell by my mother's body language. She lifted her head at the sound of the word, tilted it up, rested her elbows on the conference table as if she were suddenly Somebody.

"You'd be great, Helen, really great," Terwilliger added. "Please say you'll do this. For our employees on the assembly line, those hardworking ladies you mentioned. And, of course, for the mothers out there, the ones you stand for so articulately and valiantly."

"Oh, *Frank*," she said. They were on a first-name basis now? "For years I've been sending out my complaint letters, hoping to create a better world in my own modest way. I suppose it *would* be nice to have a larger platform, to be able to reach so many people at once through the medium of television, to have my opinion matter for a change."

*To have my opinion matter for a change.* That was a dig at me, obviously, because I'd ignored her advice for so many years. But was she actually saying yes to them? Accepting their offer? Agreeing to star in a national TV commercial? Maybe a series of national TV commercials?

"Sounds like we've got a new ad campaign," said Terwilliger, a big smile on his face as he offered his hand to my mother and helped her rise from her chair. "I, for one, couldn't be more pleased. How about you, Helen?"

She beamed right back at him, and pledged that she would take her role seriously and work as hard for Fin's as the women who cut the bones out of the fish.

"Here's to Helen," the creative supervisor shouted, as the rest of them cheered and clapped.

I continued to sit there as if I'd been hit by a truck. Who would have believed this? I asked myself. How had a trip to a tuna fish cannery evolved into a life-altering experience for my mother (and, by extension, for me)? And why wasn't I happier about it? After all, I'd been urging her to get a job, volunteer, do anything other than pester me day and night. And now she'd gotten a job–a great job, as a matter of fact–so what was my problem? What kind of a daughter was I that I wasn't jumping for joy on this day that had turned out so serendipitously for her? Why wasn't I thrilled, the way you're supposed to be when something fabulous happens to someone else, especially to someone you love?

Okay, I knew damn well why. My mother was starring in a television commercial that I wasn't even asked to audition for and I was jealous. Yeah, jealous of the woman who gave birth to me. It's embarrassing to admit, but it was true. *I* was the actress in the family. *I* was the one who should have been hired. *I* was the one who had trained and paid my dues and earned the right to appear on television sets across the country, and yet *she* was the one they wanted.

Couldn't she have gone out for the senior women's golf circuit? Couldn't she have gotten involved in saving the whales? Couldn't she have written one of those books of helpful hints? Did the arena she decided to enter have to be *my* arena, for God's sake?

If there was fairness on this earth, I failed to see it.

# Chapter
# Ten

★

OH, COME ON, Stacey. So it's one measly thirty-second commercial that nobody will ever see," said Maura, after I called to tell her the news. "It's not as if tuna fish companies advertise on the Super Bowl. They don't have huge budgets like Coke and Pepsi."

"I realize that," I said. "It's just a weird feeling having my mother vaulting into *my* profession. It's as if we're in competition all of a sudden."

"Not really. She'll do the commercial for Fin's and that'll be the end of it, while you'll go on to have the acting career you always dreamed of. And remember that you asked for this, Stacey. You kept saying, 'If only she'd find something other than me to occupy her every waking moment.' Well, now she's found that something. You're getting exactly what you wanted, so be gracious about it, huh?"

Maura was right. I should be gracious about it. I *was* gracious about it. I was so gracious about it that I called my mother a few days after the trip to the cannery and offered to take her to meet my agent, Mickey Offerman. She would need representation, I figured, someone to deal with the financial side of things. She was a novice in the business, and I would do her a favor and show her the ropes.

"I already have an agent, dear," she trilled after I'd made the overture. "Peter at the ad agency set me up with Arnold Richter."

I was speechless. Arnold Richter was the hottest agent in town. I couldn't have gotten a meeting with him if I'd chained myself to his desk.

"Arnold's a lovely man," she went on. "He told me he's very close to his mother."

Like he even had a mother. Agents like Arnold Richter were too consumed with dealmaking to have mothers.

"He's got quite a reputation as a slick talker," I warned, trying to be protective of her. "If you want me to, I'll come with you the next time you meet with him."

"Oh, not to worry," she said breezily. "I've got a great manager now, Karen Latham. She'll check over everything Arnold does. She handles the actor who plays Joe Isuzu, so she's very familiar with the kind of work I'll be doing."

"Okay, fine. Then you don't need my help at all."

Sheesh, another conflict of emotions. On one hand, I was relieved that she was being taken care of. On the other, I was hurt—well, not hurt, exactly, but definitely a little put out—that she hadn't come to me for advice. Now that I thought about it, she hadn't called me since the trip to the cannery, hadn't stopped by my apartment, hadn't bossed me around. Hallelujah. Sort of.

"What's the next step with the commercial?" I asked, swallowing the odd little lump in my throat. "When are they shooting it?"

"Peter said it should take about two weeks for the agency to do the storyboard and then maybe another few days for Fin's to approve it, and then the storyboard goes out for bids to different production companies and then away we go. I think I'll be on the air in six weeks, because they're not flying me to some exotic location for the shoot. They're just sticking me at a kitchen table and letting me speak my piece."

"Very exciting, Mom," I said, forcing the words out. "Very, very exciting." I *was* excited for her. Excited and nauseous.

"What's new with you, dear?" she asked. "Anything percolating?"

"Not right this second." Not right this eternity. While Mom was gearing up for her big break, I was sliding further into obscurity. Mickey hadn't sent me on an audition in days, so I'd been putting in extra time at Cornucopia!, which padded my bank account a bit but did nothing for my morale. It was hard to be chipper when those Brentwood babes sashayed into the store and hit you with: "Can you watch my kid while I drop a thousand dollars on a set of dishes?" I mean, was I supposed To sell merchandise and iron linens and vacuum carpet *and* be a day-care worker?

My absolute nadir at Cornucopia! came a few weeks after my mother's hiring as Fin's' pitchwoman. Cameron, the owner, had just given the sales staff a refresher lecture about how we must never, under any circumstances, make reference to a celebrity customer's movies or TV shows, in order that all the celebrities who frequented the store would feel comfortable, anonymous, under no obligation to be "on." This lecture had been triggered by Arnold Schwarzenegger's appearance in the store the previous day and the fact that Sarah, a part-timer like me, had fawned over him to the point of being pathological, and he'd fled without making a single purchase. "Treat them with courtesy, but allow them their space," Cameron admonished us after explaining that Sarah had been fired. "Either that or find another job."

So there I was, ears still ringing with Cameron's threat, when who walked in, on the arm of a fetching redhead, but Jack Rawlins, God's gift to film criticism—the little shit who'd labeled me Sledgehammer Stacey. He was his tweedy, oh-so-smug self, moving among the merchandise as if the very notion of commerce were beneath him. "Who would ever buy this?" I overheard him say to his lady friend, referring to a desk clock that provided the time on three continents. I wasn't sure I disagreed about the clock, especially not at the outrageous price Cornucopia! wanted for it, but it was his attitude that was unbearable, the same attitude that had ruined my career.

"Stacey, go over and see if they need any help," whispered Cameron, nodding at our illustrious customer and his gal. "And remember: no mention of his television show."

"Couldn't someone else help him?" I pleaded. "I was just about to take my lunch break." Not mention his television show? It was all I could do not to grab him by the lapels and tell him what I thought of it–and him.

"Take your lunch break after you help him," she said. "Everyone else on the floor is busy."

Fine. Great. Done. I took a deep breath, fluffed my hair, smoothed my sweater, and strode over to the darling couple.

"Is there anything I can help you with or are you just looking today?" I asked, glaring at Jack Rawlins, daring him to remember me from *Pet Peeve*, daring him to atone for his Sin.

"We're just looking," said the redhead, fondling a five-hundred-dollar chenille throw.

"How about you?" I said to Rawlins. "Are you just looking, too? Because we have a beautiful pair of sterling silver nose-hair clippers."

Okay, so we didn't carry sterling silver nose-hair clippers. I couldn't resist baiting him, saying something that would get a rise out of him.

He looked at me for a long second or two, as if genuinely trying to place me. When he couldn't, he said with a smirk, "I'm not in the market for the nose-hair clippers, but have you got any sterling silver nipple rings?"

"Jack!" The redhead pretended to be shocked by him and tousled his hair, as if he were a bad little boy. She turned to me. "He's got a wicked sense of humor. Don't mind him."

"Oh, but I do mind him," I said, because I couldn't stop myself. "Excuse me?" she said.

"I meant, I do mind that I can't come up with the right item for him."

Rawlins lowered his tortoiseshell eyeglasses so he could see me better. "The right item for me? What might that be, do you think?"

"Well," I said, as the redhead wandered off. "What about a letter opener? You get mail, don't you?" Hate mail, probably.

"I do," he said, "but my assistant takes care of it."

"Ah, then I should come up with something more personal," I said. "What about a mirror?" Or is it too hard for you to look in the mirror after you rip peoples' reputations to shreds?

"Nope. A mirror isn't on my shopping list today," he said. "But you're extremely enterprising. Has anyone ever told you that?"

"No, but someone once said I had the subtlety of a sledgehammer." I let the words hang there, just to see if there would be a glimmer of recognition. There wasn't.

"Whoever said that must not have understood the demands of your job."

"He didn't."

"Well, then to hell with him."

"My sentiments exactly."

At that moment, the redhead returned and indicated that she hadn't found anything she wanted to purchase but was ravenously hungry. "How about the sushi place down the street?" she suggested to Jack.

"They're doing construction," he said. "I think they're closed."

"Speaking of construction," I said, insinuating myself into their conversation but focusing my gaze exclusively on him. "You know how that obnoxious person told me I had the subtlety of a sledge-hammer?"

Jack nodded absentmindedly.

"He also told me that I should think about going into the construction business. He said—well, why don't I give you his direct quote—'Stacey Reiser uses her precious few moments of screen time to pound us over the head with her lines. She has the subtlety of a sledgehammer and should consider applying for a job in construction.' I'll bet *you'd* never say anything as insensitive as that, would you?"

"What on earth is she talking about?" mused the redhead.

It took a few beats, but the remark finally registered with Jack Rawlins. I could see it on his face, which dropped the ha-ha-ha expression he'd worn during our banter and went serious. Yeah, he remembered me now. And he was ashamed. Or, if not ashamed, then a tiny bit chastened. It's one thing to trash people from behind the safety of a camera; it's another to have one of the trashees confront you face-to-face.

"Jack, I'm starving," whined the redhead, as she tugged on his sleeve. "Can't we *go?*"

He continued to look at me, trying, I think, to formulate a response—perhaps even an apology—but in the end he said nothing and slunk out of the store.

Way to go, Stacey, I complimented myself, loving that I had thrown the jerk's malicious review right back at him without ever violating Cameron's edict. I'd never so much as mentioned Jack's stupid television show or even that I was aware that he hosted one.

Feeling in control of my life for the first time in months, I actually whistled as I walked into the stockroom to grab my sandwich out of the refrigerator.

"Stacey, I noticed that Jack Rawlins didn't buy anything the whole time he was in here," said Cameron, who was chomping on a baby spinach leaf. "Tell me you didn't embarrass yourself with him, not after I just explained my policy toward our celebrity customers."

I was dying to tell her that the piece of spinach between her teeth was a bigger turnoff to her celebrity customers than asking them for an autograph, but I decided against it. "I didn't embarrass myself with Jack Rawlins," I said instead. "As a matter of fact, Cameron, I gave Mr. Rawlins the treatment he richly deserved."

# Chapter
# Eleven

★

THE NIGHT BEFORE the Fin's commercial was scheduled to be shot, I called my mother and asked, for the third time that week, if she wanted me to drive her to the studio.

"I know how nervous you are about the freeways here," I said.

"That's sweet of you, dear," she said, "but, as I've already told you, the agency is sending a car and driver to pick me up."

"Right," I said. "But why don't I come along for moral support? This is the first time you'll be acting in a commercial and, let me tell you from experience, your stomach will be tied up in knots. I remember the first time I shot—"

"Both my agent and my manager will be there, remember?" She cut me off, the way I used to cut her off. "And the agency people have promised me they'll do everything they can to provide me with a safe environment, so I can get in touch with my creativity. Besides, they explained how I can use my fear to tap into my inner realness."

I held the phone away from my ear and stared at it. Was this *my* mother speaking? Safe environment? Creativity? Inner realness?

I mean, sure, okay. The acting thing was a novelty for her, and it was only natural that she'd start parroting the way everyone in the business talked. But to not want me along on her very first shoot? Perhaps she didn't understand how daunting it is to have a director fire commands at you—where you should stand and how you should move and, most crucially, how you should deliver your lines. Perhaps she didn't understand that lecturing a bunch of suits in a conference room is a far cry from performing in front of a camera. Yes, I should insist that I go with her, I thought.

"I'll ride in the car with you, Mom," I said. "You're new to the business and you don't realize how brutal it can be."

"I won't hear another word about it, Stacey. You've been telling me for years how you're too busy to take a whole day off to spend with me, and now I finally understand. So listen to your mother: Go to work at your store or run off to your auditions, and don't worry about me."

Well, there was no point in arguing about it. "Fine, but I'll have both my cell phone and my pager with me, so if you want some advice or words of encouragement, call me. Okay, Mom?"

"Yes, yes. I will," she said. "And now I'd better go to bed. They told me to get a good night's sleep because tomorrow is bound to be exhausting for me."

"I was about to suggest the same thing," I said. "Oh, and here's a tip: you might want to lay off the dairy products in the morning. Skip the cereal and milk and have some toast and tea instead. Dairy can cause phlegm buildup in the throat, and your voice has to be perfectly clear tomorrow."

"Actually, dear, the director already told me that. I haven't had dairy for the past week."

"I see. Did he tell you about the voice exercises? To limber up your vocal cords?"

"You mean, *'ahhhh'* and *'eeeee'* and *'ooooo'*?"

"Yes." Gee, I couldn't tell her anything she didn't know. "And be careful when you get into makeup. Sometimes they use the same brushes on everybody and you can pick up bacteria, especially when it comes to mascara. Maura is the expert in that area, so if you want, I can have her call you tonight and–"

"What I want is to hang up and go to sleep, dear," said my mother, the person who never–I mean, never–used to let me off the phone. It was I who had to invent stories (the UPS man is at the door, the water on the stove is boiling, the police have to question me about the robbery down the street) to extricate myself from our conversations, and now she was in a hurry to get off with me?

"Okay. Sleep tight," I said, trying to adjust to this role reversal. "I'll be thinking about you all day tomorrow, wishing you good luck. I love you, Mom."

"I love you, too, Stacey. Nighty night."


My mother did not call me the day of the shoot, because she did not need advice or words of encouragement or anything of the sort. When I finally reached her later that night, she explained that the shoot went without a hitch and that everyone involved was pleased with her performance.

"Tell me, tell me," I said excitedly. "What did they have you do?"

"Basically, it was a problem-solution type of ad, just as they'd planned in the storyboard. I sat at a kitchen table wearing one of my nice dresses–the dark green one with the bow under the collar– and I looked straight into the camera and told the public what happened with the bone."

"You're kidding. I never thought they'd really go with that."

"Oh, they went with it. They told me to be myself, so I was myself. I said how shocked I was about finding the bone. I lashed out at companies that don't take their quality control seriously. I spoke up for all us faceless consumers, mothers in particular. But then I recounted how Fin's invited me to inspect their cannery and how I met their employees and how I was so impressed with their operation that I agreed to come and work for them. The commercial ends with a close-up on me saying, 'Fin's is the name you can trust—for taste, for freshness, for *honesty*.' And then I wag my finger at the camera and say, 'And if they slip up, they'll have *me* to answer to. Make no bones about it!'"

"Hey, that sounds very cute," I enthused, remembering what Maura had said—that the commercial would probably air during times of the day when no one would see it and that life would return to normal. My mother would go back to being my mother, and I would go back to being the actress in the family.

"Cute? It's a possible award-winner, according to Peter at W and W. Everybody's so thrilled with it that they're considering putting me in a whole series of commercials. They're waiting for the focus groups to weigh in, then for the commercial to run. If there's a big bump in sales, your mother could become a household name, Stacey. What do you think of that?"

"I think you shouldn't get your hopes up," I said gently. "I'm a veteran of this business, Mom. One day you're hot. The next day you can't get arrested. That's just how it is."

She laughed. "Such a pessimist, my daughter."

Wait. *She* was always the pessimist. *I* was always the one who said anyone could be a star if they were persistent enough. "I'm only trying to protect you," I said, as further evidence of how we appeared to have traded places.

The feedback on the commercial was overwhelmingly positive, according to my mother. Focus groups said they loved her authenticity, her credibility, her *realness*. They said she was a refreshing change from all the phonies on television. They even remarked about her Cleveland accent, how her wide vowels made her seem more trustworthy. They also responded to her age—that she wasn't a kid but a straight-talking sixtysomething, nor was she a model on loan from a cosmetics commercial. And they got a kick out of the fact that she was grumpy. "Helen Reiser is Everywoman," one of them wrote on her comment card. "Helen Reiser is Everymother," wrote another. "Helen Reiser speaks for me," wrote a third, who also wrote that she thought my mother should run for Congress.

The commercial aired in prime time as well as in day time, and the reaction was sensational. Sales of Fin's Premium Tuna increased by some ridiculously high percentage, and W&W promptly ordered up three more spots starring my mother.

How did I feel about that? Proud, truly I did. After all, it's not everyone's mother who becomes a successful pitchwoman for a tuna fish company, right? Besides, I had pretty much come to terms with the jealousy I'd felt in the beginning, made peace with the fact that she had landed a terrific gig on television. It wasn't as if we'd ever be competing for the same job, so what was the big deal, I decided.

And then it became a big deal. A huge deal. A monster deal that sent me running to Maura's house on a Friday night—without calling first. Yup, I just showed up without an invitation, which was not the sort of thing I'd ever done before but was the sort of thing my mother used to do all the time. Without meaning to, I was turning into the very person whose behavior had driven me crazy.

"Oh. Stacey," said Maura, looking startled. She was wearing a bathrobe and clutching it tightly around her, her cranberry hair sticking up in all directions, her lipstick smeared across her left cheek. Clearly, I had interrupted something.

"Whoops. You're not alone," I said. "I'll go."

"No, you will not." She grabbed my arm and pulled me inside. "It's just Rick. You know. The actor who plays Donald on *Days*. We see each other every once in a while."

"But Maura. That guy's old enough to be your–"

"Shhh. He's in the bedroom sleeping. One roll in the hay and it's lights out for the Rickster."

Whatever works, I thought. If she liked them old, that was her business, as long as they didn't traumatize her by dying in the saddle. "You sure you don't want me to leave?"

"Positive. Tell me why you're so upset."

We sat on her sofa. After I apologized over and over for barging in on her and Rick, I unburdened myself.

"It was one thing for her to invade my personal space by moving here," I said, referring to my mother. "It was another for her to invade my professional space by acting in commercials. But now there's a new plot twist. Apparently, Corbin Beasley, the PR director at Fin's, isn't the ineffectual doofus I thought he was when I met him at the cannery. Based on the favorable response to the commercial, he's sending my mother on a publicity tour. Are you ready for this? He's booked her on Leno. He's booked her on Regis. He's even booked her on–brace yourself–*Oprah*."

Maura gasped, finally comprehending the enormity of what I was telling her. "Oprah?"

I nodded.

"But she only does segments about lifting your spirit."

"Apparently, my mother is going to lift everyone's spirit by chronicling her rise from obscurity to celebrity, thereby assuring women of all ages that they can 'make it.'"

"But once she appears on Oprah, she'll be insufferable."

"She's always been insufferable, Maura. Now she'll be impossible."

* * *

And she was. On Leno, she sat on the couch next to the band members of U2, barking at Bono to get a haircut and grilling him about being nice to his mother. On Regis, she was asked to mug for the camera, wag her finger at the audience, and say the last line from her commercial, the one that ended "make no bones about it," because, according to Reeege, it was becoming the popular culture equivalent of "Wassuuuup!" And on Oprah, while she shared the spotlight with other women who found success late in life (her fellow guests included novelist Belva Plain and Missouri Senator Jean Carnahan), she was heralded as someone who ventured into a world in which she never imagined she'd find herself and discovered she was more than up to the challenge. She talked about my father and how much she missed him; about me and how my leaving the nest took its toll on her; and about her newfound visibility as an actress and consumer advocate and how she felt productive for the first time in years. By the end of the show, there wasn't a dry eye in the audience, including mine.

It was the power of those television appearances that put the name Helen Reiser on everyone's lips. She had leapt into the public consciousness, become the flavor of the month. School-age kids were "doing" her, imitating her grouchy line "Make no bones about it." Magazines were knocking themselves out to interview her, even those with demographics more appropriate for an interview with, say, me. And—this was the final straw—the movie people were calling.

"Woody wants me for his next picture," she said one night at Chadwick's, the Beverly Hills eatery owned by Harrison Ford's son Ben. The place was much too pricey for me, but Mom was treating. She was a big spender now and enjoyed frequenting all the celebrity hangouts, enjoyed soaking up the attention. Cameron Diaz stopped by her table one night and Robert Wagner stopped by her table the next night and Shaquille O'Neal stopped by her table the night after that (she didn't know who he was, but she was thrilled when he bent down and kissed her hand). She took to being fawned over in a way I'd never anticipated. For years she'd branded Hollywood as the land of moral turpitude, but now she was clearly in its thrall.

"Woody Allen wants you to be in his movie?" I said, trying not to choke on my lamb shanks. It had always been my dream to be in one of his movies. I know, I was supposed to get over myself and be happy for her. The stumbling block was the suddenness of her stardom, the randomness of it. On one hand, it gave me hope that if she could become a hit so easily, I could, too; that if she could go from complaining about a tuna fish bone to winning the hearts of Americans, anything was possible for me. On the other hand, it confirmed how unlikely it was that I'd ever go further in the business; that success in Hollywood was all about being the new face in town (even if the new face was sixty-six) and not about having talent. I couldn't remember ever feeling so confused about my path, so conflicted about my goal. Was it realistic for me to continue to plug away at my chosen profession? Or was my mother's overnight success a wake-up call telling me to find a new career?

"That's right. His people called my people," she said. "We're in discussions."

"Your people?"

"Yes. Arnold, Karen, and Jeanine."

"Who's Jeanine?" I knew that Arnold was her agent and Karen was her manager, but I hadn't heard this Jeanine person mentioned before. The entourage was growing.

"Jeanine's my publicist. Arnold and Karen didn't think Corbin could handle the avalanche of media requests I'm generating."

"But he got you on three national TV shows."

"I know, dear, and he's fine for the Fin's-related appearances, but my reach is broader than that now. I've become—well, I hate to sound immodest—an icon."

You see? I wasn't overreacting when I'd told Maura my mother would be impossible. An *icon,* she called herself. No one in their right mind calls themselves that. Not unless they've started believing their own press releases. Fame is a slippery slope, no question about it, but I just didn't figure my no-nonsense, straight-talking mother to be seduced by it. It occurred to me, as I sat there listening to her yammer about taking a meeting with this one and granting an interview to that one, that we really had switched places, she and I. It was my turn to look after her, I realized. Yes, it was up to me to make sure that fame wasn't the only thing she was seduced by.

# Chapter Twelve

★

I GUESS YOU'VE FORGOTTEN your own daughter," I said to my mother's answering machine, since it had been days since she and I had connected. "Or am I supposed to go through Jeanine to get to you?"

Actually, my mother hadn't forgotten me at all. It just felt that way. She had tried to call me several times, but we never managed to make contact other than to engage in a frustrating game of phone tag. She was so busy now, was on such a crazy schedule, that I worried about her health. And so I kept leaving messages for her that went like this: "Are you getting enough sleep?" "Are you taking your vitamins?" "Are you drinking your Metamucil?" Sound familiar? Yes, I was nagging her, the same way she used to nag me, and my excuse was the precise excuse she'd always fallen back on: I cared.

I mean, how would I know if she was all right? I may have been her daughter, but I hadn't seen her in weeks. Not in person, anyway. The last time I'd caught a glimpse of her was on *Hollywood Squares* (she sat in the center square). Shortly thereafter, she'd flown to New York to shoot a small part in Woody Allen's movie, then participated in a segment on *Good Morning America*, during which different celebrities cooked their favorite dishes with Diane Sawyer. (Mom made tuna noodle casserole using canned Fin's premium solid white albacore.) Her fame was spectacular, her presence felt everywhere. In one week alone, she was a clue in *TV Guide*'s crossword puzzle, mentioned in Maureen Dowd's op-ed piece in *The New York Times*, and photographed by Annie Leibovitz for a *Vanity Fair* spread entitled "Women Who Rule." Oh, and Tim Russert invoked her name on *Meet the Press* after a politician wagged his finger in response to some policy question and said, "Make no bones about it."

Yes, the circus surrounding my mother was breathtaking in its scope, and turned my life upside down. Not only did I feel dwarfed by all the attention she was getting—both personally and professionally—but I just plain missed my mommy.

Yup, you read that right. I missed her pestering, missed her showing up and rearranging my kitchen, missed her sticking her nose into my business. I never would have thought it possible, but I yearned for the good/bad old days when I cringed at the mere sound of her voice.

Of course, there was one moderately amusing aspect to having a newly famous mother. Suddenly, people were nicer to me. For example, Cameron, the manager at Cornucopia!, had begun to treat me less like her cleaning lady and more like the lady of the house. I nearly fainted when she instructed another member of the sales staff, a woman whose mother wasn't famous, to vacuum the store every night so I wouldn't have to anymore. And there was Mickey, my agent, who saw an opportunity to cash in on the Helen Reiser phenomenon and put the word out to all the big casting directors that I was her daughter. "Maybe you can get back in the game now," he offered, instead of his usual: "You gotta let the dust settle for a few years." And finally there was Ethan, the Welsh hairdresser with whom Maura had fixed me up months before, the one who'd fled after my mother had barged in on us that night. Out of the blue, he called and asked me out. As with our first date, we went to dinner and came back to my place and kissed wildly on my sofa—until we were interrupted yet again.

"Was that the phone?" I asked, pulling away from Ethan, who was breathing heavily and quite flushed.

"I didn't hear anything," he said and proceeded to draw me back into his embrace.

"Yes. It is the phone," I said, pulling away again.

"Let your machine pick it up," he said, drawing me closer again.

"But it might be my mother," I said. "I need to talk to her."

Ethan practically shoved me off the sofa. "If it's your mother, you should get it," he said. "She could be calling from some celebrity party. Maybe she wants us to join her."

While Ethan preened, in the hope of mixing and mingling with the A-list, I answered the phone, but it was not my mother calling. It was a wrong number.

"Why don't you ring her up then, Stacey?" he suggested. "Maybe she'd like to join us tonight. We could meet her someplace, have a nightcap, just the three of us."

Funny you didn't want her around before, I thought, hating Ethan suddenly and showing him the door.

Feeling empty and rather melodramatic, I plunked myself back down on the sofa and balled my body into the fetal position. No, I did not suck my thumb, but that's certainly the mood I was in. As I said, I missed my mother. I wanted her back the way she was. Not, I realized then, because I was jealous of her success, but because I needed her love. That's the weird thing about mothers: no matter how much they get on your nerves, they're the ones who love you when no one else does.

*   *   *

I had just come home from having my first mammogram—the technician who was squishing my breasts confessed that she, too, had dreams of going into acting—when I noticed I had a couple of messages on my answering machine.

The first was from my mother, who apologized profusely for being out of touch but promised we'd have dinner as soon as she was back from Cleveland, where she was throwing out the first pitch at the Indians' baseball game.

The second was from—no. It wasn't possible. Absolutely not possible.

I hit the play button again to make sure I wasn't hallucinating.

"Hello, Stacey," said a sonorous male voice. "This is Jack Rawlins, the host of *Good Morning, Hollywood.* I hope you don't mind my calling you directly instead of going through your agent or publicist—the manager at Cornucopia! was kind enough to give me your home number, in case you were wondering—but ever since you waited on me at the store that day and forced me to confront the harsh words I used in connection with your performance in *Pet Peeve,* I've had terrible pangs of guilt. Truly, I have. I'd appreciate the opportunity to make amends, Stacey. In person, preferably. I realize that you must have less than fond thoughts of me, but I'd relish the chance to apologize for any damage to your career. I'm learning that I don't review films in a vacuum; that there are living, breathing people behind them and that they get hurt by what I say. So please give me a call back and let's schedule a meeting. I promise you I can be a fairly decent guy when I work at it."

The message ended with Jack Rawlins leaving me his direct line at the office. As if I'd ever use it.

"What do you mean you're not calling him back?" Maura demanded later that night while we were scarfing down pizza at her place. She'd had a date with a seventy-year-old TV producer, but he'd died earlier in the week, so the date was canceled.

"Why should I?" I said. "The guy's a nightmare. You heard what he told a television audience about me."

"But he's sorry. He wants to apologize to you in person. You must have made quite an impression on him at the store that day."

"All I did was throw his review right back in his face. If he feels guilty, so be it."

"Obviously, he feels guilty or he wouldn't have tracked you down. This could be an incredible opportunity for you, so don't blow it."

"An incredible opportunity? To sit there and listen to him pontificate about what a swell guy he really is? Please."

"Listen, Stacey, let's say he *is* a jerk and a snake and a creep, and, other than being great to look at, he has virtually no redeeming qualities. Still, he's a powerful man in the movie business. Becoming his acquaintance—particularly now that he owes you a favor—wouldn't be the worst thing that could happen to you. So you despise him. So what. Use him. Use his guilt. Use his clout. You've been waiting for a break for months now, waiting for something to put you back on the fast track. Well, maybe Jack Rawlins's phone call is that something."

I smiled at her, at how she never ceased to amaze me with her positive spin on life. And she didn't even take Zoloft.

"So I should call him back," I said warily.

"Of course you should. Have lunch with him or a drink with him. Just get together with him and see what comes of it. Maybe he'll mention you to some studio executives. Maybe he'll engineer some meetings for you. Maybe he'll do neither of those things, but you won't know unless you call him."

I took her advice and phoned Jack Rawlins the next morning. I did not reach the Great One himself. I spoke to Kyle, his assistant, who was far less off-putting than his boss.

"Hey, Stacey. Jack said to ask you which of these dates are convenient for you." He rattled off several days and times. "He also said I should be very nice to you, which leads me to believe he's added you to the list of people who dream about punching him out?"

I laughed in spite of myself. "He gave me a rotten review and I'm still smarting from it, I must admit."

"Sorry about that," said Kyle. "I've worked for Jack for two years now, and I've learned the drill: he serves up the reviews and I smooth things over with the reviewees—or try to."

"You play good cop to his bad cop, you mean."

"Yup, only Jack's not the bad cop you think he is. Really. Underneath the I-can't-get-over-myself façade beats a heart of gold."

I said I'd keep that in mind but wasn't buying it for a second. Jack Rawlins was a self-serving son of a— I stopped myself, remembering that I had an agenda in meeting with him. I was hoping to use him to resuscitate my career.

"So you're free for drinks with Jack at the Four Seasons next Tuesday?" said Kyle.

I took a deep breath. "That would be fine," I said.

# Chapter
# Thirteen

☆

THE BAR at the Four Seasons in Beverly Hills is a lively spot where industry folk mix with wannabes, and nobody makes eye contact with the person they're with because they're too busy checking out everybody else. It's a scene, in other words, and I spent as much time preparing for it as I would for an audition. I labored over my makeup and fixed my hair in an elaborate half-up/half-down 'do, and I wore a very tight, very short black skirt with an equally clinging black turtleneck and high, skinny-heeled black sandals. (If you want to get noticed at the Four Seasons, you have to go with either a slutty look or a filthy rich look. Since I was low on funds, I went slutty.) My goal was to appear as different from my wholesome receptionist role in *Pet Peeve* as possible, in order that Jack Rawlins could see my versatility and pass the word along to his big-shot friends.

Okay, so where are you, you pompous ass, I thought, scanning the room and not finding him.

I glanced at my watch. I was right on time.

Oh, I get it, I said to myself as I continued to peruse the place.

You're the power guy so you're gonna keep me waiting, is that it? Well, guess again, because I'm only hanging around for ten minutes, tops, and then I'm outta here.

Tough talk, I know, especially from someone who really needed this meeting to happen, but the very idea of Jack Rawlins, just the image of that arrogant windbag with his florid sentences and preppy wardrobe, got me going.

Another tour around the room. And another. No Rawlins, the bastard. If this was his way of apologizing, I was unimpressed.

I did one more sweep of the room, was about to storm out of there, when I spotted him at a table outside, in the bar's patio area. So *he'd* been waiting for *me?*

Fine, so he's punctual, I thought, as he got up from his chair and waved me over. Punctual *and* pompous.

"Hi, Jack," I said in my perkiest voice when I reached the table and shook his hand vigorously. I was determined to be charming and memorable, determined to take advantage of this guy's guilt over having trashed me.

"Thanks for coming, Stacey," he said, pulling out my chair for me. Such a gentleman. "I was delighted when Kyle told me you'd called."

"Well, when someone says they're sorry for what they did, it's only right to forgive them and move on." I smiled widely.

"I was hoping you'd feel that way," said Jack, who, by the way, was a canvas of earth tones. He was wearing a brown corduroy blazer, beige shirt, and khaki slacks, and the clothes, combined with his reddish-blond hair, ruddy complexion, and tortoiseshell glasses, made me think of soil or sand or maybe just dirt. "I've ordered myself a scotch. What can I get for you?" he asked.

"A martini," I said. "Very dry. Onions and olives, please." I never drink martinis, but I wanted to appear sophisticated, worldly, movie star-ish to this man. Also, I was nervous.

He ordered my drink and returned his attention to me. "So," he said, "should we have me expand on my apology for a few minutes or should we try to get to know each other better? How would you prefer to spend the time?"

"How about a little of both," I said, because while I wanted to advance my cause and promote myself, I also wanted to watch the guy grovel.

"All right. Let's start with the apology. I'm very, very sorry that I hurt you with my review of your movie. I have a tendency to go for the wisecrack instead of simply offering up my opinion, because it makes for better television."

"Wait, so are you saying that you're sorry you compared me to a sledgehammer but that you hated my performance?"

"I'm not saying that at all. I just think your performance lacked—well, let me rephrase—I thought, as I was screening the film, that you were a promising actress who'd been badly directed."

"Oh." The waiter brought the martini, thank God. I popped the onions and olives into my mouth, not wanting to drink on an empty stomach, and took a much-too-big sip, which caused me to make a slight slurping sound, regrettably. "Then let me understand. You hated my performance but you decided it wasn't my fault?"

"Stacey, it's the director's job to guide you into doing the best work you can. You weren't well served in *Pet Peeve*. Now that I've seen you in other roles, I'm convinced of that."

"Other roles? What roles?"

He smiled. "I'm nothing if not thorough. I was curious about you after our exchange at Cornucopia!—it's not every day that a subject of one of my reviews taunts me with it—and so I asked Kyle to get me tapes of everything you've done."

My, my. So he had researched me, done his homework on me. I was amazed. Flattered, too. "And?"

"And I came to the conclusion that you were wonderful."

I gulped more of the martini and sat back in my chair. "Wonderful in what, for example?"

"The *Ally McBeal* episode," he said. "The *Boston Public* episode. All the television work was first-rate, Stacey. Honestly."

Jack Rawlins is really handsome. I thought this either because he *was* handsome or because he was praising my acting or because I was sliding into inebriation. "I appreciate that. Too bad you missed my Irish Spring commercial. I gave a bravura performance in it."

He laughed. "I'll bet you did. I'll bet if you'd been directed by someone who knew what he was doing, you would have given a bravura performance in *Pet Peeve*, too."

"Here's a question for you, Jack," I said, starting to feel pretty peppy now. "Why are you such a snob about movies? *Pet Peeve* wasn't *Citizen Kane*, but it wasn't meant to be. It was meant to be a goofy, fluffy piece of escapist entertainment. What's wrong with that?"

"Nothing, if it's well made. But I'd rather talk about what a capable actress you are, not about what a snob I am. Can we do that?"

"No argument here. Go ahead."

"For starters, I think you have a very natural quality on camera, a compelling vulnerability about you. And you're beautiful, of course."

Of course? Since when? "I don't know what to say, Jack." Another sip of the martini was in order. "I certainly don't consider myself beautiful, and my agent thinks I'm better suited to character parts than leading lady parts, but maybe he hasn't been pitching me in the right way."

"Maybe not."

At that point—it must have been the booze that had loosened me up—I spontaneously unburdened myself to Jack Rawlins, told him the story of my struggles as an actress. I left nothing out, not even the anecdote about the Tic Tac commercial and the saga of the

Monster Cold Sore. He seemed fascinated by every gem that came out of my mouth, murmuring in sympathy, patting my hand in a gesture of commiseration, even agreeing to offer to help me revive my career. "I'd be happy to do whatever I can, since you're having trouble getting the roles you want—the roles you deserve," he said. "I could make a few calls, drop your name around, 'create some heat around you,' as they say in this town. It's my job to keep my ear to the ground, so if I hear of anything, I'll do my best to get you involved."

"That would be fabulous, thanks," I said, feeling both giddy with the drift the conversation had taken and queasy from the martini, which I'd polished off entirely too fast.

"Would you like another one of those?" asked Jack, nodding at my empty glass.

"I'd better not," I said. "But a ginger ale would be great."

Jack signaled the waiter, who brought the soda right away.

"So, are we friends?" he said, running his fingers through his hair. He had nice hands, I noticed. Nice wrists, too. Come to think of it, there wasn't anything about Jack Rawlins that wasn't attractive. Now that I had seen this other side to him, this sensitive, generous side, I found myself feeling rather drawn to him.

"Yes, we're friends," I said, wondering about the redhead suddenly, the one he'd had on his arm at Cornucopia! "But enough about me, Jack. Tell me about you, about how you became a movie critic."

"I became a movie critic because I love movies," he said. "I love to watch them, think about them, talk about them, talk to the people who make them, all of it. When I was a kid, I'd spend whole weekends in theaters, seeing everything that came out, even the crap. Movies were a safe haven, I guess."

"From what?"

"The usual: adolescent angst. My parents had a poor excuse for a marriage and my younger brother had a lot of physical problems. Our house wasn't the most festive place in the neighborhood."

"I'm sorry," I said.

He shrugged. "Everybody's got a story. The point is, I buried myself in movies the way other people bury themselves in books. When it was time to start earning a living, it seemed only natural that I'd go into the business."

"The business of reviewing movies?"

"The business of covering the movie industry. I was a better-than-average writer, so my first gigs out of college were with the trades; first *The Hollywood Reporter*, then *Variety*. Eventually, I moved into reviewing movies for consumer magazines, which led to the local television show, and now the syndicated version."

"You must be thrilled that you've gone national, Jack. You've got an audience of millions now."

"It's been exciting, no question about it, but when you're at the top, there's only one place you can go from there—down. There's a lot more pressure on me than there was when I was writing my columns. I can't just review movies anymore. I have to interview guests, too, and the problem with that is that I'm competing with the other entertainment shows for the same guests. It's all about the 'get' now; how you can't let *Entertainment Tonight* or *Access Hollywood* or *Extra!* air a segment with Tom Cruise before you do. It's the proverbial jungle out there."

"It must be."

"So the trick, I'm finding, is to snag the most interesting guests as opposed to the most famous guests—the ones who aren't just out there plugging their latest film but who genuinely have something to say." He paused to swallow the last of his scotch, and as he did, it occurred to me that he might be on the verge of asking *me* to be a guest on his show. Well, why not? True, I wasn't a big name, but he'd just gotten through telling me what a good actress I was, plus he had seemed so captivated by the trials and tribulations of my career. Most importantly, he had promised to help me raise my profile, and wouldn't putting me on his show be the most efficient way to do that? Maybe he was considering doing a segment on up-and-comers or down-and-outers or actresses-who've-plateaued. Maybe he'd decided that *I* was someone who wasn't just out there plugging my latest film but who genuinely had something to say. Maybe he was dying to invite me on the show but was hesitant because of the sledgehammer thing.

"Sounds like you've got quite a challenge with the new and improved *Good Morning, Hollywood*," I said, "but I think your vision for the show is absolutely right, Jack: interesting guests, not the usual suspects."

"Exactly," he said. "So, since you have such a keen understanding of what I'm up against, I'd like to ask you a question, Stacey."

"Ask away," I said, my excitement growing. Yes, he definitely wanted me for the show. He'd been searching for undiscovered talent and stumbled onto me. God, I couldn't wait to tell Maura, without whom I wouldn't have had the foresight to even meet with Jack Rawlins. To think of it! An appearance on *Good Morning, Hollywood* would totally change my life! Every producer, never mind casting director, would see me. It would be the opportunity of all opportunities. I could hardly contain myself.

"I feel a little uncomfortable asking you," he said, "given the rocky start to our friendship, but now that we've cleared the air, I don't see why I can't do you a favor and you can't do one for me. That's how this business works, isn't it? One hand washes the other."

"That's how it works," I agreed, eager for him to pop the question already.

"All right," he said. "What I'm asking is if you would–"

"Yes!" I couldn't resist jumping in. I was just too charged up. "I'd *love* to be a guest on your show, Jack. I think your producers could come up with a great segment where you interview me about my day-to-day routine of trying to make it in Hollywood. I think your viewers would enjoy it and I'm available to do it. So let's schedule it." ·

He looked puzzled.

"Is something wrong?" I said.

"Uh, I'm afraid there is," he said. "I wasn't asking you to appear on the show, Stacey. I was asking you to get me your mother."

"What did you say?"

"Listen, before you react, let me explain the situation. I need her for the show, Stacey. It's a ratings issue. The producers have been falling all over themselves to convince her to come on, but she won't, thanks to my *Pet Peeve* review of you and the grudge she's got against me because of it. They suggested I talk to you, to see if you'd persuade her that I'm not such a terrible guy after all."

Well! I was so angry, so humiliated, so undone, that I couldn't breathe at first. I just stared at Jack Rawlins, who was no longer handsome to me in the slightest, and tried to figure out how in the world I could have been so gullible, how in the world I could have believed his apology, believed his interest in me, bought his act. Of course he was a sneaky son of a bitch. Of course he was an ambitious asshole. Of course he was using me to get to my mother. (It was entirely beside the point that I was using him to further my career.) I mean, the nerve of the guy. The sheer audacity.

I stood, swaying a little from the martini and the rage, grabbed my glass of ginger ale, and said, "But you *are* a terrible guy after all." And then, because I was out of control and no longer cared what sort of an impression I made on anybody, I splashed the soda in his face.

"I guess the answer is no?" he said, as he reached for his napkin to mop himself up. "You won't talk to your mother for me?"

"I guess the answer is no *way*," I said and headed for the exit.

# Chapter Fourteen

★

"YOU DID WHAT?" said Maura after I told her about the ginger ale shower I gave Rawlins. We were sitting in the spare bedroom she'd turned into a studio, and she was applying color to one of her wigs. In addition to using the studio for makeup sessions with private clients, she stored her wigs and costumes and stage props there and rented them out to make extra money. Needless to say, she cleaned up on Halloween.

"I threw my drink at him," I said. "I was beyond angry."

"If you ask me, you overreacted."

"Overreacted? That jerk lures me to the Four Seasons, letting me believe he's interested in me, in my career, when all he wants is to get to my mother? Come on, I think I was justified in feeling used."

"Why? You were using him, too. From what you tell me, you solicited his help in getting jobs. And then he solicited your help in getting your mother. Favor for favor."

"That's exactly what *he* said." Was Maura really taking Jack's side? My Maura?

"Stacey, you're going to have to adapt to your mother's success, to the fact that she's in demand right now. Besides, you of all people know how fleeting fame is. There'll come a day–probably sooner rather than later–when your mother's phone won't be ringing anymore and no one will be cozying up to you to get to her. This is her moment. She's sixty-six years old and she never expected to find herself in this position. So let her have fun with it. Tell her it's okay with you if she does Jack's show. She may never have the chance again, and you'd hate it if you were the one who deprived her of that chance, wouldn't you?"

"I never thought of it that way." I had to admit that Maura had a point. Just because I had a grudge against Jack Rawlins didn't mean my mother shouldn't have her day in the sun. This *was* her moment. This *was* her time to take advantage of all the offers that were coming her way. This *was* the opportunity of her lifetime, and I'd be selfish if I let my petty hurts ruin it for her. If anybody understood how quickly her good fortune could evaporate, it was I.

"He must think I'm the Wicked Witch of the West," I mused, "losing my temper the way I did."

"He probably does," said Maura. "You might consider apologizing."

"Yeah, right. Maybe he didn't deserve the soda in the face, but he's still a rat. Don't forget that he pretended to praise my television work, softening me up before zooming in for the kill."

"What if he was sincere about your acting? What if he meant it when he said you were wonderful on *Ally McBeal* and *Boston Public?*"

"He didn't mean it."

"How do you know?"

"Because the only reason he even looked at those tapes was to set me up, so I'd coax my mother into doing his show."

"Maybe, but it's possible that when he did look at the tapes, he liked what he saw."

I dismissed what Maura said. She always viewed the glass as half-full, as I've indicated, so what good was her opinion anyway?

My mother came over to my apartment the next day. It was one of her rare visits since stardom hit, and she looked terrific. The woman who never wore anything but dresses and skirts was sporting a black Armani pants suit, and the streaks in her brown hair were no longer gray but a flattering shade of red. Apparently, there had been yet another addition to her entourage–a stylist–and she now wore whatever *Eve* told her to wear.

"You look great, Mom," I said as she eyed my messy kitchen but refrained from rushing around to straighten it up. This was the new Helen Reiser, the Helen Reiser who had much too much on her plate to worry about mine.

"Thanks, dear. You look great, too."

See? No: "You need a haircut." Or: "There are dark circles under your eyes." Or even: "Watch your posture."

I offered to make us lunch, but she already had a lunch date–with a writer for *Good Housekeeping*.

"This is just a quickie visit, so I can spend a little time with you," she said, hugging me. "Come, let's sit down so you can tell me what's going on."

We sat. "Nothing much is going on," I said. "I'm still working at the store a few days a week and going out on auditions. But there is something I'd like to talk to you about."

"What? You're not sick, are you? I was in the greenroom at the *Today* show last week and everyone had these horrible, hacking coughs. Even Katie Couric had a cough. She's very nice, by the way."

"I'm thrilled to hear it. Actually, what I'd like to talk to you about involves another show: *Good Morning, Hollywood.*"

She scowled. "Why would I want to talk about that show? The host insulted my daughter."

"Because it has a huge audience, Mom, and it would be the perfect vehicle for you."

"That's what Jeanine says. She's been inundated with calls from some producer over there. I keep telling her to say no to him."

"I think you should say yes to him, Mom. They've changed the format of the show, so you'd have lots of air time. Jack Rawlins isn't on my list of favorite people, obviously, but he's a really good interviewer, an intelligent interviewer, and he'd give you the kind of exposure that'll keep you in the limelight." I didn't add that she should grab every invitation she could get, because there was no telling when the media would tire of her and move on to the Next Big Thing.

She shot me one of her are-you-crazy looks. "I'll do that show over my dead body. Not after how he treated you, dear."

"Maybe that's exactly why you should do his show," I said, remembering Maura's words of wisdom, that I shouldn't let my grudge against Jack deprive my mother of her chance to shine. "You should go on with him and then give him a hard time. Remember how you wanted to write him one of your complaint letters after his review of *Pet Peeve?* Well, now you can badger him face-to-face, on national television."

She cackled. "I hadn't thought of that."

"Well, think of it, although I didn't mean you should discuss me during the interview. I meant that you should take him on, the way you took on Fin's. Make him earn his money, ask him some tough questions, engage him in a lively dialogue about whatever subject he brings up. It would be great television, great for your career, and great for me."

"Why for you?"

"Because I'd get to watch him squirm, Mom. You're brilliant at making people squirm."

She cocked her head, considered my proposition. "I suppose it would be fun to go one-on-one with that rascal."

"Of course it would. So will you do it? Will you have Jeanine call his producer and book the interview?"

"Now that you've put a different slant on it, yes, I will. I'll have her call this afternoon and set it up."

"Great. But will you also promise me something?"

"What?"

"Swear to me that you'll tell Jack Rawlins that the reason you finally relented and agreed to do the show was because Jeanine twisted your arm."

"But you're the one who–"

"I know, but you have to tell him it was Jeanine and that she persuaded you over my objections. The point is, you can't mention that I was in favor of it. Not a whisper. Are we clear?"

"Yes, but why the secrecy?"

"I'd just like to stay out of it, that's all."

The last thing I needed was for Jack Rawlins, the dirtbag, to find out I'd caved in and done what he'd asked me. I may have lost my composure with him, but I was not about to lose my pride, too.

My mother taped *Good Morning, Hollywood* two weeks later, and the show aired a few days after that. It was a ratings winner, one of those once-in-a-lifetime interviews that everybody remembers, because it was so provocative, so compelling, like watching two evenly matched heavyweights duke it out until the final round. Jack kept trying to get straight answers out of my mother, and she kept dishing out fabulously crabby barbs in return, and at the end of the interview, he knelt down in front of her and literally begged her for mercy. The clip was played and replayed on all the other entertainment shows, which brought my mother the kind of visibility I would have denied her had I not convinced her to do the interview. I felt good about that, surprisingly good.

My own career took an interesting turn shortly after my mother's appearance on Jack's show. Mickey called to say that Hal Papush, a director of small, independent films, was casting a new comedy and wanted me to come in and read for the part of a woman who steals the parking space of the main character.

"It's not a big part, kid, and they don't have much of a budget, but it's something," said Mickey.

"You bet it's something," I said, delighted by this development. "How did he hear about me?"

"According to his assistant, he saw you in *Pet Peeve* and remembered your spunk. Like I said, it's only a scene, maybe two, but it puts you back in the ball game."

Back in the ball game indeed. So *Pet Peeve* wasn't a noose around my neck anymore, in spite of Jack Rawlins's review.

I went and read for the role of the parking space thief and, miracle of all miracles, snagged the job. It occurred to me that the fact that I was Helen Reiser's daughter probably nudged the director into hiring me, but I didn't care. I was thankful for the part, ecstatic to have it. Unfortunately, my ecstasy was tempered when my mother called one night, sounding oddly girlish, and hit me with stunning news.

"I'm in love," she announced, following several seconds of giggles.

"What do you mean?" I said, because my mother hadn't used the "L" word in connection with any man but my father, not for my entire adult life.

"Oh, Stacey, I didn't want to tell you until I was sure. But now I *am* sure. Victor loves me and I love him."

"Who the hell is Victor?" I said. It was true that since my mother had become as famous as Madonna, I didn't see or speak to her as often as I used to, but she had never even mentioned that she was dating anyone, never even mentioned that she was in the market for a man.

"He's a catch, that's who he is," she cooed. "He's smart and rich and sooo handsome, and he treats me like a queen. Oh, and he's terrific in the sack."

"Stop!" This was crazy. My mother had never talked about sex before, except to warn me not to have it without a ring on my finger. She may have been vocal about other subjects, but when it came to sex, she was so uptight she'd wouldn't even say the word out loud; she would spell it, as in: "I heard Gloria Marx's daughter had s-e-x with her tennis pro." And now here she was, extolling her new boyfriend's prowess in the bedroom? "What I mean is, I think you should slow down and start from the beginning. How did you meet this guy?"

"Through Arnold. Well, not really *through* Arnold. I was sitting in the waiting room at Arnold's agency, and Victor was sitting there, too, and we struck up a conversation."

"Is Arnold his agent?" I asked.

"No. Victor was there to see one of the other agents. Oh, Stacey, it was straight out of a movie. Pure magic. He approached me in that waiting room, very much the gentleman, and said, 'I hope you don't mind the intrusion, Ms. Reiser, but I get a bang out of your television appearances. You're so unique.' I was flattered, naturally, and said, 'I don't mind the intrusion at all.' Then he introduced himself and we continued talking and before I knew it he was inviting me to lunch."

"Does this Victor have a last name?"

"It's Chellus. Victor Chellus. He's in his late sixties–sixty-seven, I think–and he's retired."

"From what?"

"Oh, my, he did a little of everything, from the sound of it. He was a producer, a real estate developer, an investor in different businesses, and who knows what else. Everything he touched turned to gold, judging by the mansion in Beverly Hills. And to think that he could have any woman in Hollywood and he picked me. It's amazing, isn't it?"

"Amazing" wasn't the word for it. "Suspicious" was. Not that my mother didn't have her charms. But, as I've said, the men in this town tend to go for women my age or younger. It wasn't the norm for one of them to fall head over heels for a matronly midwestern sixtysomething like Mom, no matter how successful she'd become. Not unless he was broke.

"You say Victor has money?" I asked, feeling yet again that my mother and I had swapped roles. In the old days, she was the one who'd quiz me about the state of my boyfriends' finances.

"I told you, dear. He lives in an enormous house in Beverly Hills. He has staff, he has limousines, he even has his own movie theater right off the living room with a chaise that converts into a bed. The first time we made–"

"When do I get a look at him?" I cut her off before she could utter another syllable about s-e-x. I was having enough trouble absorbing the romance part.

"Whenever you say," she replied. "I've told him all about you, of course. He feels as if he knows you."

"Well, he doesn't know me and I don't know him. Which is why I don't think you should rush into anything here, not until I've checked him out."

She laughed. "So you're the mother now, Stacey? You don't trust me to bring home a good one?"

"It's not that I don't trust you, Mom. It's just that your life has changed dramatically since your first Fin's commercial. You've become a household name. People want things from you, want to hang around you, and their motivations might not be legitimate. I'd hate to see you get taken in by–"

"Oh, so you don't think a man could want me for *me*?"

"I didn't mean that, Mom. I meant that you're not in Cleveland anymore. People in Hollywood aren't always what they seem."

"Stacey, Stacey. Don't be such a party pooper. Listen to your mother and be happy about this. You'll meet Victor and you'll love him as much as I do. Maybe he's even got a handsome young friend for you. Wouldn't that be nice?"

Incredible. Not only had my mother eclipsed me in the professional arena; she had now outdone me in matters of the heart. In meeting this Victor person, she'd been able to accomplish what I hadn't: she'd found a man to love. Yes, she had a boyfriend and I did not, and I'd be lying if I said that didn't suck.

Still, she'd urged me to be happy for her, and I would certainly try to be. It was entirely possible that Victor really was the gem she'd made him out to be, in which case I would be the quintessential Miss Congeniality around him, nothing but supportive and encouraging of their relationship.

But if he was a bad guy, I'd nail him to the wall.

# Chapter
# Fifteen

★

I HAD A GOOD EXCUSE for not meeting Victor just yet. I was rehearsing for and then shooting my one scene in *Money*, the arty little comedy directed by Hal Papush. Since the film's budget was about six cents, I didn't get to do any traveling–we did my scene on Highland Avenue in the Hancock Park section of L.A.–but it felt great to be in the company of actors again, great to be among the technical people, great to be working.

The star of the film was an Australian actor named Alex Hart, and he was funny and sweet and very generous to me, complimenting me on my approach to the scene, offering suggestions, making me feel as if I were truly engaged in a collaborative effort.

Basically, my part called for me to parallel park my car into the space that Alex was simultaneously backing his car into, for our cars to collide, and for us to storm out of them and hurl obscenities at each other, with him ultimately turning on the charm and convincing me not to call the police. What my character didn't know was that Alex's character was in the midst of a jewelry heist and that my character was fouling things up for him. Anyhow, the scene went well and Alex told me to stay in touch, and as I packed up for the day I was in excellent spirits.

Before going home, I lingered on the set to chat with Hal Papush, the director, who was friendly to me in spite of the fact that he was the big cheese and I was an actress with only a handful of lines. At one point, I said, just fishing around for a little positive feedback, "So, Hal, your first look at my work was in *Pet Peeve*, the Jim Carrey movie?"

He had lots of people vying for his attention at that moment, and so when he replied, "I never saw *Pet Peeve*," I assumed he was merely distracted and not focusing. Mickey had told me that the reason Hal had asked me to read for the film was precisely because he'd seen me in *Pet Peeve*. I remembered the conversation clearly.

I tried again. "Hal, you did see *Pet Peeve*. You—or maybe it was the person who does casting for you—said to my agent, Mickey Offerman, that you thought my performance had spunk."

He glanced at me, eyebrow arched. "You've got me confused with somebody else."

Strange. "But if you didn't see me in *Pet Peeve,* why did you hire me for *Money?*"

Before he could answer, one of his assistants commandeered his attention briefly. When he was free again, I posed my question once more.

"I hired you because you've got friends in high places," he said with a wry smile.

I tried to process this. So he hadn't seen *Pet Peeve* but had hired me because someone had asked him to? Someone with clout? Someone with the same last name as mine, perhaps?

Yup. That had to be it. He'd hired me because of my mother, not because of my work. Well? What was I supposed to do? Cry about it? Make a stink? Demand that he unhire me? Of course not. So my mother had exerted her newfound power and gotten me a break. Maybe Arnold was Hal's agent as well as hers, and she'd asked him to call in a favor to his other client. As I said, I'd suspected it was something like that, deep down. I was the daughter of America's Most Famous Mother now, so there were bound to be times when I'd be riding her coattails. But you know what? I was finally at the stage where I accepted the situation instead of resented it. Yes, I was grateful for the job, very grateful, even if it did come through her. "It was sweet of my mother to intervene on my behalf," I said, as much to Hal as to myself.

"Sorry, but I have no idea what you're talking about," he said.

Was he distracted again? "I meant that I'm okay with having my mother pull some strings for me," I said. "I realize how lucky I am to have 'friends in high places,' as you put it."

He laughed. "I've seen your mother do her thing on television, and I think she's outrageously funny—a total original—but she's not the one who whispered in my ear about you."

"No?" Now I was really confused.

"No, it was Jack Rawlins. For whatever reason, the guy loves my films and enjoys helping me discover new talent. When he heard I was making *Money*, he suggested I get in touch with your agent."

Jack? Jack Rawlins? I felt my heart explode, so unprepared was I for this bulletin. So he was the one who helped me land the job? The ambitious little prick actually did me a favor?

I tried to act cool, to *not* hyperventilate, but I was caught off guard and had a zillion thoughts running around in my head and couldn't—

Oh, wait. I got it. Yeah, I understood it now. When my mother was a guest on his show, she must have let it slip—despite my begging her not to—that I had encouraged her to schedule the appearance. In response, he must have figured he owed me one. This was just the favor for favor he'd talked about, the one-hand-washing-the-other business. Well, at least he'd kept his part of the deal, I had to give him that. "So Jack called you—what?—like a few weeks ago? Right after my mother was a hit on *Good Morning, Hollywood*?"

"Hey, as I said, I think your mother's a riot, but I have no idea when she did Jack's show. He called me about you a while ago. He told me he'd had drinks with you the night before and that you were someone I should take a look at."

Jack had called Hal Papush the day after I'd thrown the ginger ale in his face? Before my mother had even done his show? What was *that* about?

"Uh-oh. I just remembered that I wasn't supposed to tell you all that," Hal added with a semi-embarrassed chuckle. "Jack specifically asked me not to mention that he was the one who gave me your name."

"He did?"

"Yeah, and I blew it. Oh well." He shrugged, as if betraying confidences is no big deal, which, in Hollywood, it isn't. "So what's the story with you two? Does he have the hots for you or something?"

The hots for me. Right. "No, no. It's not like that." Then what was it like? Jack had not only given Hal my name but asked to remain my anonymous benefactor. I didn't know what to make of it, but I was definitely intrigued.

I decided to write Jack a thank-you note. I figured I could control what I'd put down on paper much better than I could control what I'd say on the phone, so it seemed like the best course of action.

I was appreciative in the note, as well as apologetic about my behavior at the Four Seasons, and I expressed a desire for us to bury the hachet and be friends.

The very day I mailed the note, I received one from Jack.

How odd, I thought when I opened it. Talk about being on the same wavelength as another person.

It, too, was a thank-you note. Apparently, my mother *had* let it slip that I was the reason she had done his show, but she'd led it slip to Jeanine, her publicist. The little tidbit had only recently made its way from Jeanine to one of the show's producers to Jack himself, which was why he was writing to me at this late juncture to thank me.

He was appreciative in the note, as well as apologetic about his behavior at the Four Seasons, and he expressed a desire for us to bury the hachet and be friends.

"On the same wavelength" was an understatement! We had used the identical language in our notes, the identical tone, too. The combination of the similarity in our approaches and the timing of them was more than intriguing. It was downright thrilling.

When Jack received my note, he called, laughing. "I think it's official: we must have been separated at birth."

"Right. The nurses dubbed us the Thank-You-Note Twins before they sent us to live with different families," I said, laughing, too. I also noticed that he had placed the call himself, instead of having Kyle, his assistant, handle it, and I took that as a sign that we had moved into new territory.

"Well, I, for one, am glad the separation's over," he said. "How about dinner Saturday night?"

This Saturday night? Well, I should say I'm busy, I thought. Play hard to get. Let him think I'm declining dinner invitations by the dozens. "I'd love to," I said instead.

"Great. Should I bring a change of clothes or am I safe from another drink in the face?"

You should bring a change of clothes, I thought, my mind leaping instantly and wildly into a fantasy in which Jack Rawlins took me to dinner, brought me home, made love to me, and spent the night. Had such stirrings been there, lurking inside me, from the very beginning of our "relationship"? Or was I newly turned on by the fact that he had shown me such kindness? "You're safe," I said. "No more temper tantrums. You'll be getting the Good Stacey as opposed to the Evil Stacey." I wondered suddenly about the redhead, the one he'd been cutesy with at Cornucopia! Were they dating? Was his interest in me purely professional? Or did he find me as attractive as I found him, now that we were no longer mad at each other?

"Actually, I'm looking forward to seeing whichever Stacey shows up," he said in a rather husky, suggestive voice that answered my questions without my having to ask them.

# Chapter

# Sixteen

☆

IN SPITE OF the passionate and often X-rated images that danced in my head (Jack rushing over with a huge bouquet of flowers, Jack declaring his undying love for me, Jack ripping off my clothes before we even made it into the bedroom), I was determined to take this one slowly–this relationship, this romance, this professional association that had grown personal. In the past when I'd meet a man who held the promise of genuine boyfriendhood, particularly after a long dating drought, I would hurl myself into the relationship, just jump right in, regardless of the possible consequences. I was too willing, too eager, too dumb, and the result was always the same: the "I love you, Stacey" would be followed, three months or so later, by the "There's something I need to talk to you about, Stacey." I was like roadkill when it came to men. I'd never see the tractor trailer coming.

But this time it would be different, I vowed, as I got ready for my dinner with Jack. I would be available and open and responsive, but I would not rush things. If my mother wanted to hurry love, that was her business.

"You look great," said Jack when he arrived at my door to pick me up.

Swell, I thought. He kicks off the evening with a compliment and I'm not supposed to rush things? He was the one who looked great, by the way. He looked great, smelled great, had great teeth. I'd never noticed the last one before, never been as close to him as I was at that moment.

"Thanks," I said and invited him in. I had spent as much time spiffing my place up as I had spiffing myself up. My mother would have approved. "Can I get you a drink?"

He pretended to flinch, protecting his face with his hands. "Come on. You promised."

"I meant a *drink* drink, silly. Scotch, isn't it?"

"It is. I'm flattered that you remember."

I remember almost everything about you, I thought, trying to rein in my hormones, settle myself down. It amazed me how my grudge against Jack had so suddenly and unexpectedly turned to— what? Lust? Infatuation? Respect? Gratitude? All of the above? Or was I kidding myself? Had I felt something for him right from the beginning, when he'd sauntered into Cornucopia! and we'd sparred for the first time? Or had the feelings surfaced at the Four Seasons when Jack had let down his guard and told me about his childhood, and was that why my subsequent angry reaction that night had been so over the top? Because my humiliation was more about my attraction to him than it was about his wanting my mother on his show?

I fixed Jack's drink and a glass of wine for me and brought them out to the living room, where he was inspecting my collection of videos.

"I see you like old movies," he remarked, thumbing through such classics as *All About Eve, Some Like It Hot,* and *A Letter to Three Wives.*

"I do," I said. "I can watch them over and over and never get tired of them. Why is that? Were actors just better then?"

"Probably, but it's the writing that sparkled in those films. It was sharp and funny and never lazy. The reason we remember Bette Davis's 'fasten your seatbelts' line in *All About Eve* is because it was fresh, not some warmed-over, cliché-ridden drivel."

"Like the dialogue in *Pet Peeve*, you mean?"

Jack smiled. "Why don't we make a pact not to talk about that movie ever again," he said. "I don't want to be reminded of how much my review hurt you, and you don't want to be reminded of how much my review hurt you, so let's stick with *All About Eve*."

"Deal," I said.

"Want to watch it tonight? Or one of the others?"

Tonight? "I thought we were going to dinner. You said you made a reservation someplace."

"We were. I did. But the idea of spending a quiet night here with you, watching a movie we both love, just struck me as being a much better idea. We could order in or rustle up something from your kitchen."

I groaned. "All I have are a gazillion cans of Fin's premium tuna, and I can't even look at them."

"What about popcorn? Got any?"

"Yeah, I do."

"Then I'll cancel the reservation and you make the popcorn and we'll spend the evening at the Stacey-plex Theatre."

"Okay." Why not? Jack probably went out to restaurants all the time. Staying home would mean he wouldn't have to sign autographs or run into people from the industry or be the guy with his own TV show. It would also mean I'd get to sit next to him on my sofa with the lights off.

I microwaved the popcorn and set the bowl on the coffee table. "Which movie are you up for?" I asked.

"How about *A Letter to Three Wives*. I'm in the mood for romance, and that movie has three of them."

He was in the mood for romance. Well, that made two of us. Still, I was not going to rush into anything, as I said. Jack Rawlins was bright and successful and wonderful to look at, and he was clearly interested in me, judging by his words as well as his actions, but I was taking this one slowly, no matter how great the temptation not to.

I popped the tape into the VCR, dimmed the lights, and settled onto the sofa—onto the other end of the sofa from where Jack was sitting.

"It's not contagious," he said with a laugh.

"What isn't?"

"Whatever you think I've got." He patted the cushion next to him, indicating I should slide over and sit there.

"Oh. Fine. I just thought you might want to spread out." I moved over next to him, affecting nonchalance.

As I hit the play button on the remote and the opening credits rolled, I was so conscious of Jack's physical presence that I could hardly concentrate on anything else. Nevertheless, I watched the movie, munched on popcorn, sipped some wine, and behaved myself.

And then, a little over halfway into the film, my resolve suddenly and irrevocably deserted me.

We had gotten to the part of the story that chronicles the relationship between Linda Darnell and Paul Douglas. Jack leaned over and said, "Look at the chemistry between those two. She's determined to act as if she doesn't love him and he's determined to act as if he doesn't love her, and the audience is fully aware that they're crazy about each other."

His arm grazed mine as he made his point, and my body jerked involuntarily, the way your leg jerks when the doctor taps your knee to test your reflexes.

"She has to act as if she doesn't love him," I said, hoping he hadn't noticed. "She's protecting herself."

"And he's protecting himself," said Jack, "which is what creates the sexual tension between them." He made serious eye contact on the words "sexual tension," and I made serious eye contact back at him, and there was no denying the electricity right there on that sofa.

"What?" I said, thinking he had said something else.

"Nothing."

"Oh."

We refocused on the movie.

A split second later, Linda Darnell and Paul Douglas engaged in a steamy (for the 1950s) kiss, a kiss that confirmed all their pent-up emotions. Jack turned to look at me at the precise instant that I turned to look at him and, like two love-starved maniacs, we went for each other, just flew at each other in that darkened room, the flickering black-and-white images on the TV screen our only light.

"Listen," I managed, as he was kissing me with such ardor that I had trouble breathing. "I hardly know you. I don't want you to think I do this all the time." Okay, so maybe I had been known to make out with guys on a first date, but never like this. Never as intensely or fabulously as this.

"So if you're not promiscuous," he said as I sucked on his cheek, his chin, his lower lip, "it must mean that you really like me."

"Not necessarily," I said as he stroked my thigh. "It might just mean that I like your cologne."

"I'm not wearing any," he said after a luscious duel between his tongue and mine.

"Then I can't account for it," I said, my body a mass of exposed nerve endings. "But please don't stop what you're doing."

What he was doing was rubbing up against me while he was kissing me. If it was possible to die of arousal, I could have.

"I've wanted to do this since I saw you at the store," he said in a low moan.

"I don't think the redhead would have approved," I said.

"The redhead's a friend," he said. "Didn't you notice how platonic we looked?"

"I didn't have time to notice," I said, ecstatic with this news. "I was too busy hating you."

"Do you hate me now?" As he asked the question, he had his hand up my sweater and was unhooking my bra.

"No."

We kissed some more. I couldn't get enough of him. I loved the way he inhaled me with every kiss, loved how he stopped every few minutes to look at me, to take me in, loved how he said my name in a soft, whispery voice.

"You know what would be great?" he said.

"What?"

"If we could do this all night."

"I don't have a curfew. Do you?"

"No."

"There's just one problem," I said. "I want to take this slowly. In fact, I'm determined to take this slowly."

"I'll go very, very slowly," he said, unzipping my slacks and slipping his hand inside them.


When I woke up at two o'clock in the morning, we were still on that sofa. I was stark naked and being spooned by Jack, who was stark naked, too, and drooling on my shoulder. The television was still on and the popcorn was still sitting in its bowl, and our clothes were strewn haphazardly on the floor.

My first thought upon surveying the scene was that I had done it again: rushed in instead of heeding my own advice, and that I would pay the price. Sure, Jack and I had created real magic in the sex department, but what if it had meant more to me than it had to him? What if he was a love-'em-and-leave-'em type? And, speaking of types, why couldn't I be one of those dopey *Rules* girls?

I slipped out of his arms and stepped back into my clothes, resigned to the fact that my hoped-for romance would likely become a giant flameout, based on past experience.

As I was turning off the TV, he stirred, then peered at me, not quite awake but getting there. Here it comes, I thought, preparing myself for the awkwardness, the weirdness, the feeling of wanting to crawl down a drainpipe. Brace yourself, Stacey. He's going to say what a nice evening he had and promise to call you, then grab his clothes and head for the door.

In that instant, I decided that I wouldn't give him the chance; that the smarter thing to do—the most self-preserving thing to do—would be to thank *him* for a nice evening and then kick *him* out.

"Jack," I said, handing him his clothes. "That was fun, but I have an early day tomorrow. I hope you understand."

He laughed. "Get over here, would you please?" He threw his clothes back onto the floor.

"I'm serious," I said, handing them to him again. "I really enjoyed our time together, but it's better if you leave now."

"Why?"

"I already told you. I have to get up early."

"For what?"

"For an audition."

"Tomorrow's Sunday. What are you auditioning for, a church choir?"

"Oh. Stupid me. What I meant was that I have to get up early for work at the store."

"Really? Don't most stores open later on Sundays?"

"Yes, but the salespeople have to come in early. We have to set up, make sure the merchandise is displayed properly, the usual."

"Stacey?"

"Yeah?"

"You're pulling a Linda Darnell."

"Meaning?"

"You're acting as if you don't care about me, so you can protect yourself."

"That's ridiculous."

"What's ridiculous is that you're standing there with your clothes on. Take them off and come over here, would you?" He held out his hand to me, pulled me back onto the sofa, and finger-combed my hair off my face in a gesture that was exquisitely tender. "You know, there are no guarantees in life, especially when it comes to relationships, but I think things are going pretty well between us so far, don't you?"

I nodded reluctantly.

"So what do you say we play this out, see where it leads? I'd like us to do that, Stacey. I'd really like us to do that."

He kissed me soulfully on the mouth, purposefully. It was a wet, damp, humid kiss, and it sapped all the resistance out of me.

"You win," I said, taking off my clothes.

"We both win," he said. "There's just one little matter before you get comfy."

"What?"

"Do you have a bedroom? With an actual bed in it? This sofa's hell on my back."

"Yes, I have an actual bed," I said. "Follow me."

# Chapter
# Seventeen

★

OVER THE NEXT FEW WEEKS, Jack and I embarked on the kind of feverish romantic adventure that was as exhausting as it was exhilarating. Sleeping was out of the question, thanks to our incessant and extremely satisfying lovemaking, and eating was merely a means of survival, since the very act of falling in love triggers an odd sort of nausea. Discovering tiny details about each other, however mundane (Stacey to Jack: "You had a little red truck when you were a kid? That's so cute." Jack to Stacey: "You were on the girls' field hockey team in high school? How athletic."), was like unearthing buried treasure. On a more serious note, Jack confided that he was now estranged from his parents, who were as distant emotionally as they were geographically. He also confided that he was in constant contact with his younger brother, who, it turned out, had suffered a spinal-chord injury as a child, was in a wheelchair, and was supported not by his parents but by Jack—a revelation that made me admire him all the more. I confided that I had always been at odds with my mother, given how domineering and intrusive she was, but that I was beginning to appreciate her positive qualities and, as a result, was more accepting of her than I was irritated by her. I also confided that, while I had dreamed of being an actress since I was five, I was slowly coming to the conclusion that I was probably not going to "make it" in a major way and that I would have to find another career at some point–a very tough admission.

There were a lot of confessionals between Jack and me in those early days. We filled in the blanks, rounded out the picture, shared information both personal and professional. Everything we did and said seemed miraculous to us, as is the case with new lovers, and we spent an inordinate amount of time discussing how thrilled we were to have found each other, particularly after our bumpy start.

Of course, there was the real world to contend with. Jack not only had his show to tape once a week, but he regularly screened movies and boned up on the guests he had to interview and took meetings with a variety of industry types. And I continued to go on auditions–getting a job here, a job there–and to work part-time at the store. Still, we stole as much time together as we could. No matter how hectic our days, there were always the nights–those precious hours when it was just the two of us, getting to know each other, getting to touch each other, getting to trust each other.

One night, we were stretched out in bed at my place. Jack was reading the notes his producer had prepared in anticipation of an interview with Jeff Bridges, and I was reading the latest issue of *People* in the hopes of understanding the appeal of Jennifer Lopez.

I looked up and said, "Oh, by the way, I'm finally meeting my mother's boyfriend tomorrow night." While Jack hadn't seen my mother since her appearance on his show–he and I had been keeping a low profile, not ready to go public just yet–he had certainly expressed interest in her.

"How are you feeling about her having a man in her life?" he asked, putting his notes aside and sliding across the bed to be closer to me.

"Conflicted. I want her to be happy, obviously, and, while no one can replace my father, she deserves to be with someone, especially after so many years on her own. On the other hand, I don't know anything about the guy, so I can't help being a little wary."

"What's his name? You never told me." He was massaging my shoulders as he asked the question, and my knots of stress melted with every stroke of his fingers.

"Victor," I said dreamily. "Victor Cheever. No, Chester. No, wait. His last name is like cello or something. *Chellus.* Right, it's Victor Chellus."

Jack brought a halt to the massage. I turned to glance at him.

"What's the matter? Got a cramp in your hand?" I said.

He shook his head. "Just taking a break."

"Good, because I was enjoying that. So, have you ever heard of this Victor Chellus? My mother claims he's a producer—or used to be. According to her, he's a man of many talents."

"The name's vaguely familiar," said Jack, resuming the massage, "although everyone in Hollywood claims to be a producer."

"You're telling me. But you're not aware of any specific projects he's produced?"

"Nope. Sorry."

"Maybe you could ask around about him. Would you do that, Jack? My mother isn't the brightest bulb in the lamp when it comes to dating, and I don't want her getting mixed up with some phony. Any background stuff on him would be much appreciated."

"I'll see what I can find out. Meanwhile, why don't you and I concentrate on us." Jack moved his hands from my shoulders to the small of my back and began to knead my muscles there.

"Hmm. That feels wonderful," I purred. "To think that you're brilliant and a skilled masseur, too. I only hope my mother's as lucky with her man as I am with mine."

*  *  *

I met Mom and Victor at Il Pastaio, an Italian restaurant in Beverly Hills that's impossibly crowded every night of the week. This particular Thursday night was no exception. People were stuffed into the place, our table for three shoehorned into a tight corner, and the noise level was ear-splitting. Before her celebrity, my mother would have bitched and moaned. ("Don't they know there are fire codes? Don't they give you any elbow room? Don't they care that it's hot enough in here to roast a chicken?") But because the waiters treated her with the utmost unctuousness and because the clientele gawked and pointed and regarded her as the icon she had indeed become and because–this was the key–it was *Victor's* favorite place to dine–Il Pastaio was the site of our introductory dinner.

"Ah, Stacey! We meet at last!" he boomed in a deep baritone of a voice, punctuating every word with an exclamation point. He also stood to greet me, and instead of shaking my hand, which would have been appropriate for an initial encounter, he opened his arms and folded me into a bear hug. Clearly, he was the affectionate type. He was short, only an inch or so taller than I am, and chubby around the middle, and he wasn't handsome in a conventional sense. What made him attractive was his air of playfulness, the impishness in his hazel eyes, the way he threw back his head of wavy, shoe-polish brown hair when he laughed. His wardrobe left something to be desired–his outfit represented nearly every color in the Crayola box–but I attributed this garishness to exuberance. Of course, if one of my boyfriends had ever appeared at our door decked out in a red blazer and a green shirt and a Dodger blue baseball cap, my mother would have been appalled. How times had changed.

"It's nice to meet you, too," I said, sitting down.

"Your mother and I have ordered drinks. What about you?" he said, raising his bushy eyebrows, which were dyed to match his hair.

I told him I'd like some water. I intended to keep a clear head.

"Well, well," he boomed again, as if he were speaking into a bullhorn. "So you're Cookie's daughter, her pride and joy."

Cookie?

"Victor calls me that," my mother explained with a shy little giggle. "It's a pet name. Because I'm as sweet as a cookie."

My mother wasn't the sort of person to whom you'd give a pet name. And "sweet" wasn't an adjective I'd ever heard used in connection with her, but never mind.

"I'm Stacey, yes," I said to Victor, wondering if she had a pet name for him and, if so, whether it was Shrimpy. "My mother tells me you're retired now, but that you used to be a producer?"

He nodded, sipped his vodka on the rocks. "I've put together a few projects over the years," he said. "Producing is really about squeezing money out of people, and I'm pretty good at that."

"Victor's been in several businesses," said my mother, patting his arm. "He's a genius when it comes to spotting a potential money-maker and turning opportunity into reality."

"Now, come on, Cookie," he said with a chuckle. "Don't oversell me to your daughter. I'm hardly a genius. I just enjoy a challenge."

"You *are* a genius," she said. "And a handsome genius to boot."

"What about that face of yours?" he protested. "I'm not supposed to gloat that I landed the most beautiful woman ever to come out of Cleveland?"

"Some beauty," she said with a shr ̄

"Beauty and brains," he added. "A     ̄umor and maturity."

I smiled tolerantly as they made goo-goo eyes at each other and spoke in baby talk. I couldn't believe I was watching my own mother. She'd never been a sappy romantic, certainly not when she was married to my father, so this behavior of hers was a surprise, to put it mildly.

"Tell me more about yourself, Victor," I said, when they'd finished their back-and-forth about how handsome/beautiful they found each other. "Do you have children? Brothers and sisters? Any family here in L.A.?"

"Regrettably, I don't," he said.

"Victor was married years ago, dear," said my mother, jumping in, "and his wife passed away without bearing children." She looked at him with sad, adoring eyes, as if his pain were hers now.

"I'm sorry," I said to him.

"It was very difficult to lose her," he acknowledged, noisily enough so the diners at the next table turned around to look at him. I wondered if he might be hard of hearing, but decided he was just one of those people who compensates for being short by being loud. "But time does heal, as they say. I'll never fully recover from her death, of course, but at some point I had to pull myself together and carry on." He misted up here, causing my mother to pat his arm again. "Now," he said, clearing his throat, "let's not dwell on unpleasantness. We're here to celebrate tonight, thanks to my first meeting with Stacey."

Basically, that's how the evening went. Victor was solicitous of my mother and of me, and, in contrast to his goofy wardrobe, he had a sensible, self-deprecating way about him that was rather charming. I liked him, I realized halfway through dinner. Despite my initial reservations and whatever subconscious allegiance to my father I harbored, I actually liked the guy. He wasn't a braggart, didn't monopolize the conversation, wasn't one of those me me me types that are ubiquitous in Hollywood, but showed an amazing restraint when it came to talking about himself and his accomplishments. Moreover, he didn't throw himself at me in an attempt to make me accept him as my mother's boyfriend. He simply expressed how attached he was to her, how much he cared about her well-being, and how he hoped I would be fine with that. He wasn't an overt sleaze, in other words.

"I don't want you to worry about your mom," he said as he was paying the check. "I know she and I have only known each other for a few months, but she's in good hands with me, Stacey. Really."

I left the restaurant feeling fairly reassured.

When I got home I called Maura. Since I'd started seeing Jack, I hadn't spoken to her as often as before, and I missed her, missed her habit of putting things in their proper perspective.

"Hi. I just had dinner with Mom's new sex slave," I said when she picked up.

"And?" she asked.

"He's not bad at all," I said. "I was prepared for some total operator, but he seems genuinely interested in my mother. Of course, she's mad about him. And why not? He treats her like a goddess."

"It should only happen to me. So what's he like? Good-looking?"

"Sort of. He's short and he's got a little paunch and he desperately needs a wardrobe consultant, but he has a great smile and nice eyes, and he falls all over my mother. "

"Tell me this heartthrob's name?"

"Victor Chellus."

*"Victor Chellus?"*

"Why? Do you know him, Maura?"

"Know him? I slept with him."

"I don't believe it!"

"Believe it, because it's true."

Well, Victor was the right age for Maura, and everyone knows everyone in L.A. Still, it had never occurred to me that she would know him in the biblical sense. "When did you sleep with him?" I said. "A long time ago?"

"About four months ago," she said. "It was just a one-nighter, nothing serious, but he's got a great house in Beverly Hills with a screening room and a chaise that converts into a bed."

"My mother told me all about the house," I said, "and the *chaise*." God, this was too creepy for words. "How did you meet him?"

"At a party. He picked me up with some lame line like, 'You're too pretty to be standing here all by yourself.'"

"Yuck. What made you fall for that?"

"I was lonely. And he was attentive. And I go for the geezers, you know that."

"And he obviously goes for women younger than my mother. You say you were only with him that one night?"

"Yeah. He took me back to his place and we watched a movie and fooled around and then he had his driver take me home."

"Did he call you after that?"

"No. I figured he met someone else."

"He *did* meet someone else: *my mother!*"

"Boy, this is small-world stuff, even for L.A."

"That's not the point," I said. "The point is that four months ago, Victor was at a party picking up a woman in her thirties, and then, a mere month later, he was at a talent agency picking up a woman in her sixties—a woman he's got wrapped around his stubby little finger at this very moment. Something's wrong with this picture."

"Very wrong. The night I met him he was coming on to every chick in the place—every young chick. And now he's madly in love with your mother? I hate to say it, but he could be after her for her money."

"But he has his own money, Maura. You just told me about the fancy house in Beverly Hills."

"Doesn't mean a thing. The bank could be foreclosing on the place for all we know. I've learned a lot about the people in this town, and the most important thing I've learned is that most of them aren't what they seem and appearances are deceiving and you can't tell a producer from a putz. I'd advise your mother to go slowly with this guy, if I were you."

"As if she would listen to anything I had to say," I scoffed. "She's as impulsive as I've always been, now that she's Ms. Fin's Premium Tuna Fish."

"Then *make* her listen. If Victor was such a hot producer, how come there isn't a single credit for him on the Internet Movie Database?"

"You checked?"

"Yup. Right after our date. He's not listed anywhere on that website."

"Well, he did say he was in other businesses, like real estate and financial investments. Maybe most of his money comes from those sources."

"Maybe and maybe not. Just keep an eye on him, would you?"

"Maura, you're scaring me. You're supposed to be the one who views the glass as half-full all the time. Where's the eternal optimist when I need her?"

"I'm here," said my friend. "But I'm telling you that guys who try to score with women our age typically aren't interested in women your mother's age. Unless they have an ulterior motive."

"And you think that ulterior motive is money?"

"Could be."

"Then why would he chase after my mother? She's done very well very quickly, but she's not exactly the richest woman in Hollywood."

"No, but she's probably the most gullible. She's new to all the nonsense, Stacey. For all her bluntness and bluster, she's totally naïve when it comes to the kind of manipulating that goes on here. In other words, she's easy prey."

I sighed. "Victor was awfully nice at dinner."

"Look, it's possible that he *is* nice and that we're overthinking the situation."

"You're right. In the meantime, I'll try to do some nosing around about him. Oh, and Jack promised to make some inquiries."

"Speaking of loverboy, how are things between you two?"

"Pure bliss. I've never been happier, Maura. I know the relationship is still young, but Jack is different from the others, I can tell. It's Victor I'm worried about."

"Then make it your mission to get all the information you can about him. Your mother would do that for you, if your positions were reversed."

They *are* reversed, I thought, not for the first time.

# Chapter

# Eighteen

☆

'LL TAKE THESE cocktail napkins," said the woman, a walking Ralph Lauren logo. There was a Polo man on her turtleneck, a Polo man on her jeans, and a Polo man on her handbag. There was even a Polo man on her Yorkshire terrier, who was encased in a tiny tartan plaid sweater. She was a regular customer at Cornucopia! and, despite the expensive wardrobe, she was hilariously cheap. "This is a house gift, so make sure you put a *really* big bow on it." The napkins were paper, not cloth, and cost a whopping five dollars, but she was trying to impress her hostess by going heavy on our free wrapping.

"I'll be right back," I said, taking the napkins into the stockroom.

I was wrapping the package and putting a *really big* bow on it when I overheard Cameron sucking up to a customer just outside the stockroom door. A male customer.

"Why, it's Mr. Chellus. How nice to see you again," she said.

I stopped what I was doing, obviously, and craned my neck to get a better listen. At first I assumed Victor had come to the store to see me, figuring that my mother had told him I worked there. But he didn't ask for me or even mention my name.

"Nice to see you again, too, Cameron!" thundered Victor, who was either a very good customer of Cornucopia! or an acquaintance of Cameron's. Perhaps more than an acquaintance. "How's business?"

"Great," she said. "We're so busy we can hardly keep our salespeople from collapsing." She had that right. "What brings you here today? A gift for one of your lovely ladies?"

*One of his lovely ladies?*

"One lovely lady," said Victor with a chuckle. "It's not her birthday. I'd just like to surprise her with a treat of some sort, to show her I was thinking of her. Any ideas?"

Cameron took his arm and guided him around the store, out of earshot, damn it. I tried to at least follow them visually, from my post in the stockroom, but the customer with the Ralph Lauren obsession kept yelling, "Where's my package? Do you people hire the handicapped to wrap your gifts or what?" Very politically correct. I wanted to strangle her with the gold ribbon I was winding around my right hand.

"I'll be right out," I shouted back, hoping to shut her up.

Meanwhile, Cameron led Victor to this counter and that section, and within minutes he had made a selection. Cameron came running into the stockroom with a set of English bath soaps and body lotions and told me to wrap them as a gift.

"But I've got to give this to the customer who's been waiting," I said, nodding at the cocktail napkins.

"I'll take them to her. You start on the bath products, and bring them out when you're done," she said, grabbing the napkins and turning on her heel.

Well, there was no point in hiding in the stockroom, I decided, no point in keeping my presence a secret from Victor. So I wrapped his items, took a deep breath, and walked over to him.

"Stacey!" He seemed very surprised to see me, which confirmed that my mother hadn't told him where I worked. "What an unexpected pleasure!"

"I'm a part-timer here," I explained, as I handed him his gifts. Today's wardrobe involved a lime green blazer with pale blue slacks. It would have been over the top for most Angelinos, for whom black and beige were the rule, but it was sedate for Victor. "So you've been shopping?"

He pressed his forefinger to his lips. "Promise you won't tip your mother off? I'm giving this to her tonight, before we go out for dinner."

"I promise."

"I thought I'd buy her a little treat. She resists the sort of lavish gifts I'd prefer to give her, so I have to keep coming up with more mundane presents. Bath soaps!" He laughed. "Cameron's idea."

"I'm sure my mother will be very appreciative," I said, "since she's a bath person, as opposed to a shower person." But then he must have known that, given that the two of them were, uh, intimate.

Victor and I chatted about nothing–he was friendly and, once again, disarmingly self-deprecating–and then he took off.

He seems like such a decent guy, I thought, trying to make my impression of him jibe with Maura's information about him. And then there was Cameron's remark, indicating that he often bought gifts for his "ladies." What was the deal with Victor? I had to know, had to find out for my mother's sake, before he broke her heart.

The minute Cameron ducked out of the store to run some errands, I hurried over to the computer, where all the customers' names and addresses were available on a database, along with the items they'd purchased and the dates they'd purchased them.

Okay, where are you, Victor? I thought, scrolling down through the As, Bs, and Cs.

Bingo. There he was, between Robin Charon, the customer who'd ordered enough stationery to wallpaper the entire store, and Ellen Cheppel, the customer with an apparent addiction to table linens.

My eyes widened as I saw what a good customer Victor was. Too good a customer. Long before he'd met my mother, he'd been buying English bath soaps and other goodies for women. And his purchases weren't just ancient history; his most recent one actually overlapped with the time period during which he'd started seeing Mom.

This did not make me happy, and so I tried to excuse away what was staring me in the face. Maybe Victor was merely one of those generous types who routinely hands out thank-you gifts to his secretaries and cleaning ladies, as well as others among his support staff. Or maybe the purchases were business gifts; if he really had produced movies, it wouldn't be out of the realm of possibility for him to have bought pretty little trinkets for the female studio executives he was trying to win over. Or maybe he'd just dated a lot of women before he met my mother. Maybe he'd been depressed, being a widower with no children to dote on, and he'd sought to ease his emptiness by bestowing gifts on members of the opposite sex. But now he had found my mother and they were a loving couple and his randy, runaround days were behind him. Righty-o, Stacey.

I brought all of this inner turmoil home that night and dumped it in Jack's lap. He and I had just enjoyed a thrilling roll in the hay, speaking of randy, and while we were putting our clothes back on, I reported on what I'd learned about Victor.

"What do you think?" I asked. "Is he using my mother?"

"I doubt it. Just because he dated your friend Maura and a series of other younger women doesn't mean he isn't sincere in his affection for Helen. Maybe he was a lonely widower who wanted to play the field before jumping back into a committed relationship with a woman his own age."

"Maybe. By the way, you promised to ask around about him. Any feedback?"

"Not so far."

"But he said he used to be a producer."

Jack shrugged. "He could have been more of a fund-raiser—the schmoozer type who ropes his friends into throwing a few thousand into a picture and then walks around telling everyone he's a producer."

"I suppose that could be the case. In fact, his precise words to me the other night were: 'I'm pretty good at squeezing money out of people.' He was involved in a lot of businesses, apparently."

"See?"

"Yeah, I just don't want the latest person he squeezes money out of to be my mother."

Jack drew me to him, wrapped me in his arms. "I understand that you want to protect Helen, but if Victor Chellus isn't the saint you'd like him to be, she'll find out in time. She's a grown woman, Stacey. She can take care of herself."

"No, she can't. She's very vulnerable right now. She might as well be a teenager for all the experience she's had with men."

"I take it she was protective of you when you were a teenager?"

"Protective? She used to frisk my dates."

He laughed. "Are you sure she wasn't copping a feel?"

"I'm positive."

"What was she checking them for? Condoms?"

"No. She was checking them for wallets. In those days she wanted me to marry well. Now she just wants me to marry, period."

He laughed again. "You realize that by snooping around Victor, you're meddling in her life the way she meddled in yours? I think you ought to let him be, just let his relationship with Helen play out."

Yeah, sure. My mother didn't raise me to be a woman who lets things play out. She frisked my dates and I was going to frisk hers, figuratively speaking.

About a week later, my mother suggested another dinner with Victor. I agreed and invited Jack to come along. He declined, citing his workload, even though I pleaded and cajoled and tried to make him feel guilty (I inherited this trick from Mom).

"I'll make it worth your while," I teased. "We can fondle each other under the table."

"I'd rather fondle you without your mother hovering," he said.

"I know, but I really want you to meet Victor, so you can give me your unbiased opinion of him. I also want my mother to get to know you better."

"And why's that? Are you thinking of keeping me around a while?"

I blinked in response to his question. He made it sound as if our continuing on together was *my* choice—an entirely new concept for me. Based on my previous romantic disasters, I had come to believe that it was up to the man to either love me or dump me; that I was just this passive blob who had no say at all in matters of the heart. I'd fall hard, hope the feeling would be mutual, and end up disappointed, so where was my power, my *choice*? Was Jack telling me without telling me that he was in the relationship for the long haul and that if we were ever to part company, it would be up to me to say good-bye? Inconceivable.

"Yes, I'm thinking of keeping you around a while," I said. "So would you please come to dinner? You've just got to witness the love fest that goes on between my mother and Victor. He actually calls her Cookie, and you don't want to miss that, do you?"

"Stacey, you know I'd come if I could, but I'm under the gun with the show and I just can't take the time. You go and tell me all about it, okay?"

Reluctantly, I let him off the hook and went to dinner with the twosome myself. Once again, we landed at Il Pastaio, and once again everybody stopped by our table to fawn over my mother, tell her how much they enjoyed her, and give her the "Make no bones about it" line, imitating her nasal, crabby voice.

Victor laughed at everything she said and told her how beautiful she looked and generally behaved like a man who was smitten.

"See how they adore you, Cookie," he said of the gawking pas- sersby. "You've won their hearts as well as mine."

Brother. I could have been invisible for all the attention they paid me, although Victor did ask about Jack, about why he couldn't be there.

"He's very busy with his television show," I said. "He wanted to come, really."

"Well, I was looking forward to seeing him," said Victor. "He and I have so much in common."

Not your taste in clothes, buddy. (Victor was a vision in a yellow- and-orange striped sweater and navy slacks.) "So much in com- mon?"

He smiled. "Yes, the two Reiser women."

"Right."

"Yes, I was really hoping to dine with the toast of Hollywood," he went on. "Wait. Let me amend that. The *other* toast of Holly- wood." He leaned over and kissed my mother. "I watch his show religiously."

"I'll tell him," I said. "He can be a pretty tough critic on that show—*I* ought to know—but it's all because he has a genuine love for movies and has since he was a child."

"Since he was a child? How interesting," said my mother.

"How did he get into television?" asked Victor. "Did he cover the movie business in print first?"

"Exactly," I said, surprised that he had guessed Jack's route to success. "He used to write for *Variety* once upon a time."

"The Bible of the industry," Victor mused. "I bet he knows where all the bodies are buried in this town."

"What an odd thing to say," my mother remarked.

He patted her hand. "Just an expression, Cookie, like talking about skeletons in the closet. No harm meant, right, Stacey?"

"Right," I said. "I'm sure Jack does know who's done what to whom in Hollywood. But he's discreet. Too discreet, if you ask me. He never gossips about people in the business, and it's so frustrating."

We all laughed.

"Maybe Jack remembers when you were in the movie theater business," Mom said to Vic. She turned to me to explain. "Victor owned a small chain at one time, dear. Such a mogul."

"You owned movie theaters?" I asked him.

"I did," he said offhandedly, "along with other businesses. I bought companies at rock-bottom prices and sold them after they reached their potential."

"He's a magician with money," my mother chimed in. "I've been begging him to take charge of mine."

I knocked over my wineglass. "You already have a financial advisor," I reminded her. "You hired him right after you hired Arnold and Karen and Jeanine and Eve. Any more in the entourage and you'll have a baseball team, Mom."

"No one is the financial wizard that Victor is," she said. "What's more, no one *cares* about my money the way Victor does."

That's what I'm afraid of, I thought. "Yes, but why burden Victor with money issues when the two of you are having such fun?"

"You're absolutely right, Stacey," he said. "I keep telling Helen that she shouldn't rush an important decision like that. She's fine with the investment advisor she has."

Well, at least he wasn't pressuring her. Maybe he really did care about her. And maybe I still couldn't stop obsessing about all those bath soaps he'd been buying.

After we'd finished our entrées, my mother and I got up to go to the ladies' room. While we were at the sinks, washing our hands (she'd just delivered a speech about the importance of hand washing in public rest rooms), she said, as if she were a girl with a high school crush, "Isn't Victor wonderful?"

"He's very nice," I conceded.

"He *is* very nice, especially when you consider all that he's been through. He could have turned into a bitter, angry man after his wife died so tragically, but he's retained his humanity, his zest for life. He puts on his outlandish costumes every day and goes straight out into the world, saying, 'Here I am, ready for anything.'"

"Wait. Wait. Wait. What do you mean his wife died tragically?"

"She was in an accident, a horrible accident."

I tried to act as if this were merely a bit of trivia as opposed to the scary news bulletin it was. "What kind of an accident?"

"Well, she was an avid sailor. She and Victor had a boat in Marina Del Rey and they used to sail all over the place. One day they took the boat out, and a storm hit, and poor Mrs. Chellus—Elizabeth, her name was—fell overboard and drowned. Victor was devastated, naturally."

"How awful. Did they ever find his wife's body? I mean, did it wash up on the shore somewhere? You always hear about kids who go fishing and find these bodies—"

"I didn't ask about her body, Stacey. There are things I simply wouldn't broach with Victor."

Like what? I wanted to say, perplexed by her reluctance to pry more information out of Vic. Before falling for him, there was nothing she wouldn't ask men. She was unafraid of intimidating them or pissing them off. As an example, she had practically tortured the president of Fin's Premium Tuna the day she met him, absolutely assaulted him with questions, but now she couldn't confront her new boyfriend about his past? What was up with that?

"So you have no idea if they recovered the body and whether they did an autopsy on it?" I said.

She was aghast. "Don't be a fresh mouth, young lady," she said, hands on hips.

"I was only wondering how an avid sailor would fall overboard and drown. Aren't you at least a *tiny* bit curious?"

"Of course not! This entire subject is downright ghoulish, Stacey. I don't appreciate it and neither would Victor."

"Okay, okay. I'll stop."

"Good. You see, what made Elizabeth's death even more traumatic for him was that he had only been married to her for a matter of months. Of course, the fact that she was a wealthy woman with no family other than Victor put an additional burden on him, because he was stuck managing her estate."

I tried not to let my eyes bug out when she said this. "You're telling me he was a newlywed when she died and that she left him all her money?"

She nodded, oblivious to my drift. "Now can you understand why I fell in love with this man? Look at his indomitable spirit. Look at how he rebounded instead of giving up. Look at how he not only goes on with life after the terrible blow he's been dealt, but how he relishes life. He's such a role model for me, Stacey. There I was, a widow in Cleveland who lived only for the occasional phone call from her daughter in Los Angeles. I had given up on the idea of ever finding love again after your father died, but Victor's changed my whole attitude. He's changed *me*. You've noticed that, haven't you, dear? How much I've changed?"

You bet I've noticed, I thought miserably. The old you would have run like crazy from a guy with a rich wife who died under suspicious circumstances ten seconds after she said "I do." But now you've let fame and fortune make you soft in the head, and I've got to do something about it before it's too late.

# Chapter
# Nineteen

★

"Victor chellus? Yeah, I've heard the name," said Mickey Offerman, my agent. I had gone to see him in hopes of strategizing about my career, as well as picking his brain about Victor. They were contemporaries and had both lived in L.A. forever, so it occurred to me that their paths might have crossed.

"What have you heard?" I said, trying to stay out of Mickey's line of fire, breathwise. He'd eaten something with onions prior to our meeting, and the by-product was bringing tears to my eyes.

"Rumor has it he's had business reversals."

"Really?" And my mother had said he was whiz with money.

"Yeah, he's been in and out of financial trouble, I think. There was a chain of movie theaters that had problems, some real estate that went sour, that sort of thing."

The movie theaters had problems? It hadn't sounded that way at dinner. "Well, he seems perfectly solvent now," I said. "He's living in the lap of luxury in Beverly Hills."

"What's new about that? Some people are up one minute, down

the next, up again the next. He's probably got a little gambler in him."

"Swell. He and my mother are an item."

"No shit." Mickey laughed. "The Tuna Lady's in love?"

"Apparently, and it's not funny."

"Why? Because Chellus took a dive or two in the market?"

"Speaking of diving, have there been rumors about his personal life? His wife drowned in a boating accident."

"Like that's a big deal around here. Look what happened to Natalie Wood. The thing is, everybody in L.A. is the star of their own drama, Stacey. This one's mother threw herself out a third-story window and that one's daughter was shot and killed by her drug-addicted boyfriend, and on and on it goes. So Chellus's wife went overboard on their boat. Doesn't make him an ax murderer."

"No, I guess not. It's just that this is my mother we're talking about. If I find out Victor's bad news, I'm breaking them up."

"Isn't it her decision whether or not to be with the guy? Why should she listen to you about it?"

"Mickey, Mickey." I sighed. How could I explain that my mother had raised me to be a meddler and that I was only doing what she'd taught me. "Let's move on and talk about my career."

He shrugged. "What's to talk about? Nothing's cooking at the moment."

"Nothing?"

"Nada."

"What should I do?"

"Keep working at that store."

"What else?"

"Ask your boyfriend Jack Rawlins to help you."

"He *has* helped me. But I feel I should get jobs on my own."

"Then have your boobs done, like I told you when you first came to see me. You're the only one in this town without hooters, kid."

"I already have *breasts*, Mickey. I just don't have the kind that are the shape and consistency of basketballs. Besides, there are plenty of actresses who haven't had theirs done. Meg Ryan, Sandra Bullock, Nicole Kidman. None of them is especially well-endowed."

"They're movie stars," he said. "They don't need hooters. You, on the other hand, are a woman who's pushing thirty-five and still waiting for her big break."

"Maybe if you started thinking more like an agent and less like a plastic surgeon, I wouldn't be waiting," I said.

"Maybe if you'd drop the I'm-so-talented-I-don't-need-tits act, we wouldn't be having this conversation," he countered.

Dear Mickey. After I left his office, I stopped at a drugstore to buy some Advil for the headache he'd given me. I tried to pay, but the young woman behind the register was too engrossed in *Variety* to take my money.

"Excuse me," I said, holding up the Advil. "Can I please pay for this?"

"Oh, sorry," she said. "It's just that I'm hoping to break into the business."

"Don't tell me: you want to be an actress," I said, my head throbbing.

"Doesn't every girl in this town?" she said, stating the obvious.


My mother went to New York to shoot an episode of *Sex and the City*. Yeah, I should have been the one appearing on that show, given that I was the thirtysomething single girl, but they wanted her to play Sarah Jessica Parker's bitchy aunt, so off she went.

While she was gone, Victor invited Jack and me over to his house to watch a movie. Jack begged off again, saying he had too much work to do, but I accepted the invitation, figuring I could use the evening alone with Victor to learn more about him.

His house was north of Wilshire Boulevard in a very tony area of L.A. known as the Beverly Hills flats. Set back behind tall hedges on one of the city's prettiest and most desirable streets, it was an elegant, traditional-style estate, more reminiscent of the grand mansions of the East Coast than the mazelike contemporaries of California. It was tastefully decorated, too—like a spread straight out of *Architectural Digest*—with expensive antiques and solid brass fixtures and French doors everywhere you looked.

Victor must have given his interior designer a sky's-the-limit budget, I thought, as I forced my tongue back into my mouth and tried not to compare my crummy apartment to his palace. Of course, the other thought I had was that, business reversals or not, Victor had enough money to afford one of the choicest properties in town. The question was: Did he do something illegal to get it and keep it?

And how about all the members of his staff that were bustling around? How was he paying for their services? For example, I was greeted at the door by Carlos, a strappingly handsome Latino, who welcomed me inside and offered me a beverage. He was Victor's "manservant," his majordomo, the guy who made sure everybody was well tended to. (It's a status symbol in L.A. for the super-rich to have a manservant, as opposed to a butler, even though they do essentially the same job. Perception is everything here.) And then there was the similarly Spanish-accented Rosa, Victor's personal chef, who was also Carlos's wife. They were hired as a "package deal," he explained to me at some point during the evening, and had been with him for many years. There was also Vincent, the beefy and always beaming chauffeur. He doubled as Victor's "security man," which is L.A. speak for bodyguard. And, of course, there were the housekeeper and the man who took care of the grounds and the full-time projectionist, whose domain was Victor's fabled screening room. Such lavishness. No wonder my mother's head was spinning. When we lived in Cleveland, she had a cleaning lady to help out once a week, but that was it in the way of "staff." This new lifestyle to which Victor had introduced her must have made her feel like a queen. It just seemed too good to be true—all of it.

"Well, isn't this cozy?" Victor said as we sat at opposite ends of his football field–length dining room table. Cozy it wasn't. "If I can't be with my Helen tonight, at least I get to dine with her baby."

"Thanks for having me," I said after taking my first bite of Rosa's chicken with roasted red peppers. It was delicious, and I complimented her on it as she served me some rice. A slim, pretty woman with big dark eyes and long dark hair tied in a ponytail, she smiled and thanked me and offered to give me the recipe. As she was talking, I allowed myself a brief fantasy in which I was a huge movie star with my own personal chef—a chef and a chauffeur and, of course, a manservant, not to mention a manicurist who made house calls.

"So tell me, Victor. How do you pass the time now that you're retired or semiretired or whatever? Are you a golfer?"

"Yes, but a very mediocre one," he said, doing his self-deprecating number again. "And I travel quite a bit—when I'm not chasing after your mother, that is. I like to keep an eye out for possible business ventures."

"Was it a business venture that brought you to Arnold Richter's talent agency the day you met my mother in his waiting room?"

"Oh, that." He chuckled. "I was there to see one of the other agents, Tony Linton, about a screenplay Vincent wrote."

"Vincent? The man who works for you?"

"Yes. Nice fellow and honest as the day is long. I promised him I'd show it around. Unfortunately, Tony didn't think much of it."

So Victor was out there peddling a script on behalf of his chauffeur/bodyguard. Well, that was pretty decent of him, wasn't it?

"Helen offered to read it," Victor mused, "which was very generous of her. She takes the cake, your mom."

"She does," I agreed. "Is she very different from the other women you've dated?"

"God, yes. For starters, she's not young enough to be my daughter. I have to admit that I was on a youth kick before I met her."

Wow. So he was being truthful about his dalliances with Maura and women her age. That made me feel a tiny bit better about him.

"And I can have an intelligent conversation with her," he went on. "She's well-informed about many, many issues, and isn't shy about sharing her opinions."

And he not only doesn't mind that my mother is opinionated, he actually likes that about her.

"Mostly, I love how real she is," he said. "There's no phoniness, no attempt to be someone she isn't. Do you know how rare that is in this town, Stacey?"

I do, I thought. But are *you* attempting to be someone you're not? And if you are, how do I find out what you're up to?

We chatted about my mother for a few more minutes before I decided to plunge in and probe the touchy subject.

"Tell me about your wife," I said. "If it's not too painful for you."

"It's not painful at all," he said. "I relish the chance to talk about Elizabeth. She was the light of my life, and the time we spent together is a beautiful memory for me." He paused, as if conjuring up just such a memory. "I was immediately attracted to her, to her dark beauty and her trim, athletic figure, but it was her wit that hooked me. She was lively and funny and very, very blunt, much like your mother. She also cared about her fellow man, serving on a number of charities."

"She didn't have a career?"

"No, but she worked hard for her various causes. She had inherited a great deal of money from her father, and so she didn't need a paying job."

Neither did you after she died, I thought, wondering if the bundle she'd left him had been squandered in one of his failed business deals. "And she died in a boating accident?"

"Yes. She adored being out on the water. She was a skilled sailor and taught me what little I know about the sport."

If she was so skilled and you were such a novice, how come she drowned and you didn't? "My mother said you were practically newlyweds when she died. You must have been devastated."

"I was. I kept hoping that I would wake up and discover that the accident had been a bad dream—a typical reaction, I've been told. But it wasn't a dream, and Elizabeth was never coming back, and I spent years grieving for her."

"Well, you seem to be doing much better now," I said.

"Thanks to your mother," he said. "She's given me a reason to get up in the morning."

"How sweet."

"It's true. She's helped me to look ahead to the future," he went on, "instead of dwelling on what might have been with Elizabeth. She's an amazingly positive force, your mother."

We shared a few chuckles over Mom's tendency to make her presence felt.

"Your attitude is remarkable, Victor. A lot of people would have dealt with the sudden loss of a spouse by saying, 'That's it. I'm not going to let myself care for anyone again.' But now here you are romancing the famous Helen Reiser. How do you explain that?"

"I explain it by admitting that I didn't let myself care for anyone for a very long time, and it was easy, because I dated women who weren't suitable for me, women to whom I'd never form an attachment. Then I met Helen and she touched my heart. I decided I'd been alone long enough. I had to move on."

Brother, I didn't know what to believe about Victor Chellus. He had a way of making everything sound so plausible. Yes, his wife had died tragically, but bad luck happens. As for the fact that she was rich when she died, well, good luck happens, too, right?

Before adjourning to the screening room, he excused himself to have a word with Rosa. "I'll be a few minutes," he told me before heading into the kitchen. "Give yourself the grand tour if you like."

I took him up on his invitation. I was halfway through the tour, in the master bedroom, when I spotted a phone and decided to call Maura, to give her a quick report on my evening.

"So far he hasn't revealed much," I said after she picked up.

"Did you ask him about his wife?" she said. "You were going to see if you could find out any more about how she died."

"I know I was, but I chickened out. He seemed very genuine in his grief, so I asked a few harmless questions and left it at that. He did admit that Elizabeth was very rich."

"Elizabeth? Who's she?"

"The dead wife. Who else?"

"Well, now I'm confused. When I had my date with Victor, he told me his dead wife's name was Mary. It was 'poor Mary' this and 'poor Mary' that all night long."

"That's strange. Are you sure?"

"Positive. My sister's name is Mary, remember? I tend to pay attention when someone else has that name."

"But he told me his wife was Elizabeth, Maura. I swear he did."

"Hey, I warned you to check this guy out, didn't I? There's something off about him. Like he's demented or just incredibly slippery. Who knows? Maybe he was married to two women, not one, and they both died and left him money."

"You really think that's it? That he was married to Elizabeth *and* Mary and blurted out a different name to each of us in a moment of weakness?"

"Could be. Look, if I were you, Stacey, I wouldn't hang around that house by myself. I don't care how much Victor says he cares about your mother. I saw him in action and he's a letch, among other things. It would be completely creepy if he came on to you while Helen is out of town."

"Oh, God. That delightful thought never occurred to me."

"It occurred to me. You're supposed to watch a movie with him in his screening room, right? Well, don't forget about the chaise in there, the one that converts into a bed."

"The chaise. *Yech*. I'd die if he got anywhere near me."

"So go home now, before anything happens. Visit him again when your mother's with you. Then you can confront him with the Mary-Elizabeth thing."

"Good idea."

I hung up the phone, scampered downstairs, and ran smack into Victor, knocking a brandy glass out of his hand. I apologized profusely, then told him I'd developed a monster headache and needed to pass on the movie.

"But I was looking forward to the two of us getting comfy," he said, pouting.

That's what I'm afraid of, I thought, and beat a hasty retreat.

# Chapter Twenty

☆

I DIDN'T GO STRAIGHT HOME after all. I drove to Jack's house in the Hollywood Hills. I knew he'd be there, because he'd given me a big speech about how he couldn't possibly come to Victor's for dinner with the pile of notes he had to go over. I hoped he wouldn't mind the interruption, but I just had to tell him about Victor's Elizabeth-Mary bit, plus the business reversals Mickey mentioned, and get his reaction in person.

His house was a 1940s bungalow with a gorgeous pool–not a palace, like Victor's, but a private hideaway in a hip location that had been tricked out with new kitchen appliances, hardwood floors, and a sexy master bath. The only downside to the house was that Jack was a serious pack rat, the type who saves every single scrap of paper–for years! As a result, his place was ridiculously cluttered. Okay, a mess would be more accurate. Everywhere you looked there were magazines and newspapers and stacks and stacks of books, never mind videos and DVDs and Post-it messages from Kyle, his assistant. It was a miracle he didn't break his neck just trying to navigate from room to room. It was a miracle *I* didn't break my neck whenever I slept over, which was becoming more and more often.

I pulled up to his front door, rang the bell, and, while I waited for him to answer it, thought about how grateful I was that he was in my life, pack rat or no pack rat. My career was going down the toilet and my mother was going off the deep end, but I was happy. I woke up in the morning knowing there was a man who cared about me. I went about my days fortified with the certainty that I was in love.

Yes, love. Well, that's no surprise, is it? That I had fallen in love with Jack so quickly, even after my vow not to rush things between us? It was simply my nature to fall hard and fast; there was nothing I could do about it. Moreover, I honestly believed the outcome would be different this time. I felt that I had matured significantly since my past bust-ups and that I was a better judge of character now, was more discerning when it came to choosing a romantic partner. Besides, I kept reminding myself of what Jack had said the first night we were together: there were no guarantees in life but that he and I were off to a damn good start. He hadn't told me he loved me, but I trusted that it wouldn't be long before he made the declaration.

He opened the door and looked both surprised and delighted to see me, which made me love him all the more. When you show up at a guy's house unannounced, you're definitely taking your chances.

"I know I should have called first, but I had to talk to you," I said, feeling safe and protected in his arms.

"I take it that dinner with Victor wasn't a success?" he said, holding my hand as we went inside. It was a good thing he *was* holding my hand, because I nearly tripped over a mountain of *Entertainment Weekly*s.

"Pour me a glass of wine and I'll tell you," I said as we made our way into his kitchen.

"Okay, but let me run into the den and shut off the VCR."

"What were you watching?"

"A double feature," he said. "*Mildred Pierce* and *Stella Dallas*. I'm interviewing the author of a book about movies that focus on dysfunctional mother-daughter relationships. I've been studying up."

"Perfect. You're about to hear my sob story on the subject."

"What's it called? *Hollywood Mom?* Or maybe *No Bones About It?* Or how about *Mother's Tuna Helper?*"

"Funny. Very funny."

He kissed the top of my head, disappeared for a few minutes, and returned to pour me some wine.

"Now," he said, leaning against the kitchen cabinet. "I'm all ears."

I gave him a blow-by-blow of my evening with Victor, including my phone conversation with Maura. "Isn't that weird?" I said when I'd finished my saga. "I mean, it's bad enough that his wife drowned right after they got married, leaving him a rich man—a rich man who lives like a king, travels all the time, and yet doesn't seem to have a job. But the fact that he told Maura the dearly departed's name was Mary and then told me her name was Elizabeth is beyond bad. It's totally bizarro. The point is, I'm convinced my mother's better off without this guy, and I've got to do something about it."

He shook his head at me. "Stacey, Stacey."

"What? You're not impressed by all this?"

"Well, for starters, there's no proof that Victor is rich because of his wife. It's more likely that he had his own money from his various business investments, questionable though they may be."

"What do you make of the rest of it?"

"Truthfully?"

"Of course."

"I think you're overreacting."

"Victor has a dead wife whose name he can't remember or keep straight, and you think I'm overreacting? It's distinctly possible, Jack, that the reason he said the wrong name to me or to Maura is because the woman meant nothing to him. She was a meal ticket—a way for him to cover his business reversals, which he did by taking her out on that boat and pushing her overboard. Or—and I know you'll think this is a stretch—maybe he had two wives, Mary and Elizabeth, and pushed them both overboard."

"Would you please listen to yourself? Victor may not be everyone's idea of Mr. Right, but there's no evidence whatsoever that he's a homicidal maniac."

"How do you know? You're not a police detective. You review movies for a living."

"And I'm fairly sure I've just seen the movie you're describing. In *Mildred Pierce*, the daughter is fixated on her mother's boyfriend."

"Right, but the reason she's fixated on him is because she wants him for herself. I want Victor like I want a case of food poisoning."

Jack smiled. "Maybe you and Helen are the subject of a movie that hasn't been made yet. It's about a daughter who decides to turn the tables on her domineering mother and torment her about her choice in a man."

"Oh, I get it. So you think I'm just paying my mother back for all the times she disapproved of my boyfriends?"

"Aren't you?"

"No!"

"Stacey, you've told me again and again how she used to involve herself in every aspect of your life. Isn't it possible that, by rushing over here with these wild accusations, you're doing to her what she did to you? That you're instigating trouble between her and Victor in order to shift the balance of power between you two?"

"Pardon me, but when did you get a degree in psychology?"

"No degree necessary. Anybody can see what's going on here."

"Really?"

"Really."

So was I just leaping to nutty conclusions? Had I taken the facts about Victor and distorted them because I wanted to be the boss of my mother for a change? Had I insinuated myself where I didn't belong because *she* had become the successful actress and *I* had become the one with too much time on her hands?

"I'll grant you, it's odd that Victor used two different names to refer to his wife," Jack conceded, "but that's hardly a crime."

"Fine. But doesn't it concern you that Elizabeth or Mary or whatever-her-name-was died under suspicious circumstances?"

"They're only suspicious according to you. Victor wasn't arrested. There was no murder trial. And, most importantly, your mother loves him. Can't you let her lead her own life, just as you always wished she'd let you lead yours?"

I sighed. "He's not right for her. Even if he's not a lunatic, he's not right for her. If she weren't the famous Tuna Fish Lady, she'd realize it. She'd realize that he's got a pot belly and that he talks with a mouth full of food and that he dresses like a fool. I'm telling you, if she were back to her normal self, she wouldn't give him the time of day."

Jack drew me into his arms. "But she is the Tuna Fish Lady and she's mad about the guy, and the best thing you can do is step back and leave them alone. That first night we spent together, you confided to me how your most fervent hope was that she get a life of her own. Now she has one. Why not let her live it?"

"So I shouldn't tell her how tacky his wardrobe is?"

"She's not blind, Stacey. If she's not upset about the way he looks, why should you be?"

Because she's not running on all cylinders, I thought. Because she's too caught up in her commercials and her talk show appearances and her movie and television roles to deal with the truth about Victor, just like Joan Crawford couldn't deal with the truth about Zachary Scott in *Mildred Pierce*.

"So you won't help me investigate Victor?" I asked in a tiny, defeated voice.

"Investigate him? What on earth is there to investigate? Come on, Stacey. Remember when you told me how Helen used to frisk your dates? Well, wouldn't investigating Victor have the same negative connotation? Wouldn't delving into his background make you feel as if you and your mother had switched roles?"

Sure we had switched roles, but it was never more apparent than when she returned from her New York trip and stopped by my apartment for a visit. For three solid hours, I was as big a pain in the ass to her as she had always been to me, criticizing her, pestering her, offering her my opinion whether it was soliticited or not.

She arrived in her chauffeur-driven limo wearing a dress that was cut extremely low and, thanks to her new Wonderbra, revealed honest-to-God cleavage—a complete departure from the prim and proper style she'd once adopted.

"That outfit cheapens you," I said, sounding like the old her.

"Too bad. I love it," she said, sounding like the old me. "What's more, who asked you?"

"And your hair," I said. "It's falling in your eyes. Want me to snip off the uneven ends?"

"I don't need a haircut," she said. "It looks fine the way it is."

"Maybe it's your face. You're too thin, Mom. How about sitting down and letting me make you something to eat?"

"I'm not hungry, but I could go for some soda. Do you have any Coke or Pepsi?"

"I don't think you should be drinking soda, not with all that sugar in it."

"And I don't think you should be telling me what to do," she said. "If I want a soda, I want a soda."

"But soda is full of empty calories. There's absolutely no nutritional value in it, and at your age you really should watch what you eat and drink. So listen to your daughter and have some fruit juice."

The second the words were out of my mouth–"listen to your daughter"–I thought, Stacey, you haven't switched roles with your mother; you've actually *become* your mother.

This realization was so frightening to me that even the possibility of Victor being the Wacko Widower paled in comparison. I decided then and there that if the two of them were determined to be Hollywood's golden couple, they were on their own.

# Chapter
# Twenty-one

★

FREED OF MY RESPONSIBILITY to hover menacingly over my mother's social life, I rededicated myself to my pursuit of an acting career. Deep down, I knew full well that the clock was ticking and there was precious little time left for me to make my mark in the business at my supposedly advancing age. Part of me was looking forward to the day when I would give up the dream and establish a more sensible game plan—the part of me that was exhausted and deflated and numbed by having to measure up to an impossible standard of beauty; the part of me that was sick of hearing about the need for larger breasts or perkier breasts or breasts that bespoke a ripe, wanton persona I didn't have, with or without them; the part of me that was terrified of eating too many Reese's peanut butter cups. It was the other part that kept me hooked—the part that clung to the belief that someday I'd be famous, that someday I'd be sought after, that someday I'd fulfill the expectations of my high school drama teacher.

It was that latter part that prompted me to jump at the chance to play the role of an eccentric cat owner on an episode of the TV show *Just Shoot Me*. When Mickey called to tell me about the read-ing, I was so thrilled that I neglected to reveal to him that I am powerfully allergic to cats.

I auditioned for *Just Shoot Me*'s casting person and was very con-vincing as the eccentric cat owner—so convincing that I was called back for a second reading with the producers. I was convincing in their opinion, too, and landed the job. Hooray for me. The only tiny wrinkle was that when they asked me if I had any problem with cats, I said, "Are you kidding? I'm great with cats." I showed up on the set a few days later to film my scene, which involved me going on a date with Finch, played by David Spade, and insisting on bringing along Yankee, my cherished tabby, and his feline broth-ers Doodle and Dandy, and then getting into a "cat fight" with Finch's old girlfriend, who happened to be seated at the bar next to me. Okay, so it wasn't Shakespeare. It meant visibility on a hit show, and I was determined to give it my best shot. I had taken a Benadryl before leaving the apartment and had even given myself a squirt of one of those bronchial inhalers, so it wasn't as if I went to the set unprepared. It was just that neither meds worked. The instant I cradled the cats in my arms, my eyes began to drip, not to mention itch, and don't even ask about my lungs, which filled with what felt like motor oil and left me gasping for air. Thank God one of the cameramen had the good sense to drag me outside into the parking lot, away from Yankee, Doodle, and Dandy and their dreaded dan-der, and allow me to catch my breath.

"I think it was a sign," I told Jack later at my place. "I think I'm destined to quit this acting thing and get a real job."

"I'm not convinced of that," he said, trying to comfort me. "Maybe the sign was that you're a dedicated actress who goes out for roles even when she might be allergic to them."

I laughed ruefully. "You should have seen the producers. There I was, wheezing and coughing and choking to death, and all they cared about was how long it would take to recast the part. It made me feel warm and fuzzy about this business, I'll tell you."

"Look, why don't you let me help," said Jack, who helped simply by existing. He and I were growing closer every day, despite the fact that his star had risen and mine had just about dropped out of the sky. "I could get in touch with more directors, to see if they're shooting anything worthwhile."

"That's very sweet, but when you asked Hal Papush to hire me, you and I weren't a couple yet. We weren't even speaking, as I recall. I had no qualms about taking favors from you, because you were up there with your own television show and a powerful position in the Hollywood hierarchy and I was struggling to pay my rent. We were strangers to each other then, and the inequities between us didn't matter. But it's different now, Jack. They do matter, because you and I are–well–in a relationship. I want you to view me as an equal, as a partner, not as someone who needs you in order to survive. What I'm saying–and I've said this to my mother, too–is that if I'm going to make it, I have to make it on my own, not to sound too Mary Tyler Moore–ish about this."

"But people in this town never make it on their own, Stacey. It's all about networking here, about picking up the phone and calling everyone you know."

"I've been picking up the phone since I got to L.A.," I said. "And now all I'm getting is a busy signal. No, I've got to do this myself. It'll be my last hurrah, my final grab for the brass ring. If I don't make any progress within the next few months, I'll become the civilian my mother always wanted me to be."

A few days later, Mickey called about a possible part on the top-rated sitcom *Will & Grace*. I was so excited I almost cried.

"I can't believe it, Mickey," I said, then went on a gushing binge, telling him how much I appreciated his loyalty through the years and how, when the day finally came for me to stand up on that podium to receive my Emmy or my Oscar or even my People's Choice Award, he would be the second person (after my mother) I would thank.

"Yeah, well. You're a good kid," he said. "So. About the audition. You're gonna read for the part of a lesbo."

"Oh?" Mickey was loyal but crude, never mind politically incorrect, as I've indicated.

"Yeah, a gay girl," he said, in case I didn't get it the first time. "You hire Grace to redecorate your apartment, and while you two are yakking about fabric swatches, you're gonna come on to her."

"Come on to Debra Messing?"

"You got it, kid. Does Mickey Offerman get you the juicy parts or what?"

Okay, so I would have to flirt with another woman, perhaps even engage in some physical display of affection. I was an actress. I was up to this or any challenge involving my craft. I would tackle a same-sex scene with the same dogged professionalism that I displayed in my scenes playing a straight person. Besides, Debra Messing wasn't exactly chopped liver.

I did well in the audition with the show's casting director and got called back for a reading with Debra Messing herself. Apparently, she was a little squeamish about the scene and wanted to feel comfortable with the actress who'd be putting the moves on her. That was the good news. The bad news was that there were six other actresses that were called back, and one of them was my old nemesis, Brittany Madison.

As we all sat in the waiting room, studying the portion of the script we'd been given, Brittany performed her usual stunts meant to break our concentration. She pulled her "*ahhhh, eeeee, ooooo*" nonsense. She shouted into her cell phone every five seconds. And she paced back and forth, her heels *click-click-click*ing on the tile floor. So annoying.

When she saw she wasn't getting a rise out of anybody, she plunked herself down in the chair next to mine and leaned over.

"Well, if it isn't Stacey Reiser," she said, her tone mocking. "I didn't expect you to be here."

"Oh? And why is that, Brittany?" I said.

"Because the last time I saw you, you were flunking out of Gerald Clarke's acting class."

"Sorry to burst your bubble, but I didn't flunk out. I walked out."

"What I remember is that you couldn't get in touch with your sexuality and Gerald made an example of you in front of everybody. You do know that the part they're casting today is for a lesbian. A homo*sexual.* A woman who's totally out of the closet. Doesn't that scare you, Stacey? I mean, considering how inhibited you are, I can't believe you're even giving this audition a shot."

I smiled to myself as I tuned her out. Yup, she was playing her usual head games, no doubt about it, but I was not about to let her get to me. I knew exactly what she was up to: she was trying to make me feel so inadequate about my acting that I would figure I had no chance of landing the part and leave. That was always her strategy: to discourage the rest of us from staying and competing, so that she would win by default. Well, not this time.

I'll show her, I thought, plotting my own strategy. I was going to get in touch with my sexuality—or, rather, the character's sexuality—and push the envelope, go for broke, make edgy, creative choices with the script.

When it was my turn to read with Debra Messing, however, instead of sounding edgy, I sounded cheesy, delivering my lines with a sort of "hey-baby" lecherousness.

Debra: "I've been thinking about doing your walls in pale yellow."

Stacey (with lip curl and eyebrow arch): "I've been thinking about you, period."

Debra (looking surprised): "What do you mean?"

Stacey (moving closer to Debra): "I find you extremely attractive, Grace. I'm hoping you feel the same way about me."

Debra (looking shocked now): "Uh–*no*. I'm sorry if I gave you the idea that I–"

Stacey: "Look, Grace. You don't have to play coy with me. I know you live with a gay man and, while I understand that there are some lesbians, particularly lipstick lesbians, who try to keep the act going, I also understand that you deserve–no, *need*–to be fulfilled sexually."

Debra (horrified now): "You've really made a mistake here. I enjoy working with you and I'm happy to redo your apartment, but–"

Stacey (standing seriously close to Grace): "But what? You aren't interested? Are you sure?"

At this point, the script has Grace struggling to talk her way out of the situation. She doesn't want to insult me, because I'm her client and I'm a wealthy woman with great connections and she's nervous about losing my business, but she's not a lesbian, lipstick or otherwise, and she's freaked out by my advances and she's dying to bolt out of my apartment. What is not in the script is what I do next: I pull her into my arms and kiss her. Well? I was determined not to be the wimp Brittany had accused me of being, right?

There was bedlam, pure bedlam. The casting director yelled at me, demanding to know why I'd made such an edgy choice. The producers yelled at me, demanding to know why I'd taken it upon myself to touch, never mind brush my lips against the star of their show. And the security guard posted down the hall yelled at me, threatening to have me removed from the building if I put my grimy hands on anyone else. The only person who was nice to me was Debra Messing, who whispered, "I would have done the same thing if it meant getting the part. I've been in your shoes." I thanked her and slunk out of the studio before they had me thrown out.

# Chapter
# Twenty-two

★

NOW THAT JACK had met my mother, it was time for me to meet his brother, he decided. I took this as another indication of his as-yet-undeclared love for me.

On a Saturday afternoon, we drove to Newport Beach, where Tim Rawlins, who was in his twenties and paralyzed from the waist down as a result of a swimming accident when he was only eight years old, resided in a seaside cottage.

"How, exactly, did the accident happen?" I asked as we headed south on the freeway.

"Tim dove into the shallow end of a neighborhood pool and broke his neck. We consider ourselves lucky that it's only his legs that don't move."

"How horrible for a child to have to go through that," I said. "It must have been a nightmare for him, for everyone in your family."

"It was, but there are families who are brought closer together by tragedy. Mine wasn't one of them. My parents, who were remote even under the best of circumstances, drew even further into themselves, barely going through the motions. They got Tim the medical care he needed, but emotionally they were zeroes."

"You speak about them in the past tense, as if they don't exist."

"They don't, not for me. What kind of people abandon their disabled son to travel around the country? As soon as they saw that I was stepping up to assume responsibility for him, they flew off to the South Pacific, then changed their minds and moved to Maine, then switched gears a third time and settled in Idaho. They're still there, I think, but I have no confirmation of that."

"How do they support themselves with all this nomadic behavior?"

"They get jobs, live simply. The irony of their many years of marriage is that they can't stand each other. At least that's the way it looked from my vantage point."

"So they never call you to say how proud they are of you, of what you've accomplished in your career?"

Jack scoffed. "My father thinks movies are a waste of time, just another crutch for people who have no lives of their own. I used to lie about how often I went to movie theaters as a kid. Who needed an argument? As for my mother, she's such a lost soul that my success probably makes her feel worse about herself, about how little she's achieved. Of the two of them, she was the one with the brain. She just never bothered to use it."

"I still don't get how they could have left you and your brother to fend for yourselves, no matter how much money you were making or how vocal you were about taking responsibility for Tim. It's almost criminal."

"You're right. But remember: not everyone has a mother like yours, Stacey. She may drive you insane, but you've never doubted for a second that she loves you."

"Oh, she's been there for me, that's for sure. A little *too* there."

"Well, when she's a little *too* there, remind yourself that it could be worse."

We arrived at Tim's cozy beach house just as he was finishing up his exercises for the day. He was a handsome man, with Jack's reddish-blond hair and blue eyes, but a younger, less cynical version of Jack, more college boy than college professor. He smiled broadly when I entered the living room and teased Jack for keeping me a secret for so long.

"It hasn't been that long," Jack said, winking at me. "It's only been a few months since she threw a drink in my face on our first date."

"It wasn't our first date," I told Tim. "It wasn't even a date, although it *was* a seduction. As Jack must have explained, the one he was really after was my mother."

"I heard the story," Tim said with a laugh. "And I would have thrown a drink at him, too, Stacey."

"Aha! An ally," I said.

"An ally and a fan," he said. "I've seen you on television and I think you're great."

I gave Tim a hug. "You have just made my day," I said. "Just made my *year*."

The three of us chatted for an hour or so, then Jack went out to buy us lunch at a nearby deli. While he was gone, Tim took the opportunity to share his insights into his brother.

"He can be a know-it-all," he said, taking a loving swipe at Jack's occasional pomposity. "And he's not the most open person with his feelings. Reviewing movies gives him the perfect distance from them; he can stand back and critique them without having to be involved with them emotionally. And, of course, he gets a kick out of being Mr. Show Business—who wouldn't. But there's nobody more fiercely protective of me than he is."

"He told me about your parents," I said, "about how they're, well, absent."

Tim nodded. "Jack walked right into their role and took it over. He probably hasn't told you this, Stacey, but he pays for everything here: the roof over my head and the food I eat and the physical therapist who comes over and works out with me. Yes, I have a job, but Jack supported me before I was able to get a job. He's made huge sacrifices for me to allow me to live as well as I do—sacrifices he's much too proud to discuss."

"What sort of sacrifices?" I asked.

Tim smiled. "I'd better keep my mouth shut. As I said, they're not a subject Jack enjoys getting into."

I left it at that, but continued to wonder. On the drive back to L.A., I mentioned my conversation with Tim. "He's very grateful to you, very respectful of you," I said.

"He's a good person," said Jack. "Why wouldn't I do everything I can to help him?"

"Right, but you've made sacrifices to support him. That's what he told me."

"No big deal. Nothing I couldn't handle."

I looked over at him. There was a tightness in his voice when he spoke about the sacrifices, a clamming up, which was unusual for the usually loquacious Jack Rawlins. Tim had warned me that this was a subject Jack didn't like to talk about, and now I could see he was on target. But Jack's unwillingness to be more forthcoming only piqued my curiosity. What sort of sacrifices would he have had to make on his brother's behalf? Clearly, he earned enough money to support a sibling, but that hadn't always been the case. How had he paid for Tim's expenses before *Good Morning, Hollywood* made him the toast of the town? How had he been able to support Tim then, particularly since it didn't sound as if his parents had left him any sort of financial cushion?

\* \* \*

The answer to those questions would have to wait, I discovered, when another issue reclaimed my attention: my mother's attachment to Victor. I had been trying to reach her at home and getting her answering machine every time. Turns out she was sleeping at Victor's on a regular basis and had even moved some of her clothes into his house.

"Aren't you rushing things?" I had the nerve to say, given my own propensities.

"No, I'm following my heart," she said defensively. "Besides, I'm a grown woman and I can do whatever I want."

God, she sounded just like I used to whenever she'd boss me around. "But you're practically living with Victor. What is it you always told me? Don't give away the store before you get to know the buyer."

"I know the buyer, Stacey. Now, if you want to see your mother, why don't you come to Victor's for dinner tonight. I'll send Vincent, the chauffeur, to drive to the Valley and pick you up. Oh, and have Jack join us if he's not busy."


Jack said he *was* busy, so I went off to Victor's by myself, courtesy of Vincent, who was very soliticious—and smiley. Every time I glanced at him in the mirror, he had a grin on his face. Now there's a guy who's happy in his job, I thought.

When I arrived, I observed that my mother was wearing yet another brand-new outfit that revealed more of her than her old wardrobe ever did.

Who kidnapped Helen Reiser? I thought as I checked out her short skirt and skimpy top and strappy sandals.

I also noticed that she had taken on the role of lady of the manor, giving instructions to Carlos and Rosa and the others. "They're hardworking," she whispered to me, "but they're not used to a woman's touch around the house. So I stick my two cents in every now and then. For instance, Rosa is a lovely cook when it comes to arroz con pollo, but ask her to make a nice brisket and she's lost."

Perhaps Helen Reiser hadn't been kidnapped after all. She was still in there somewhere.

For our dinner that particular evening, Rosa had prepared tenderloin of pork with grilled vegetables—a meal so fabulous that I was dying for a second helping. I was about to take my plate into the kitchen when Mom hassled me.

"Sit, Stacey," she said after I'd gotten up from my chair. "Let Rosa bring it. That's what she's here for. Right, Victor?"

"Right, Cookie!" he boomed. "My people are at your disposal. You tell them what you want them to do and, by golly, they'll do it."

"Such a knight in shining armor," she cooed at him.

"Why wouldn't I be when my lady is the fairest in all the world?" he replied.

"You make me blush with your compliments," she said.

"You make me float on air," he said.

You both make me want to hurl, I thought, then said, "There's no need to bother Rosa. I'd rather get the food myself. I need to stretch my legs." And escape all the lovey-dovey crap in here.

I was en route to the kitchen, plate in hand, about to push open the swinging door, when I overheard Rosa speaking to Carlos in Spanish. She was saying, "Do you believe she told me that my vegetables were undercooked? Hasn't she ever heard of al dente?"

"She's from the Midwest. What does she know," said Carlos.

"Nothing," said Rosa. "Not about cooking. And not about cleaning. Did you hear how she told Betty to watch for mold the next time she scrubs the stall shower in the master bath?"

I giggled to myself. Mom was a tireless campaigner to rid the planet of mold. Mold and dust mites. Victor's caretakers were no match for her, even in her new Hollywood glamour girl mode.

"Well, not to worry, baby. This won't last much longer," Carlos reassured his wife.

I smiled again, thinking that Carlos and I were on the same page; that the romance between Mom and Victor was sure to be over soon. And then, when I heard the rest of their conversation, my smile faded.

"I'm getting the impression from Victor that she'll be next," Carlos added.

*Next?* Next what? Next to be conned into handing over her money to Victor? Next to be forced onto his sailboat? Next to *die?*

I pressed my ear against the door, straining to hear more.

"It does look as if he's heading in that direction with her," Rosa agreed. "And I, for one, won't be sorry. She's the pushiest woman I've ever met."

Yeah, yeah. So my mother was pushy. I couldn't argue with Rosa about that, but what did she mean about heading in that direction? What direction? And why should she be sorry about it?

"Life could definitely get exciting around here," said Carlos. "Maybe we should buy our earplugs now, just in case."

What did he mean by that? *Exciting* in a way that suggested police detectives and medical examiners and forensic technicians in latex gloves? And why would they need earplugs? To keep them from having to listen to my mother's screams?

I was scared now. Scared that maybe Rosa and Carlos, as Beverly Hills fancy-shmancy as they seemed, might have helped Victor kill his first wife. Yes, maybe they were his accomplices–maybe they were *all* his accomplices–and now they were gearing up for another crime with the intended victim being my poor mommy!

I burst into the kitchen. "Okay, listen up. I've got a problem."

Rosa peered at my empty plate and grinned proudly. "I can see that you enjoyed the pork. Are you here for another serving? I would have been happy to bring it out to the dining room for you."

"Skip the niceties, missy," I said. "This isn't about the pork."

"Ah, then it's more vegetables you want?" she asked sweetly.

"It has nothing to do with food," I said. "I happen to understand Spanish and I overheard your little chat before, about how you and Carlos think that my mother will be next and that her relationship with Victor is heading in a certain direction and that you're planning to buy earplugs. I want to know what you meant by all that, and I want to know right now."

Rosa looked startled. "My goodness. We weren't talking about your mother. We were talking about the secretary that Mr. Chellus hired not too long ago. She's taken it upon herself to interfere in every aspect of our work here."

"Yeah, his secretary, sure. You were talking about my mother and I know it. Remember how you said, 'She's from the Midwest'? Well, guess where my mother is from?"

"I don't know, but the secretary is from Chicago," said Rosa.

Oh. Okay, so it was possible that I had misunderstood and that they really were gossiping about another member of the Chellus household. But I wasn't sold. Not a hundred percent.

"You said you thought this secretary would be next and that you would need earplugs," I reminded them. "What was that about?"

"First let me say that I'm embarrassed for both Rosa and myself," Carlos replied. "We should never have been talking about private matters in the public rooms, not even in Spanish. But, since you did hear us, what we meant was that we expect Mr. Chellus to fire his secretary and that there's sure to be a lot of shouting when it happens."

"I see," I said. "That's your story and you're sticking to it, huh?"

They looked at each other and shrugged, as if they honestly

didn't know why I was getting so riled up. But I *was* riled up and I *was* going to get to the bottom of this little mystery once and for all.

I deposited my plate on the kitchen counter and marched back into the dining room. Before my mother could protest, I grabbed her hand and dragged her off to the library, where I slid the pocket doors shut and sat her down.

"I'll try to say this as gently as possible," I began.

"There's nothing gentle about your manners, Stacey. To walk out on Victor in the middle of a meal is so rude that I—"

"Let me continue," I interrupted. "It's for your own good."

"So continue."

"Victor is dangerous."

She giggled as she batted her eyelashes. "Dangerously sexy, you mean."

"No. Dangerous. The way *killers* are dangerous."

"What in the world is wrong with you, dear? Did you have too much wine?"

"No. I overheard Rosa and Carlos in the kitchen, and guess who they were talking about?"

"Victor's secretary?"

I was speechless momentarily. So there *was* a secretary?

"That's what they claimed," I said. "Supposedly, Victor's about to fire her."

"He very well may fire her. She gets on everybody's nerves."

"Okay, here's a question for you," I said. "Is she from Chicago?"

My mother laughed. "Not with that southern accent. She's from Memphis, I think. Or is it Nashville? What does it matter anyway?"

I jumped up from the sofa, waving my arms like a crazy person. "It matters a lot," I said. "So Rosa and Carlos weren't talking about her, just as I suspected. They were talking about you, Mom, and they didn't want me to know it. They said they thought you were pushy and that you would be next and that they wouldn't be sorry and that they were going to buy earplugs. When I asked them to explain themselves, they made up the story about the secretary. I think you're in danger, Mom. I think you should get out of here and never see Victor again—before it's too late."

"Stacey, Stacey. What's gotten into you?" She pulled me back down onto the sofa. "Maybe Rosa and Carlos *were* talking about me. So what? They don't like me, because I butt into their business. At first I didn't want to interfere with the way Victor ran his household, so I kept my opinions to myself. But lately I've spoken up about those two—they act like they own the place and neither takes kindly to a single suggestion of mine. I'm sure they wish I weren't around."

"Mom," I said. "They're not the issue. It's Victor who doesn't want you around."

"What?" Her nostrils flared. "Victor loves me and I love him and I'd really appreciate it if you'd get over this adolescent hostility of yours. You can't seem to face the fact that your father's gone and I'm moving forward with my life." She shot daggers at me as if *I* were the troublemaker.

"I do miss Daddy. You're right about that. He wasn't a saint, but he came pretty close."

"There. You see? This *is* about your father and the close relationship you had with him—the close relationship you never had with me!"

"Mom, Mom. Please believe that it's *you* I'm concerned about, not Daddy or his memory. Rosa and Carlos were talking about you, about you following in the footsteps of Victor's wife—his dead wife."

"Stop this nonsense," she snapped. "What you overheard is that Rosa and Carlos are afraid that Victor and I will get married. They don't want me supervising their duties once I'm Mrs. Chellus, which accounts for their snippy remarks having to do with me being 'next,' as in his next wife."

"But you're not planning to marry him, right? I mean, you hardly know the man."

"I know all I need to know."

"Really? Okay, here's a question you might want to ask him. How come he calls his dead wife Elizabeth one day and Mary the next? Isn't there something a little odd about that?"

"It's not odd at all. Victor's wife's name was Mary Elizabeth Biddlehoffer. Sometimes she liked to be called Mary. Sometimes she liked to be called Elizabeth. And sometimes she liked to be called by her childhood nickname, which was Binky. She came from a family of nicknamers, according to Victor. She had an uncle named Harold and everyone called him Roldie. You know how WASPs are."

Why wouldn't she listen to me? How could I *make* her listen?

"Okay, here's something else," I said. "Maura dated Victor, Mom. My thirtysomething best friend Maura Lasky. He picked her up at a party and brought her here, and they had intimate relations."

She rolled her eyes. "Victor dated a lot of girls your age before he met me. He didn't mention Maura, specifically, but it doesn't matter, because that chapter of his life is over. He and I are in love."

"But his wife died in a sailing 'accident' only months after she married him. I don't want that to happen to you!"

"Don't be morbid. Why should it happen to me? Jewish women don't sail."

I sank back into my chair, utterly spent. How do you explain to your mother why it should happen to her? How do you explain that she's putty in the hands of a smoothie like Victor? How do you explain that because she's a widow who hasn't been with a man in years, is newly rich, and is as gullible as it gets, she's exactly the sort of woman he'd target? "Mom." I touched her shoulder. "Doesn't it scare you even a little bit that Mary Elizabeth was wealthy and that Victor profited from her death so soon after they were married?"

"What scares me is your attitude, Stacey." She was really angry at me now. I was being a bad girl, and I was in for a lecture. "You have met Victor. You have witnessed firsthand how lovely and sweet he is. But you are determined not to see your mother happy. Why, I can't fathom, other than that you preferred me when I was the little Cleveland housewife whose only source of pleasure was *you.*"

Before I could refute her theory or warn her further, she had opened the pocket doors and hurried out of the room.

It was obvious to me then. My mother would not take my warnings seriously, because she was infatuated with Victor and distracted by her celebrity. If I had a prayer of convincing her that he was not the right man for her, I needed proof of his misdeeds. I didn't know how to go about getting such proof, but you do what you have to when your mother is about to make a fatal mistake, just as she would return the favor.

# Chapter
# Twenty-three

★

MAURA AGREED to be my partner in crime prevention. I couldn't go to Jack for help, since he disapproved strenuously of my poking around in Victor's marital escapades, so much so that I didn't even tell him I had decided to go ahead and do it. No, I didn't like deceiving him, but our relationship was progressing smoothly and we had passed the all-important three-month mark and I believed that he would confess his love for me any day. I couldn't afford to screw things up, not at such a critical juncture. Besides, Maura had more time to snoop than Jack did, plus she knew Victor, although marginally, and, as a result, was the ideal co-conspirator.

We began by looking into the death of Mary Elizabeth Chellus, who supposedly drowned during a sailing outing. Our first order of business was to search the *L.A. Times*'s archives for news of the accident, which we did at Maura's house on her computer.

"Anything?" I said, breathing down her neck as her fingers skipped over the keyboard. "It's possible that Mary Elizabeth died over twenty years ago, and the *Times*'s archives only go back seventeen years."

"She died sixteen years ago. Take a look."

We waited breathlessly for the article to appear on the screen.

"Boy, they didn't devote much ink to this," I said when the blurb—and that's truly all it was, six or seven short paragraphs—popped up on the monitor.

The gist of the story was that the weather on the day of the Chellus's excursion had turned threatening. Victor was at the wheel of the couple's thirty-eight-foot sloop, the unfortunately named *Lucky Lady*, while Mary Elizabeth (Victor hadn't lied to us about this; she really did go by both the Mary and the Elizabeth) was on deck trying to bring the sail down. When the boat was hit by a strong gust of wind, she slipped and fell overboard. He attempted to turn the *Lucky Lady* around in order to both find his wife and pull her back onboard, but the seas were choppy and he couldn't spot her. He radioed the Coast Guard for help. By the time they arrived, Mary Elizabeth was gone. They continued to search for her until dark without success, and it wasn't until the next morning that they made the grim discovery of her body. An autopsy was performed, the police ruled her death an accidental drowning, and Victor was said to be grief stricken.

"What do you make of it?" I asked Maura when we'd finished reading. "Other than that Victor took his sweet time getting married. If Mary Elizabeth died sixteen years ago and they were relative newlyweds at that point, he was a ripe old fiftysomething when he finally walked down the aisle. That's unusual right there."

"It sure is, although at the rate I'm going, I may not have any rice thrown at me until I'm in Depends."

"That's because your boyfriends are already in Depends. But getting back to Vic, it is odd that he waited so long to get married. I wonder what there was about Mary Elizabeth that convinced him to trade in his bachelorhood."

"Maybe he was waiting for just the right combination in a

woman," she said. "She had to have money, she had to be inexperienced with men, and she had to be easy to fool."

"My mother has money and is inexperienced with men, but she never used to be easy to fool. Quite the contrary."

"Everybody's easy to fool when they come to Hollywood and stumble on success and start believing their own press releases."

"I know. Victor must have been overjoyed when he met Mom and realized how impressionable she was."

"What's interesting is that, according to this article, no one suspected him of foul play in the drowning," Maura pointed out.

"But let's say there was foul play," I speculated, "and the police just didn't pick up on it. Let's say Mary Elizabeth didn't slip overboard on her own but that Victor caused her to slip overboard, which wouldn't necessarily show up in the autopsy unless he whacked her over the head first or shot her or strangled her. I bet he could have finagled the whole thing so that she went overboard without a single mark on her body."

"If he was professional about it, yeah," said Maura. "But that would suggest he either had help–like a hit man–or that he'd committed murder before."

"Committed murder before?" I said. "But he's only had one wife. Who else would he have murdered?"

"You're right. I'm getting off the track. The truth is, we don't have anything on Victor. We're back to square one."

"Not necessarily," I said. "Why don't we take a ride to Marina Del Rey, where Mr. and Mrs. Chellus kept their sailboat. We could ask around, see if anyone remembers the accident."

"It was a long time ago and the marina is the biggest one in the country. Who's going to remember an old boat or its owners?"

"Only one way to find out," I said.

We drove to the marina on Saturday morning, parked the car, and accosted every craggy-faced guy in a nautical shirt, asking every one of them if they remembered the *Lucky Lady* or the Mary Elizabeth Chellus accident. None of them did. Then we stopped in at all the yacht clubs based at the marina and tried to find someone familiar with the case. No success there, either. We finally found our way into the headquarters for the Coast Guard and the sheriff station, and started hounding people there.

"How can you *not* remember?" I snapped at the young coast guardsman who happened to be standing near the reception desk. I was growing frustrated and had become rather cranky. "The boat was docked right here at this marina! Yes, it was sixteen years ago, but the woman died, for God's sake!"

"I wasn't working here sixteen years ago," he replied. "I was in elementary school."

It wasn't insulting enough that I was considered too old by Hollywood standards? Now I was too old to get answers to questions that could save my mother's life? Please. "Aren't there records we could look at? Maybe there was a report filed? Couldn't you be a little more helpful?"

I must have been raising my voice and attracting attention, because someone from the sheriff's department sauntered over and asked what the trouble was. I brightened when I saw that this someone appeared to be old enough to be the other guy's grandfather.

"Sorry for the disturbance," I said. "I'm Stacey Reiser and this is my friend Maura Lasky, and we're trying to get information about a woman whose boat used to be docked here."

"Joe Harmony. How're you doing?" he said. I saw from his badge that he was a deputy sheriff. What's more, he was pleasant looking in a graying, Dennis Franz sort of way. "What's the woman's name?"

"Mary Elizabeth Chellus," said Maura, who sidled up closer to Joe. (He was her type, agewise.) "She and her husband Victor had a thirty-eight-foot sloop called the *Lucky Lady*. Sixteen years ago, they went out for a sail and she drowned. Is there any chance you remember the accident, Joe?"

He winked at her. (Apparently, she was his type, too.) "Sure do."

"Really?" I said excitedly. "What do you remember?"

"I remember that her husband was heartbroken, mostly," he said. "When the Coast Guard gave up the search for her that night, he was about as busted up as a man could be."

"Right," I said, "but what about the investigation? What, I mean is, why wasn't there one?"

"Once they got the autopsy results, there was nothing to investigate," he said. "The woman fell overboard and drowned."

"Or was pushed," I said. "Didn't anyone suspect that her husband could have *caused* her to drown?"

Joe chuckled. "No offense, miss, but I think you've been watching too much TV."

He should talk. There was a TV on in the background, and he kept sneaking peeks at it, which was not very confidence inspiring, given that he was a law enforcement officer and that what he was sneaking peeks at was an infomercial hawking women's lingerie.

"I guess what I'm getting at is that the autopsy could have been incomplete. Isn't that so, Joe?"

"Not usually and not this one. Like I said, I remember when they found the body the day after the drowning. There was no gunshot wound, no blunt trauma to the head, no strangulation marks on the neck, nothing to suggest that Mrs. Chellus's death was anything other than what her husband said it was. It was all very routine, if you can call a drowning routine. It stuck in my mind because I had a buddy whose boat was docked right next to the *Lucky Lady*. As he told it, the Chelluses were a nice couple–Beverly Hills types but not snooty. They didn't fight, didn't throw parties, didn't engage in reckless behavior. The day she drowned it was cloudy, with a forecast of rain, but nothing that would keep a sailor out of the water. My buddy said they showed up in their foul weather gear, carrying their cooler the way they always did."

"Their cooler?" said Maura.

"Yeah. Their cook made them lunch whenever they'd take the boat out for the afternoon. My buddy used to drool over all the fancy stuff they'd bring onboard. All his wife ever sent him off with was a bologna sandwich."

"So you have nothing to add?" I said, my energy flagging.

"Nope," said Joe, who smiled at Maura. "Except I wouldn't mind having this young lady's phone number if she isn't spoken for."

I left the sweethearts to themselves and waited for Maura in the parking lot. As I waited, I tried to sort out my feelings. On one hand, I was disappointed that we hadn't uncovered anything that would prove Victor's guilt. I was like a dog digging for a bone that I could bring back to my mother and deposit at her feet so she'd pat me on the head and say, "good doggie" or "good daughter" or something of that nature. I was determined to save her by giving her hard evidence that her boyfriend was a criminal. On the other hand, if my attempts at producing evidence failed and it turned out that Victor was innocent of murdering his wife, I would be embarrassed for making such a fuss but relieved that he and my mother could move ahead with their relationship and, above all, I would be happy for her, just as she hoped I'd be. What I'm saying is that I didn't *want* Victor to be guilty; I just thought he was, and if he was, it was my daughterly duty to expose him.

"Hi. All set," said Maura when she arrived in the parking lot.

"By 'all set,' does this mean you and Joe made a date?"

"What do you think?" she said with a sly grin.

"I think you should stick to boys your own age," I said. "But then you pay your shrink to tell you that, so I won't waste my breath."

"Thank you. Besides, just because you and Jack are madly in love doesn't make you the authority on what constitutes a good match."

"You're right. I'm hardly the authority. Not when I'm lying to him about this sleuthing adventure of ours. He thinks I'm working at the store today."

"Don't worry. If Victor's clean, Jack will never be the wiser about our snooping. If Victor's a rat, he'll be proud of you for rescuing your mother. It's a win-win situation, Stacey."

We high-fived each other and contemplated our next move.

# Chapter
# Twenty-four

★

AS WE WERE DRIVING out of the marina, Maura and I decided we should search Victor's house at some point, his office in particular, to see if we could find a connection between his failed business ventures and the death of Mary Elizabeth—i.e., whether his sudden influx of cash as a result of her death restored his financial health. It was a ballsy move and I was risking my mother's wrath, as well as Jack's disapproval, but the meter was ticking. If she was even contemplating marrying Vic, she could run off and do it at any moment, and I couldn't afford to take that chance.

She had mentioned in passing that in a couple of days she would be attending a dinner in her honor, hosted by W&W, the ad agency that had made her a star, and that Victor would be out of town on one of his jaunts. Seizing the opportunity, Maura and I planned our outing for the evening they would both be away from the house. I set the caper in motion by asking Mom if Maura and I could watch a movie in Victor's screening room while they were gone, and she had said she would arrange it.

Speaking of movies, after Maura and I returned from Marina Del

Rey that Saturday, Jack and I went to a preview of a romantic comedy starring Meg Ryan. Predictably, Mr. Highbrow hated it.

"It's not that I dislike Meg Ryan as an actress," he said as I was whipping up a postmovie pasta dinner in his kitchen. Lately, I'd been trying to improve my culinary skills, so he would see what an ideal partner I'd make. I wanted so much for him to tell me he loved me, tell me he was committed to me, tell me that I was the one and only woman for him. I longed to hear those words or, if not those exact words, then anything other than the dreaded: "I think we should talk."

"What is it you disliked about the movie?" I said.

"The fact that there was no story," he said. "It drives me insane when these romantic comedies are twenty minutes of plot and an hour and forty minutes of filler. Do we really need to see shot after shot of the lovers throwing snowballs at each other in Central Park or strolling down a country lane holding hands or sipping mocha lattes together by the fireplace at some cutesy country inn? I want something to *happen* in a film, and nothing happens in this one except that the audience gets ripped off. I think the people who made the movie should be chained to their chairs and forced to watch it themselves, over and over until they die of boredom. That would be a fitting punishment."

"Gee, Jack," I said with a smirk. "Why don't you tell me how you really feel?"

He calmed down a little, put his arms around me. "Was I pontificating again?"

"Big time."

"Sorry. But you know what I'm talking about. Movies are not synonymous with music videos."

"I agree." I kissed the tip of his nose. "But you know, now that I'm not appearing in the sort of movies you trash, it's kind of fun watching you foam at the mouth."

"Is that so?" He tightened his grip around my waist and pressed his body against mine.

"Yeah. It's fun watching you foam at the mouth and turn red in the face and make your eyes roll around in their sockets. Scary but fun."

He laughed. "I can't help it. I'm a purist when it comes to movies. Always was, always will be."

"I know, and I love you for it."

The instant the word "love" was out of my mouth, I felt my own face turn red. I wanted to crawl under the floor, hide behind the draperies, stick my head in the pot of pasta sauce—anything not to deal with Jack's reaction to the fact that I had just told him I loved him! Without meaning to! Without any encouragement on his part! It had slipped out, in spite of my promise to myself that I wouldn't be the one to say it first, that I wouldn't rush the relationship, that I wouldn't put pressure on Jack or make him feel icky toward me or, worst of all, repel him. It had slipped out and I couldn't suck it back in.

"Stacey, look at me," he said, tilting my chin up while I continued to die of humiliation. "It's okay."

"No, it's not okay," I said, refusing to meet his eyes. "I never meant to put you in an awkward position, Jack."

"It's too late for that."

"Swell." So I had ruined it, ruined us. I braced myself for the "You're really terrific and we've had some great times together, but I'm not ready for a serious relationship, and I think we should cool it for a while..." Blah blah blah.

"It's too late because you told me you loved me, and now I have to respond."

"There's no law that says you have to respond. Besides, I already know what you're going to tell me. I've heard it all before."

"Not from me. Please look at me already, would you?" He had my face in his hands, practically squishing my cheeks.

"All right, I'm looking."

He smiled. "I have to respond, because I love you, too."

"Say that again?"

"I love you, too, Stacey. I love you and I have since the first night we were together. I just wasn't very speedy about telling you, because of my own insecurities, I guess."

"Jack Rawlins? Insecure?"

"Isn't everyone? Not only that, I'm a guy, for God's sake. It's not in our genes to be able to say the right thing at the right moment."

"Okay, enough about insecurities and genetics. Let's get back to the love thing. I wouldn't mind hearing it again."

"I love you, Stacey Reiser. Very much."

He kissed me for a long time. The pasta sauce was drying out on the stove, and I couldn't have cared less.

"What do you love about me?" I asked at one point during a break in the action. "You're a big star, Jack, with your own show and a career that's going gangbusters, while I'm an actress who's still grappling with what I want to be when I grow up. I guess what I'm asking is, *why* do you love me? We seem like such an unlikely match."

"Not so unlikely at all," he said, stroking my hair. "But to answer your question, I love a lot of things about you. I love your humor, especially in the face of disappointment. I love your feistiness, your gift for picking yourself up after a fall and carrying on. I love the way you look, so pretty and yet not artificially or calculatedly. And I love your values."

"My values?"

"Yes, those solid, midwestern values that keep you from getting corrupted by Hollywood. Sure you want to succeed as an actress, but unlike most of the strivers here, you're only willing to go so far. You don't sell your soul, in other words. You haven't done the boob job. You haven't had your face carved. You haven't slept with every producer in town. That alone makes you a breath of fresh air."

"I slept with you," I teased.

"And I don't know how to thank you," said Jack.

"I do," I said. "You can sleep with me again."

"Now?"

"Right now."

We abandoned my poor excuse for a pasta dinner and headed for Jack's bedroom, where we undressed each other and caressed each other and showered each other with lush, Hallmark card–type declarations of love. It was a beautiful thing.

When I woke up the next morning, it seemed as if the whole world, my whole world, had changed, had opened up, had energized me. In the dopey jargon of pop music, I felt "brand-new," now that Jack loved me and I loved him and we were truly, magically going to be together forever. Although there was one tiny snag in the proceedings. While we were eating breakfast, he asked how I was handling the situation with my mother and Victor.

"You haven't mentioned the subject in a while," he said. "Does that mean you agree with me that Helen's entitled to make her own choices in a man and that your attempt to sabotage their relationship was a little neurotic?"

"I wouldn't exactly call it neurotic," I said.

"I stand corrected," he said. "But you have to admit that you did want to turn the tables on her—to insinuate yourself into her personal life because she'd spent so many years insinuating herself into yours."

"No. Actually, I was insinuating myself into her personal life because I thought there was something off about Victor. I still think there's something off about Victor. I'm very concerned that he's had a history of womanizing, that he's had financial trouble, that his wealthy wife died under suspicious—"

"Stacey, you're doing it again."

"Doing what?"

"Obsessing over Helen's romance. How about obsessing over ours instead? I don't have to leave for the studio for another hour."

"No?"

"No. What do you say we go back to bed and–"

"Yes."

And so I didn't tell Jack what Maura and I were up to. Why ruin what promised to be a fabulous hour of sex with my honey? Did I feel guilty about not telling him that she and I were planning to show up at Victor's house and rummage through his personal belongings? Yes, I did. He and I had pledged our love for each other, and loving meant trusting. On the other hand, I was a firm believer in the old adage: What he doesn't know won't hurt him. I also believed in the related adage: What he doesn't know won't hurt me.

# Chapter
# Twenty-five

☆

MAURA AND I took separate cars and met at Victor's at 7:30 on the evening of our enterprise. Since he and Mom were off doing their respective business, we were alone in the house with the staff. It was Carlos, in fact, who had answered the door and politely ushered us inside.

"He's sort of cute. A Latin lover type," Maura said as we trekked through the living room and the dining room and the sunroom to get to the screening room. "Too young for me, but cute just the same."

"He's not too young for you, but he *is* taken," I said. "Besides, I don't trust him any more than I trust the rest of the Stepford servants on the payroll here. They all seem too good to be true."

No sooner did I finish the sentence when Quentin, Victor's projectionist, entered the room and asked us if we were ready for him to begin the movie. We said sure, go ahead. We had no intention of watching it and were planning to skip out the minute he dimmed the lights.

"Maybe we should stay and see it," Maura whispered after Quentin announced he was showing the latest Jackie Chan martial arts adventure. "We could learn some self-defense moves. You never know when they might come in handy."

"They won't come in handy tonight," I said. "This mission should be pretty straightforward."

We waited for the opening credits to appear on screen, then tiptoed out, figuring that once Quentin was safely ensconced in the projection room we'd have a good two hours of snooping before we'd have to be back.

"Let's hit the library first," I said as we crept from room to room, cursing every time we'd land on a creaky floorboard and possibly alert the troops to our whereabouts. "I think it doubles as Vic's office."

Maura nodded and followed me into the large, panelled room where only recently I'd sat with my mother and tried unsuccessfully to persuade her to break up with her boyfriend.

We slid the pocket doors closed behind us and flipped on the lights.

"Where do we start?" said Maura, staring at the multitude of built-in drawers and cabinets.

"You take that side. I'll take this side."

"Fine, but what are we looking for? We're not accountants, so even if we find financial documents, we won't be able to decode them. We certainly won't be able to tie them to the death of Victor's wife."

"Probably not," I said, "but we're here and we might as well hunt for something. What about getting background on Victor's life? Let's check for photos of him and the missus, or mortgage papers for real estate he's owned, or correspondence having to do with the businesses he's run—anything that'll tell us more about him."

"Whatever you say."

We began the laborious task of rifling through Victor's drawers. After forty-five minutes, all we had to show for our trouble was a sore shoulder (me) and a paper cut (Maura).

"This is really boring," she said.

"Then go back and watch the movie," I said, slightly pissed off. "I'll do this myself if you're not into it."

"I'm never going to be as into it as you are," said Maura, who seemed pissed off that I was pissed off. "She's your mother, not mine, so you have much more at stake than I do."

"Yes, but you're my best friend," I said, "and best friends help each other out, even when the job is *boring*."

"Maybe, but you should have had a more specific plan," she said. "Then we wouldn't be wasting our time looking for nothing."

"I didn't hear you complaining when we went to Marina Del Rey without a 'specific plan,'" I said. "But that was probably because there was something in it for you–the geezer deputy sheriff."

"Don't even think about getting on my case about the men I go out with," she said, pointing at me. "You're just like your mother, the way you criticize my life."

"I am *not* just like my mother!" I said hotly. "And I don't criticize your life. I simply make observations. You're much too sensitive."

I *was* just like my mother, who used to try to neutralize me with the very same argument.

"I'm sorry, Maura," I said. "I guess I'm uptight because–"

I stopped midsentence. I heard two sets of footsteps clickety-clacking across the hardwood floor outside the library.

"Quick! Into the closet!" I flipped off the lights, then the two of us scrambled into the walk-in closet beyond Victor's desk and shut ourselves in.

We stood there huddled together, holding our collective breath, as someone pulled open the pocket doors and entered the library.

"That's strange," I heard Carlos say in Spanish as he turned the lights back on. "These doors are never closed unless Victor is having a private meeting."

"Maybe he closed them before he left," Rosa suggested. "Maybe he didn't want you sneaking in here while he was away."

He laughed. "Like I'm the one who sneaks around this place? It's a miracle he hasn't caught you sticking your nose where it doesn't belong."

I grabbed Maura's hand and squeezed it. Obviously, there was trouble in Victor's paradise.

"I don't have to sneak around," said Rosa. "I've got everything I need to protect myself against Victor."

I squeezed Maura's hand again, tighter this time. I was dying to blurt out, "Protect yourself against him because he comes on to you? Because he forces you to commit murder for him? Because he makes you cook brisket for my mother? *What, Rosa?*

"If I were you, I'd keep that little piece of evidence to myself," said Carlos. "We're going to use it one of these days. It's just a matter of time before Victor's crimes bring him down, and we're not going down with him. He can rot in jail all by himself."

Little piece of *evidence?* Victor's *crimes?* Rot in jail? This was fantastic! I finally had my proof that he was as dangerous as I suspected. I'd heard it right from the mouths of his employees, so it had to be true. No ambiguities this time. No double talk. No possibility of a misunderstanding. I couldn't wait to tell my mother and put an end to her relationship with Vic.

"Oh, I'll hang on to the evidence all right," said Rosa. "But if he ever threatens to ship us back to Mexico, he's going to be very, very sorry. We may be in this country illegally, thanks to him, but he's done more illegal stuff than either of us ever dreamed of."

Maura leaned over and whispered, "Could you please translate already? I don't understand a single word they're saying!"

"Shhh," I whispered back. "I'll tell you later."

She shrugged and waited silently for Rosa and Carlos to leave us alone.

But they didn't leave us alone. "Did I ever tell you that you're sexy when you talk about blackmail, Rosa?" Carlos teased, his tone turning playful.

"No. But you're welcome to tell me now," she said with a flirtatious giggle.

"Okay, baby, you turn me on when you even mention the word 'blackmail.' "

"And you're hotter than you were the day I married you."

"Then how about showing me," he said. "We'll close these doors, turn off the lights, stretch out on the couch, and have ourselves a good time."

I turned to Maura and mouthed the words, "They're about to have sex." She looked as taken aback as I was. Sure, Rosa and Carlos were free to *do it* whenever and wherever they wanted, but did they have to want it right then? In the same room with us?

While we stood together in that closet, horrified, embarrassed, wishing we were anywhere else, Victor's two paragons of hired help jumped each other.

"Yeah, that's good," she moaned several minutes in.

"So good," he moaned back at her.

"Now touch me here. And faster. Faster!"

"As fast as you can handle it, baby," he panted.

"Yeah, that's it. Oh, Carlos. Don't stop! Don't stop! Don't stop! Okay, stop!"

Every time we thought they had stopped, they started up again, with Rosa issuing commands and Carlos responding like the red-hot lover he apparently was. It was nearly an hour before they pulled their hands off each other, opened the doors, and staggered out of the room.

"Sheesh. I feel like some creepy voyeur," I said.

"A shower wouldn't be a bad idea," Maura agreed. "Do you think it's safe to come out or do you think they'll be back for more?"

"All I know is that Rosa is incredibly orgasmic," I said.

"All I know is that I'm incredibly claustrophic," she said. "I'm getting out of this closet whether they come back or not."

"Wait." I held her arm. "Here's what they said about Victor. He's keeping them in this country illegally, he's committed more serious crimes, too, and they have evidence of these crimes that could give them leverage against him. Whatever he did, they must be in on it."

"Wow! Maybe they helped him dispose of his wife and now they're all in bed together, so to speak."

"Maybe. Oh, Maura, we finally nailed Victor. Once I tell Mom what we overheard, she'll never spend another night in this house."

"Call her on your cell when we leave. Right now, we'd better hurry back to the screening room so Quentin doesn't miss us. The movie should be just about over and he'll be turning on the lights."

We were safely in our seats in time to see Jackie Chan kickbox the villain and "the end" pop up on the screen. We thanked Quentin for showing us the movie, told him to be sure to say hello to Victor when he returned from his trip, and scrambled for the door. Once outside, I hugged Maura and told her I couldn't have gotten the goods on Vic without her help.

"It was my pleasure," she replied, "although after listening to Rosa and Carlos go at it, I'd say they were the ones who had the pleasure."

"Didn't they though."

"The important thing is that you have concrete information to give your mother now."

"Yup, I just hope she appreciates it."

# Chapter
# Twenty-six

☆

I REACHED MOM on her cell phone just as she was climbing into her limo after her dinner with the Fin's advertising people.

"Hi, it's Stacey," I said. "I know it's late, but I've got to see you right away."

"Are you sick?" she said. "There's a stomach virus going around. Everybody's complaining of nausea, vomiting, diarrhea—"

"I'm fine." I cut her off before she went into more detail. She wasn't a hypochondriac exactly. She just enjoyed discussing medical maladies the way others enjoy discussing, say, gardening. "Would you meet me somewhere? So we could talk for a few minutes?"

"I'm heading over to Victor's," she said, then giggled. "I like sleeping there even when he's away. I can smell his smell in the master bedroom. I find it erotic."

Please.

"I'd rather not meet at his house, if that's okay," I said. "What about the Regent Beverly Wilshire? It's a convenient spot for both of us. We could sit in the bar and have a nice after-dinner drink together."

"I don't drink after-dinner drinks, you know that. They keep me up, not to mention give me heartburn."

"Then we'll have some nice herbal tea. See you soon. 'Bye."

I hung up before she could object further.

Fifteen minutes later, we were ensconced in the back corner of the hotel's bar, sitting on a plump sofa and sipping from pretty little glasses of port. I had ordered it before she arrived, figuring that chamomile was certainly not going to take the edge off what I had to tell her but that port might.

"So," she said. "What's this about? I'm always delighted to see you, dear, but you've got a problem, I gather. Is it Jack? Are you two on the outs? Tell your mother."

"It's not about Jack," I said tenderly, eager to break the news but wanting to cushion the blow. "It's about— Okay, let me start over. I know how fond you are of Victor and I can see why. He's bright and animated and treats you well."

"What is it, Stacey? Spit it out already."

"All right. There's something I've just found out about him and you need to hear it."

She glared at me. "This isn't going to be one of your fresh-mouth accusations regarding his poor wife, is it?"

"Not specifically." I cleared my throat. "While I was at his house tonight, I overheard Rosa and Carlos talking."

She sighed impatiently. "I thought I explained why they're not too fond of me. They don't like me taking over the household. They're used to ruling the roost, to cavorting all over the place with no supervision."

I flashed back on the cavorting they'd been doing in the library only a couple of hours before, and took another sip of port, hoping to drown out Rosa's "Faster! Faster!" "This time, what I overheard them talking about was Victor, not you, Mom. Maura was there, too. We happened to be within earshot just as they were having a very incriminating conversation."

"Incriminating? What's that supposed to mean?"

"For starters, they're illegal immigrants. Victor is keeping them in this country under false pretenses, which means that he's also cheating the IRS by paying them off the books. I know everybody does it, Mom, so it's not that big a deal in the grand scheme of things, but you've always been such a stickler about playing by the rules."

I waited for her to register shock or anger or disgust, but she didn't emit a single shriek. Instead, she shrugged and said, "He told me they were here illegally."

"What?"

"Sure. He tells me everything, because he's a sharer. Can you say the same about Jack?"

"Of course, but this isn't about Jack. It's about Victor and how he's harboring Rosa and Carlos."

"For your information, he has a darn good reason for 'harboring' them, as you put it. Apparently, Rosa and Carlos each have elderly parents in Mexico who are not well and who are desperately in need of money. Victor is such a generous, sweet man that he's been willing to stick his own neck out not only to let those two stay in America but to pay them in cash so they'll have more to send to their loved ones."

I blinked at her, amazed that she continued to condone Victor's shady behavior and dumbfounded that she'd bought his absurd story about the tragically needy parents.

"I'm not saying I like the idea of them being here illegally," she went on. "But I respect Victor's motives for allowing them to. He's helping them, Stacey. He's helping them because he's a wonderful, wonderful man. If only you'd accept that."

Jeez. This was going to be harder than I thought. "Mom, there's more. Take another sip of port."

"I've had enough port. I can feel the acid building up in my stomach already. I'll never get a good night's sleep now."

"Fine. Don't take another sip. Just listen, because here's the really bad news. Rosa and Carlos said unequivocally that Victor is a criminal. They said he's done a ton of illegal stuff and should rot in jail. They said they've got evidence against him. Those were their precise words. I'm so sorry, Mom, but I heard their conversation. Yes, it was in Spanish, but I understood it perfectly."

She narrowed her eyes at me. "Look, young lady, you may be my daughter, but you're not very smart when it comes to dealing with domestics. Rosa and Carlos are a couple of ungrateful idiots if they talk like that behind their employer's back. Calling him a criminal just because he's letting them live under his roof!"

"Mom, Mom. That's not why they called him a criminal. They were referring to other crimes he's committed."

"What crimes?"

"They didn't say."

"There. You see? Nonsense. Complete nonsense. I love Victor and he loves me, and everything else is immaterial."

So she was giving him a pass yet again. He had her totally bamboozled.

"Let me ask you a question," I said. "If Victor did commit a crime—something much more serious than the immigration thing—would you love him then? Or is this guy the Teflon Man in your mind?"

"I don't like your tone or your insinuation," she said, her voice rising. "Victor would never commit a serious crime, not knowingly. The only one who's guilty of anything is you."

"Me?"

"You. You've never been able to lie to your mother and tonight is nothing new. You and Maura didn't *happen* to overhear Rosa and Carlos talking. You went over to Victor's tonight with the sole purpose of snooping, of eavesdropping, of doing anything you could to poison me against him. You *were* snooping around at his house, weren't you, Stacey? *Weren't* you?"

I started to deny it, but why bother? She was right: she could always tell when I was lying, ever since I was a kid.

"Yes," I admitted. "Maura and I did go over there hoping to find some proof that the man you think you love isn't who he seems. It was for your own good. I was trying to protect you."

"I don't need protecting," she said huffily, her nostrils flaring.

"Yes, you do. I've told you before and I'll tell you again, Mom: Victor is up to his eyeballs in slippery stuff. You've got to trust me on this."

"Trust you? About men? I don't hear any wedding bells in your future, Stacey. I don't suppose Jack has asked you to marry him, has he?"

"Not yet," I said defensively.

"That's what I thought. You go through one bad apple after another and you want me to listen to you about Victor?"

"That's not fair," I said, my own nostrils flaring. "I may not have a marriage proposal on the table, but Jack is no bad apple. He's loving and sensitive and totally honest, unlike *your* bad apple. Wait, let me correct that: your *rotten* apple."

"Victor is not a rotten apple!" she said, her face reddening with rage.

"He is so! He cheats the government and sleeps with women a fraction of his age, and he just may have murdered his wife!"

"That's e-nough!" she barked, waving her arms in the air. "I refuse to listen to such disrespectful talk for a single minute more!"

With those fighting words, she rose from her chair, threw a couple of twenty-dollar bills on the table, and announced that she was leaving.

"So you can't stand to hear the truth, is that it?" I said, as angry at her as she was at me.

"Here's the truth," she said, poking her finger at me. "I consider myself lucky that someone as worldly and intelligent and attractive as Victor Chellus has chosen me. He's not an angel, God knows, but then no man is." She turned to go, but returned for one last parting shot. "Oh, and don't call me to apologize. Starting tonight, I'm officially not speaking to you!"

Gee, that went well, I thought, and polished off her port and mine.

# Chapter
# Twenty-seven

★

HAD A PAIN in my gut as I always did when I fought with my
mother. I hated it when she was mad at me, and the last thing I
intended to do was to push her away, right into Victor's arms. I
suppose I should have waited until I had more conclusive information about him, but I was desperate to protect her. Too desperate.
A case of premature explanation, that's what I had.

I spent the night at Jack's, who did not have a case of premature
anything. We made love like two people who were truly committed
to each other, and all my conflicts and fears melted away when he
was holding me. I woke up the next morning feeling optimistic; that
somehow I would wrest my mother from Victor's emotional grasp
and make up with her.

Meanwhile, I had a little project I hoped would distract me, and
I planned to tackle it the minute Jack left for the studio. Kyle, his
assistant, had called me the previous week to say that the crew of
*Good Morning, Hollywood* was throwing a surprise party the following
month to commemorate Jack's fifth anniversary as host.

"We're going to make it a rowdy, warts-and-all roast of your boyfriend," Kyle had said with a mischievous laugh. "We're crazy about the guy, you know that, but we can't wait to put *him* in the hot seat for a change."

"Great idea," I'd said. "How can I help?"

"Glad you asked. We want to dig up old videos, old clippings, anything he did when he was first starting out in the business, and use them as part of a *This Is Your Life*-type evening. Basically, we want to embarrass the hell out of Mr. Television Star by putting him back in touch with his humble beginnings as a print reviewer."

"I love it. And he'll love it, too, Kyle."

"He'd better or I'm out of a job. Anyhow, knowing how he's such a saver—does he keep his grocery lists, too?—I'm betting he's got all those old clips and videos at his place. And since you have access to them, I was wondering if you could hunt them down for me on the sly."

"Sure. You want to go all the way back to the articles he wrote for *Variety* and *The Hollywood Reporter*?"

"Absolutely. We've got to remind him that he used to be a lowly beat reporter for the trades before becoming a pompous film critic."

I'd promised Kyle I'd look for Jack's professional memorabilia the first chance I got.

Well, today's the day, I thought when I was alone in his house the morning after the blowup with Mom. Maybe I'll be more successful at digging around in his past than I was at digging around in Victor's.

I drank some coffee, then fought my way through Jack's clutter en route to his office, smiling to myself as I pictured his reaction to being roasted by his pals. Even though he took movies seriously, he didn't take himself seriously, not deep down, and so I expected him to be flattered by the party and good-natured about having his early work held up to public scrutiny.

Since Kyle had specifically asked me to pull all the old stuff, I started at the beginning of Jack's career and searched his filing cabinets for folders with clippings from both *Variety* and *The Hollywood Reporter*. I chuckled when I came upon the *Variety* file, because it was out of order alphabetically and should have been at the back of the cabinet instead of up front.

That's my pack rat, I thought as I began sifting through the bulging folder. I don't know how he ever finds anything around here.

I skimmed the articles, my heart swelling with pride whenever I read the "Jack Rawlins" byline. I tried to imagine how he must have felt all those years ago, covering stories about distribution companies and weekend grosses and studio executives who were leaving one company for another—all aspects of the business about which he couldn't have cared less. I knew he must have perceived the job as a way to gain exposure for himself within the industry, as a stepping-stone toward reviewing movies someday, as an entry into the magical world he'd worshiped since childhood.

I continued to read through the clippings, weighing which ones I'd give to Kyle for the surprise party, when the headline of one of Jack's articles caught my attention—and held it.

I stared at the headline, just fixed my eyes on it for several seconds, before the meaning of it, the reality of it, the enormity of it sunk in.

It read: "Theatre Prexy Chellus Plays Happy Tune Amid Fraud Charges."

I clutched the clipping in my hand and felt my mouth go dry. What the hell is *this*? I wondered as I tried to make sense of what I was looking at, tried to keep a clear head even though a thousand thoughts were bumping up against each other. Part of me went immediately into denial, as I formulated simple, innocent explanations for the piece, theories that would allow my faith in Jack to remain intact. The other part of me was wild with suspicion and mistrust and the certainty that whatever was in the article would absolutely wreck us, and it was that part that propelled me over to Jack's desk chair.

I sat down and began to read avidly, to pore over every word of the piece. According to Jack, Victor owned a chain of movie theaters, mostly in small-to-midsize markets, that operated under the name Victory Theatres. Not only had Vic been accused of bilking the studios out of their fair share of his profits, but he'd been rumored to be pirating prints of first-run movies, selling them overseas instead of shipping them back to their distributor. What's more, the backers of his renovation project—the upgrading of his older theaters to modern multiplexes—were hounding him for the money they claimed he owed them.

"In an exclusive interview with *Variety*," the article stated, "Chellus declared that he is innocent of all charges and said he is just one of many theater owners trying to survive in an increasingly competitive marketplace. 'This is a tough business,' he told *Variety*. 'People like to kick you when you're down. But I can assure the entire entertainment community that I've done nothing wrong.' Chellus pointed out that his theaters provide hundreds of jobs around the country—from Charlotte and Akron to Nashville and Kansas City— and that he is a longtime contributor to charitable organizations. 'I take my reponsibilities as an American businessman seriously,' he said. 'I would never even consider cheating another company, let alone break the sacred covenant between theater owner and distributor.'"

I let the article fall to the floor as I digested what I had just read. I felt sick, shaky, out of control, but forced myself to process what I'd learned.

For one thing, the fact that Victor had been accused of being such a crook years ago—in an actual magazine article, not simply in a conversation between Rosa and Carlos—was more proof that my instincts about him were correct and that my mother was indeed at risk of being conned by the man she loved.

But it was the fact that Jack had been privy to all this and not told me–Jack, the man *I* loved, the man who was supposed to love me, the man I trusted–that made me doubt my instincts. For months he denied knowing anything about Victor Chellus, despite my concerns over my mother's safety. And now it turned out that he knew plenty about Victor, including that he was implicated in not one but *three* cases of fraud. Moreover, it was Jack himself who conducted the interview for the magazine, Jack who spoke directly to Victor about the accusations, Jack who was at the center of *Variety*'s coverage of the whole Victory Theatre mess. And yet he never said a word to me. Not when I told him Mom was dating Victor. Not when I told him she was serious about him. Not when I told him I suspected him of being a no-good scumball who would end up hurting her. Was it possible that he didn't remember that he'd interviewed Victor? Of course not. But then why had he acted as if it didn't happen? And was his eagerness to keep it a secret the reason why he always begged off whenever I invited him to join Mom and Victor and me for dinner?

"Maybe he has a good excuse," said Maura after I called her on the set of her show.

"Like what? He has amnesia? That may work on *Days of Our Lives* but it doesn't cut it on *Days of My Life*."

"Are you going to confront him?"

"I think that goes without saying."

I rehearsed the scene on and off during the day. I didn't want to jump to any conclusions, didn't want to be too shrill or judgmental when Jack came home from work and I hit him with my little bombshell. On the other hand, I was terribly upset. I thought I'd finally found my soul mate, finally found a man who would be honest with me, and now it seemed I was mistaken.

"Hey, pretty lady," he said when he walked in the door that night and tossed his jacket onto the bench in the foyer. "What a wicked day I had. We had technical problems that delayed the taping and threw everybody's schedule off."

I didn't respond. His technical problems weren't a priority.

"How was your day?" he asked as he headed for the kitchen to sort through the stack of mail on the counter, next to which I had strategically placed the *Variety* clipping.

"My day?" I said, trailing behind him. "It wasn't too hot, either. I'm hoping you'll be able to make it better."

"Better?" He didn't look up from the mail. "How?"

"By being straight with me about a subject we've tried to discuss before."

He groaned. "This isn't about Victor, is it?"

"It is."

"But we agreed that you weren't going to 'investigate' him or meddle in your mother's relationship with him."

"*We* didn't agree to any such thing. *You* didn't want me to meddle. Why was that, Jack? Refresh my memory."

He finally glanced up at me. "Okay, Stacey. What's the matter? I'm totally in the dark here."

"Then let me turn on the light for you. If you check the counter, to the right of your mail, you'll see exactly what the matter is."

He pushed aside all the letters and magazines and junk flyers and picked up the *Variety* clip. After reading the headline and, presumably, recalling that he did, in fact, interview Victor and write the article, he flushed slightly but otherwise maintained his composure. A second or two passed before he said, "Where'd you get this?"

I didn't want to ruin his surprise party, really I didn't, but I couldn't very well withhold the truth from him, particularly since my principal beef was that he had withheld the truth from me. I told him about Kyle's phone call and how he'd asked me to find the old clippings and that I hadn't merely been poking around in his files in my spare time.

"I'd like an explanation, Jack. Why didn't you ever tell me you had information about Victor?"

He was silent briefly—a rarity for him. "It's complicated," he said at last.

"Complicated, huh? Well, how about laying the explanation on me and we'll see if I'm capable of understanding it."

"Please don't be sarcastic, Stacey. This is hard for me."

"Hard for you? What about me? I'm the one with the mother who's in love with the lowlife you wrote about. I'm the one with the boyfriend who keeps secrets."

He nodded, took a breath. "I didn't tell you what I knew about Victor because"—he paused, took another breath—"because it would have meant kissing my professional reputation good-bye."

"Excuse me?" I was incredulous. "You lied to me in order to protect your reputation? What on earth does your television career have to do with admitting that you once wrote an article about Victor?"

"As I said, it's complicated. Actually, I'd prefer not to go into it."

"Not to go into it? You'd rather we leave it that you were so afraid of tarnishing your precious reputation that you would jeopardize my mother's well-being by letting her fall for a man accused of cheating his business partners?"

"He *was* accused of engaging in questionable business practices, but I didn't consider him a danger to Helen and I still don't. If I did, I would have told you about the article."

"Okay, I get it now. You and Victor became buddies after you padded the article with that crap about his sacred covenant and his charitable contributions. That's what happened, right? You figured that your friendship with a crook, years ago though it was, could sink your career if people found out about it?"

"There was no friendship, believe me."

"Believe you? Why should I? Not unless you tell me the whole story, Jack."

"I can't. I won't allow everything I've worked so hard for to be destroyed."

"But you will allow everything *we've* worked so hard for to be destroyed?"

He didn't answer.

"I'm the woman you say you love, Jack. What could be so awful that you can't tell *me* about it?"

"You don't understand, Stacey. You really don't."

I was seething now and beyond crushed. I had given him a chance, given him the opportunity to unburden himself, but he wouldn't. "Here's what I understand," I said. "You had some sort of association with Victor and you don't want it to become public, because you're worried that your ratings will drop and your show will be canceled and that nobody will suck up to you anymore." I looked at him, looked at the man I adored, and wondered if I ever *saw* him. "You're a cool customer, Jack. I should have realized that after you trashed me in *Pet Peeve*. Take the way you approach movies, for example, a medium you claim to revere. You stand back and analyze films, critique them, hold yourself above them. You're the judge, the person who distances himself by making pronouncements about other people's abilities. If you ask me, you've got an intimacy problem. Maybe it's because of your parents, of how they treated you when you were growing up. Maybe your childhood turned you into someone who doesn't really involve himself emotionally in anything or anyone."

His eyes blazed. "That's not accurate and you know it. I've been involved with you emotionally in a way I've never been with anyone else. I love you, Stacey."

"When you love someone, you don't betray their trust, not about something that's important to them. But then, as I've just pointed out, your entire persona is about analyzing and critiquing others, about being right. But here's the irony, Jack: You were wrong to trash me—I wasn't all that bad in *Pet Peeve*—and you were wrong to withhold information about Victor."

I waited a few seconds, hoping he would break down and tell me what he was keeping deep inside, what he couldn't or wouldn't reveal. But he didn't. So I grabbed my purse and moved toward the door.

"Where are you going?" he asked, his voice low, drained.

"Home," I said. "I don't feel comfortable here anymore."

"Stacey?"

"What?"

"I wish I could tell you, but I can't."

"And I wish I could rewind the tape and play back the night we fell in love, but I can't."

My lower lip was quivering and my eyes were welling up, but I refused to let him see me cry. Instead, I put a pin in my pain, made myself hold it in for just another few seconds so I'd have the presence of mind to reach inside my purse for the key to his house, place it on the kitchen counter, and walk out.

Well, you're two for two, Stacey, I thought, as I finally allowed the tears to flow freely. First, your mother. Now, Jack. A swell night all around.

# Chapter
# Twenty-eight

☆

I DIDN'T HEAR FROM JACK for two days, and they were the longest two days ever. I had expected him to call the first night after I'd left his house, expected him to say he was sorry for not being more forthcoming and then to enlighten me about the "complicated" story he couldn't bring himself to tell me, but he hadn't. On the mother front, I had tried to reach Mom without success. She wasn't speaking to me, she reiterated, before slamming down the phone when I called. "We're officially estranged unless you come to your senses about Victor and me," she barked. Yeah, like that was going to happen. To say that I felt alienated from the two most important people in my life was an understatement.

But then came a break in the action. I had just returned home from a thrilling eight hours at Cornucopia! when Jack appeared at my door. He looked drawn, tired, not his cocky, dapper self. My first instinct was to wrap my arms around him and comfort him, but I resisted the impulse.

"Hello," he said softly. "May I come in?"

"If you're here to explain," I said.

"I'm here to explain," he said, and so I let him inside the apartment. As we walked into the living room, he suggested we sit down together.

"I think I'll stand, thanks." I couldn't bear to have him near me. I didn't trust myself next to him on that sofa, the scene of our first night of passion. I needed a clear head for whatever was coming next.

"Suit yourself." He sat down. "I really did come to talk."

"I'm listening."

He cleared his throat. "Let me begin by apologizing for not telling you what I knew about Victor way back when you first asked me about him. That must sound pretty hollow to you now, but it's sincere. I'm not proud of how I handled the situation."

"The situation? Jack, you outright lied to me."

"Yes, but there was a purpose to the lie."

"The purpose being to protect your almighty career."

He sighed, ran his fingers through his hair. "Stacey, I'm not the unchivalrous person you make me out to be. It's true that I wanted to protect my career, but not for the reason you think."

"Okay, then what's the reason?"

"The reason is Tim and my ability to support him. If my career went to hell, so would my income. My brother's expenses aren't insignificant, as you've observed."

"Right, and you know how much I admire you for supporting him. But I'm not making the connection here. What does supporting Tim have to do with withholding information about Victor from me? And why would an article you wrote years ago, about a guy nobody in this town really remembers or cares about, affect your career?"

"Are you sure you won't sit down?"

"Positive."

Instead of resuming his story, he handed me a piece of paper that he'd pulled out of his jacket pocket.

"What's this?" I said as I unfolded it.

"Read it. Then I'll tell you the rest."

I read what appeared to be a draft of an article, with Jack's name on the byline. It contained some of the same details that were in the *Variety* piece—how Victor was rumored to have cheated his distributors, as well as his investors, when he was running Victory Theatres—but there was no exclusive interview with him, no declaration of his innocence, no fluff about what an honest, hardworking businessman he was, nothing about a "sacred covenant," nothing about his donations to charities, nothing that let him off the hook or cast him in a positive light. Instead, it was more of an exposé about him in which anonymous sources within his company were quoted, along with executives at the studios, saying what a scoundrel he was, how recklessly he ran Victory Theatres, how his word meant zero within the industry, and how no one wanted to do business with him anymore.

I looked up at Jack. "You wrote this?"

"Yes, but I never turned it in to my editor. The piece you found in my file is the one I turned in, the one that actually ran."

"But why didn't this one run?" I said, giving him back the draft. "What happened to make you scrap it?"

He swallowed hard. "I'll start by taking you down memory lane," he said. "When I got the job at *Variety*, I was young and ambitious and chomping at the bit to write about movies. A few months in, I realized that I was bored to death, because I wasn't writing about movies, I was writing about the movie business. Still, I thought the job would lead somewhere, so I kept at it. And then one day my editor assigned me a story about a troubled company named Victory Theatres and its flamboyant president, Victor Chellus. I was bored, as I said, so I took it upon myself to do a little more digging than necessary for a trade piece. I spoke to people within Victory. I spoke to distributors who'd dealt with Victor. I fancied myself as a regular Woodward or Bernstein, even though the level of wrongdoing was hardly on a par with Watergate. Victor, I discovered through my interviews, was a sleazy businessman—no more, no less—but I was going to make a name for myself by exposing him. If *Variety* couldn't use the material, I was going to try to sell it elsewhere."

"Then why didn't you?"

"Because I got a telephone call—a call that changed everything."

"It was from Victor. That's what you're going to say, isn't it?"

He nodded.

"Did he threaten you?"

"Not at first. He invited me over to his house. 'For a friendly chat,' he said."

"And you went?"

"Sure. I thought it was my big break, my shot at getting an in-terview with the key player in the story I was chasing. Imagine my surprise, my naïveté, when this little eager-beaver cub reporter ar-rived at Victor's and discovered I wouldn't be getting an interview after all. Not a legitimate one anyway. After some pleasantries—I think he actually offered me a cigar—he asked me if I was interested in taking a bribe."

"A bribe? You? You'd never—"

"Yeah, I'd never." He laughed ruefully. "Victor said he'd been hearing rumblings that I was asking a lot of questions about him around town. So he hired someone, a private detective, I guess, to check into my background. He said, 'Jack, I understand that you've got a brother named Tim living in Newport Beach and that he's disabled from an accident. Swimming, wasn't it?' I was stunned, completely thrown. It never occurred to me that the weasel would dig up information about *me*. 'What's your point?' I said to him.

'People in wheelchairs cost money,' he said. 'Rumor has it that you're the one who takes care of his bills. Must put a lot of pressure on you, son, especially since you don't earn a helluva lot at your job. I'd like to help out if you'll let me.' "

"That dirty son of a bitch!" I said. "You told him to shove it, right?"

"I think you should sit down."

"I'm not sitting down! Just finish the story."

"Okay. The answer to your question is: no, I took his money—in exchange for burying the article I was planning to write and substituting the puff piece you saw in my file."

I literally gasped. After a second or so, I decided I'd better sit down, and parked myself on the sofa. "Go on," I said, wide-eyed.

"I took the bribe, the payoff, whatever you want to call it, Stacey. I took it because I was killing myself trying to make enough money to support Tim on my salary. I took it because I felt I had to."

I shook my head. "This is a disgrace."

"What is? That your boyfriend was capable of doing something so low?"

"No, that my mother's boyfriend was capable of doing something so low." My God. So he took the money to protect his brother, I thought. He took the money and then carried the guilt around for years. How awful it must have been to be put in such an untenable position. No wonder he'd denied knowing Victor. There was too much at stake for him not to deny it. It all made perfect sense to me now. "Oh, Jack. I wish you'd told me this months ago, but I understand why you couldn't. I think it's noble what you did for Tim. Noble and loving. I know you must feel ashamed and scared and worried that your career could come apart if people ever found out, but they won't find out. Why should they?"

He shrugged. "Maybe they won't, but now that I've gotten all this off my chest, the prospect of people finding out isn't so frightening, oddly enough. I lied to you, to keep the story a secret, and now I'm actually glad I told you."

I slid over to him, folded him in my arms, and smoothed his hair back off his forehead. It was wonderful to touch him again, to re-establish physical contact with him. I had missed the feel of him during the two days we'd been apart.

"Does Tim know what you did?" I asked.

"He does. Why?"

"The day you brought me to his house, he mentioned that you had made great sacrifices for him. Now I understand what he meant."

Jack nodded, squeezed my hand. "Remember how you accused me of being afraid of getting involved the other night?" he said. "You were right, as it turns out."

"No. No. I had no idea what Victor put you through."

"There was truth to what you said, Stacey, about how I distance myself from people, run from intimacy, stand in judgment of others. Except for Tim, I never told anybody the story I just told you. I *have* been isolated, *have* set myself apart from people. Your words really hit home. But I don't want to be the person you were describing. What I'm saying is that if you need me to help with the Victor situation or anything else, I'm here for you. As a matter of fact, I think you should go and see Helen right away. Tell her every-thing."

"I can't."

"No, really. It's okay. I'm not afraid of Victor anymore or what he could do to my career. Go ahead and tell her. I want to be *involved.*"

I hugged him. "It's not that. My mother isn't speaking to me, Jack. She won't listen to a thing I have to say, especially if it's neg-ative about Victor. She won't let me out of the deep freeze until I accept him or stop hassling her about him or whatever. So I need proof that he's a crook if I have any hope of getting her away from him—evidence that's not hearsay or something you wrote. If I sent her your article, she'd just accuse me of roping you into the conspiracy."

"Then we'll find your proof. Together."

I looked up at him. "We will?"

"Count on it. I told you: I'm here for you, no matter what. Okay?"

Well, it was more than okay, obviously, and I indicated that to Jack by stroking his cheek. "I think this is the part where we kiss and make up," I said.

"The part where the guy gets the girl and they live happily ever after?"

"That's the one."

# Chapter
# Twenty-nine

☆

AFTER I RECOUNTED to Jack how Maura and I had overheard Rosa and Carlos making derogatory remarks about Victor, Jack suggested that they might hold the key to our plan.

"They're close to the situation," he said, "so our job is to get close to them."

"How about if I cozy up to Rosa?" I said. "I'll make up a story about how I'm playing the role of a chef on an episode of *Law and Order* or *Frasier* or *Buffy the Vampire Slayer*, who cares. I'll explain that I'm not much of a cook, which is true, and that I'd like her to be my technical advisor."

"I think you're onto something. If you can spend time with her in the kitchen, whip up some refried beans together, engage her in a little girl talk, we might get information out of her."

"I'll do it. She can cook more than refried beans, by the way. She's actually a pretty talented chef. Mexican, French, Italian—you name it, she can make it."

"Great, but the main thing is to schedule all this for a time when Victor and your mother aren't around."

"Right."

When I made my pitch to Rosa, she was flattered. "I'd love to be your technical advisor, whatever that is," she said and told me to come by the house that very next day.

"Are you sure you'll have time to spend with me?" I asked. "I wouldn't want Victor or Mom to be upset with you."

"Mr. Chellus will be playing golf," she said. "And your mother will be doing one of her tuna fish commercials."

"Perfect. See you tomorrow."


"No, *this* is how you hold the whisk," she instructed me as we stood together in Victor's kitchen, studying a bowl of egg yolks.

Even I knew how to hold a whisk, but I was feigning total ignorance in order to stretch out my meeting with her. I had asked her to show me how to make a soufflé–the hardest thing I could think of–also in the hope of keeping her talking. "Okay. I see now. Thanks, Rosa. My character is supposed to have trained at one of the best restaurants in France, so your input is essential."

"My pleasure," she said. "I'm very excited to be involved with a television show. Will I get to visit the set while you're shooting your scenes?"

"I'll ask the producer and get back to you," I said.

"I appreciate that. I might as well admit that I've always wanted to be an actress."

"You've always wanted to be an actress?" God, was there *any* woman in Hollywood who didn't?

"Yes. Carlos and I acted a little bit before we were married. We would give anything to do it again."

I dropped the whisk, a lightbulb going on in my head. They'd give anything to act again. That's what she'd said. *Anything.*

I tried to remain calm as my mind danced with possibilities. "Is that how the two of you met Victor? Through your work in the movie business?"

"Yes. I was an extra in a movie Carlos was in—the one and only movie he was in—and Mr. Chellus had something to do with the financing. The movie never got finished, because the money ran out, but Mr. Chellus offered us part-time jobs and we were grateful to have the security, knowing how difficult it is to earn a living as full-time actors."

You're telling me. "And you've been with Victor ever since?"

"Yes. Our part-time jobs here became full-time jobs." Suddenly, her eyes moistened and her cheeks flushed. I had struck a nerve, apparently.

"What is it, Rosa? Is everything all right?"

She shook her head, fought back tears.

I patted her hand. "You can tell me. Is it that you want to leave your job here but can't for some reason?"

She nodded, then pointed to the egg yolks. "They're getting runny. We should continue to whisk them."

"Forget the eggs," I said. "Why can't you and Carlos leave your jobs here and pursue your dreams in show business?"

"Because..." She censored herself.

Well, I knew about the illegal immigrant thing, but surely that wasn't what was keeping them under Victor's roof. Or was it? "Go on," I encouraged her. "Maybe I can help. Are you afraid of leaving Victor because you think he might turn you in to the immigration authorities?"

Her eyes widened. "How did you know about that?"

"It was just a guess," I said. "Breaking the immigration law is so common in L.A."

"It is," she agreed, "but if he turned us in, we'd be out of work and out of money."

"Not if you got other jobs—jobs in acting, for instance."

She brightened. "That would be wonderful, but how? We're in this country illegally, remember."

"Victor must have wrangled phony documents for you, didn't he?"

She nodded sheepishly.

"Then what's the problem? Hollywood is full of people with phony *something.*"

"Also, we're not young anymore. We don't have much practice at acting. And, as I said, Mr. Chellus could be so angry if we left him that he'd have us arrested. He threatens to do this on a regular basis."

He's good at threatening, I thought, flashing back to Jack and the horrible way Victor had treated him. And then I recalled that Rosa had mentioned some sort of "evidence" that night when Maura and I had overheard her in the library—evidence she could use against him if he threatened her. What was it and how could I get her to confide in me about it?

"Look, Rosa. I'm going to be honest with you. There's no time to pussyfoot around."

"Pussy what?"

"Never mind. What I'm saying is that I might as well come clean."

Again, she seemed puzzled and handed me a paper towel. I realized that, despite the many years she had spent in America, she hadn't solved the mysteries of American slang.

"The point I'm trying to make is that I sense that you and Carlos have a more complicated relationship with Victor than one would suspect and that, while he exerts a certain hold over you, you have evidence that could incriminate him, too. Am I right?"

Now she sobbed in earnest. I handed the paper towel back to her, so she could wipe her face with it.

"Why are you interested in such things?" she said during a break in her crying jag. "Your mother and Mr. Chellus are close to marrying."

"That's exactly why. I'm looking for a way to prove to my mother that Victor is all wrong for her, and your evidence could be the answer. Please tell me what it is, Rosa. What do you have on him? You've been dying to use it. Why not give it to me and let *me* use it?"

Sob sob sob sob sob sob. I wished she'd stop already so we could wrap up the conversation before Vic came home from his day on the links and Mom came home from her day on the set.

"It's true about Mr. Chellus," she said. "He's a bad man. But Carlos and I have been bad, too. He made us do bad things."

"Like what?"

She waved me off.

"Okay, let's go back to the evidence. I'm begging you to give it to me."

"If I gave it to you, it would help your mother but not Carlos and me. We'd be out on the street once Mr. Chellus was punished for his crimes."

"What if I made sure you weren't on the street?" I was winging this.

"How?"

"You said you and Carlos always wanted to be actors. What if I guaranteed you jobs in a movie? My boyfriend is Jack Rawlins, the host of *Good Morning, Hollywood.* He's a famous movie critic, Rosa."

"Are you serious? Carlos and I watch his show all the time. We're his number one fans."

"Okay, then you know how influential he is. He could arrange for you two to meet with casting directors. They respect his opinion. It'll be fabulous, you'll see. You'll give me the evidence, and you and Carlos will be up there on the silver screen where you belong–a regular Penélope Cruz and Antonio Banderas. In other words, I'll help you if you help me. Or, as Jack would say, one hand washes the other."

She was confused yet again and passed me the Palmolive liquid. After I explained what I meant, she promised she'd talk to Carlos and then call me. But I knew they'd fall in line. After all, they'd had a taste of showbiz and were, therefore, seduced by even the remote possibility of stardom.

"Just one thing," she said as we were about to refocus our attention on the now-decomposing eggs.

"Yes?"

"If I went back to work in the movies, I'd need someone to give me a makeover, especially to my hair. It's long and flat and for the camera it should be short and poufy."

"Consider it done. But before I arrange for your makeover, you'll have to give me the evidence. No proof, no pouf."

I waited a couple of days for Rosa to call me with her answer. When she didn't, Jack and I decided that he would call her, to add a certain luster to our campaign.

After she gushed that she really was his number one fan, she listened to the elaborate story he'd concocted for her benefit. It involved a movie that was being shot in Vancouver by a veteran director friend of his, and its script featured two scene-stealing parts that would be perfect for her and Carlos. He went on and on about the roles themselves, about the millions of people around the world who would see the movie, including their friends and family back in Mexico, and about this once-in-a-lifetime opportunity for her and her husband to sever their ties with Victor and make a fresh start.

Rosa was sufficiently dazzled that she agreed to turn over her supposed evidence. She was, however, extremely nervous about Victor finding out about her traitorous plan, so she wouldn't allow Jack or me to come near the Beverly Hills manse to collect the incriminating whatever-it-was. She was even afraid to risk being seen with us at a public place. As a solution, we decided on a drop-off location—a bench in Roxbury Park in Beverly Hills. She would leave her goody there, in a brown paper bag after dark, and we would zip by and pick it up.

At the appointed hour, we cruised by the park and found the designated bench and waited in the car for her to make her deposit.

"This feels like a drug deal," I remarked, as we sat at the curb, engine running.

"It could be a drug deal," he said. "For all we know, Victor's into that stuff, too."

"Look, she's over there," I said, pointing at the woman who, at that very minute, was walking briskly toward the bench, the brown bag in her arms. She kept glancing to her left, then her right, checking to make sure she hadn't been followed.

When she had left the bag on the bench and returned to her car, we pounced.

"Let's wait until we get to my house to take a look at it," said Jack once we had the bag in our possession and were driving away from the park.

"Not a chance," I said firmly. "Let's pull over and take a look at it now."

"It's dark," said Jack. "Wouldn't it make more sense to be able to actually *see* it, since we've gone to so much trouble to get it?"

"Good point," I conceded.

I sat with the bag on my lap during the twenty-minute ride to Jack's. I was so curious about its contents it felt like it was burning a hole in the leg of my jeans. When we finally got there, we hurried inside, turned on the lights, and brought the bag into the kitchen.

"Here goes," I said as I opened it. What I found was your basic cheapo leatherette scrapbook into which Rosa had glued photos along with captions and assorted handwritten musings. "If this is her wedding album, I'm throwing it in the garbage."

"Let's take it one page at a time," said Jack. "She wouldn't have given it to us if it didn't link up with Victor in some way."

Ironically, it *was* a wedding album, only Rosa didn't appear in any of the photos.

"How odd," I said as we viewed the first one. It was of Victor dressed in a tuxedo and holding the hand of a bosomy blonde in a bridal gown.

"She must be Mary Elizabeth," said Jack, "the one who drowned."

I shook my head. "Victor was in his fifties when he married her, if I remember correctly from the obit in the *L.A. Times*. This picture is more recent."

"You're right," he said after reading Rosa's caption. "The bride isn't Mary Elizabeth. According to this notation, her name is Karen Sweetzer, and she and Victor were married four years ago."

I did a double take at the photo. No, a triple take. Then I read and reread Rosa's scribbles, which were in English but only sort of. Apparently, she, along with Carlos and Vincent, Victor's chauffeur, had been a guest at the wedding and was, therefore, able to give a firsthand account of the event, which, she noted, had taken place in a small ceremony at the Pfister Hotel in Milwaukee, Karen's hometown.

"What on earth do you make of this?" I asked Jack. "Victor told my mother he was only married once—to Mary Elizabeth."

"And yet he was clearly married twice. And Rosa considered the fact that he *was* married twice significant enough to give us the scrapbook as 'evidence.' "

"I know." I grabbed his arm. "So you're thinking what I'm thinking. That this wife died, too. That he *murdered* this wife, too."

"I don't have a clue. Even if they both died through no fault of his, it doesn't make sense that he'd hide having been married the second time. Why would he tell everybody about Mary Elizabeth and how much he missed her and how much he grieved for her and yet not tell a soul about Karen Sweetzer?"

"Maybe he thought we could handle one accidental death but not two. Maybe he thought we'd be more suspicious of him if he were a two-time widower."

"Maybe. As we said, there's a reason Rosa snuck us these photos."

"Right. Let's look at the rest of them, although they're probably just those cheesy wedding shots where the bride feeds the groom the cake and then the groom feeds the bride the cake and they kiss with mouthfuls of frosting."

Jack cocked his head at me. "So you're not a fan of traditional weddings?"

"No, but my mother is." I misted up when I thought of how desperately she wanted me to settle down, get married, and have kids. I hoped I would grant her that wish someday, but only if she was speaking to me.

I turned the page of the scrapbook. Sure enough, there was a shot of Victor and Karen feeding each other cake, followed by another of them locked in a disgusting embrace, followed by another in which they toasted each other with champagne.

"This is incredible," I said. "I wonder what happened to Karen. Do you think he threw her overboard during a sailing trip or did he keep things interesting by disposing of her body some other way?"

"How about this question: Did Rosa and Carlos have a hand in disposing of her body?" said Jack. "Clearly, they were involved somehow or she wouldn't have made that comment to you about how Victor forced them to 'do bad things.'"

"My God," I said. "What kind of a nut are we dealing with?"

"I don't know. I suppose there's a chance that Victor merely divorced Karen and didn't tell your mother she existed."

"But then we're back to why Rosa gave us the scrapbook. I say it's because she wanted us to see that her boss is the murderer of two women."

"But how would he have gotten away with murder twice? It's hard enough to get away with it once, Stacey."

"Maybe Rosa and Carlos helped him get away with it, as you just suggested. Maybe Victor blackmailed them into cooperating and that's why she kept a record of the crimes, as blackmail against his blackmail. In any case, I've got to show these photos to my mother immediately, whether we're estranged or not."

"Agreed."

I grabbed the phone and called Mom. "No answer at her place or on her cell," I reported after getting voice-mail messages at both numbers. "I guess I'll have to try her at Victor's."

I dialed his number and got the answering machine.

"What about calling Jeanine, her publicist," said Jack. "Won't she know where Helen is?"

"She might."

Jeanine answered after the first ring. "Your mother's gone out of town," she said, sounding apologetic, probably because she'd heard I'd been given the silent treatment.

"When will she be back?" I asked.

"Not for two weeks."

"It's not *Sex and the City* again, is it?"

"She's not working, Stacey," said Jeanine. "She's spending some private time with Victor."

*Private time?* I felt my pulse quicken. "I see. Do you know where he took her?"

"Yes." She gave me the gory details, then apologized again. I guess she was sorry to have to be the one to clue me in.

"Now what?" I said after I hung up and gazed helplessly at Jack.

"Why? What did Jeanine tell you?"

I reached out for his hand and clasped it tightly. "My mother has driven up to the San Ysidro Ranch in Montecito with Victor. Why? Because they've eloped, Jack. They've arranged to tie the knot during the last part of their stay. In other words, the same woman who told me to avoid unsuitable men like the plague has just run off to marry one."

# Chapter
# Thirty

★

BOY, DID I FEEL SLIGHTED—my own mother hadn't even invited me to her wedding. But mostly I felt panicked, so I reached for the phone to call her at the hotel.

"She'll only hang up on you," Jack reminded me. "We've got to approach this some other way."

"You're right. Let's get in the car and drive to Montecito. We'll show up with Rosa's scrapbook and stop her from making the mistake of her life."

"How will the scrapbook change her mind about Victor? He'll just explain away the photos of him and Karen. He'll make up another one of his ridiculous stories and your mother will buy every word and she'll end up accusing you of causing trouble again. The only person who can confirm that Victor actually committed a crime is Rosa. We need *her* to tell us what happened to Karen."

"Then let's get in the car and drive to Beverly Hills," I said. "With Victor gone, she might be more inclined to help us. We'll butter her up, fill her head with visions of her spectacular movie career, promise her she'll never have to cook a single meal again. If she goes shy on us, we'll ask Carlos what happened to Karen."

"Worth a try."

We drove to Victor's, rang the bell, and waited a few seconds. Eventually, Vincent, the smiley chauffeur, answered the door—a surprise, given that it was Carlos who usually functioned as the gatekeeper.

"Hi, Vincent," I said, then introduced Jack. "Is Rosa around? We'd like to talk to her."

"Sorry. She's not here. Neither is Carlos. When I arrived at the house this morning, I was told they had quit."

"Quit?" I said.

"That's what Quentin, the projectionist, told me. Since Mr. Chellus is on vacation with your mother, I wasn't able to ask him why they quit or where they went."

Jack and I glanced at each other, knowing full well they wouldn't have gone anywhere with their big show business career in the offing. What's more, it was odd that Vincent hadn't accompanied my mother and Victor to Montecito, since he was both Vic's chauffeur and bodyguard.

"It sounds as if they left very suddenly," said Jack. "And no one knows where they went or how they can be contacted?"

He shook his head. "It's strange, I agree, but they didn't leave a forwarding address, according to the rest of the staff. Everybody's upset, because those two were such popular members of the household. They will definitely be missed."

We thanked Vincent and walked back to Jack's car.

"I'm completely blown away by this," I said. "Victor must have found out that Rosa gave us the scrapbook and silenced her and Carlos."

"Which is code for 'had them murdered'?"

"I wouldn't put it past him. He could have disposed of them the way he disposed of Mary Elizabeth and Karen—the way he's planning to dispose of my mother."

Jack put his arm around my shoulders. "Try to stay calm. The bad news is that Victor could be a killer. The good news is that he doesn't kill women on his honeymoons, judging by past history, so we've got a little time to play with. Let's concentrate on what to do now."

"There's only one thing we can do, since Rosa and Carlos have disappeared and taken the truth about Karen with them: our next stop should be the Beverly Hills police."

"And tell them what? That we think the cook and the manservant at Victor's house met a violent end? That we think the woman in a scrapbook did, too? That we think your mother will be his latest victim, even though she went away with him voluntarily? They'll laugh us out of the building."

"But we've got the photos of Karen and Victor," I said hopefully.

"That's all they are, Stacey—photos of a woman Victor married, if you believe Rosa, who is no longer here to explain herself. The truth is, we have nothing the police will buy."

"Couldn't we *make* them investigate Victor?" I said.

"For what? You saw what happened when you looked into the drowning of Mary Elizabeth. You and Maura found nothing. The autopsy on her was clean. Victor wasn't under suspicion."

"But now we've learned that he lied about being married only once; that he hid the fact that he was married to another woman."

"They don't put people in jail for lying about being a two-time loser," said Jack.

I sighed, knowing he was right. "If the police won't help us, we'll have to come up with some other way of rescuing Mom," I said. "We'll have to get our own proof that Victor murdered both women and then drive up to Montecito and tell her."

\*   \*   \*

I took time off from work at Cornucopia! and got down to the business of finding out more about Victor's newly discovered second wife. Unfortunately, all my phone calls led nowhere. No one at the Pfister Hotel in Milwaukee knew anything about Karen Chellus. Her wedding to Victor was too long ago to be in their files, they claimed, which meant they had no forwarding phone numbers or addresses for the happy couple.

Next, I surfed the Internet, scouring the archives of newspapers in Wisconsin for an obituary of Karen. I found nothing, which led me to conclude that Victor must have killed her in some other part of the country, the maniac.

I reported my lack of progress to both Jack and Maura later that day. The three of us had convened at my apartment, where I had intended to cook them dinner but was so caught up in the hunt for my mother's fiancé's second dead wife that I'd forgotten to go grocery shopping. Luckily, Jack brought in Chinese.

"You did a search of the newspaper archives for Karen?" he said, passing the pu pu platter.

"I did, and I couldn't find a trace of anybody named Karen Chellus."

"There's your problem," said Maura.

"Where's my problem?" I said.

"You searched the papers by inputing her married name. You should have searched for Karen Sweetzer, too. She could be one of those women who keeps her maiden name."

What was the matter with me? Maura was absolutely right.

I grabbed an egg roll, bolted up from the table, and went straight to the computer. I combed the newspapers' websites and did searches for Karen, using her maiden name–to no avail.

"I struck out again," I reported when I returned to the kitchen. "No obit. Nothing."

"Okay, forget the obit," said Jack. "Just do a regular search for Karen. There are dozens of sites where you can find people's phone numbers and addresses."

"But she's dead," I reminded him. "Why would her phone number and address still be listed?"

"You can be dead and be listed," Maura maintained, "the same way you can be dead and get mail. I'm still getting letters at my house for the guy who used to live there, and he's been dead for years."

"Besides which," Jack added, "we don't know how long she's been dead. Victor could have killed her recently–like after he met your mother and decided he needed to subtract a wife before adding another."

"A cheerful thought," I said.

"Let's call the names at the numbers you've got there. At the very least, maybe whoever answers will tell us something interesting."

His suggestion was a stretch, and we all knew it, but, since no one had a better idea, we gathered around my phone as I prepared to dial. There were two listings for Karen Sweetzer in the Milwaukee area. The first one turned out to be a number that was disconnected.

"See?" I said dejectedly. "It's an old number. A useless number."

"There's one left," Maura said. "Call it, Stacey."

I called it. A woman answered.

"Hello," I said. "I'm trying to find out about a person who may have had this number before she died. Her name was Karen Sweetzer."

"I'm Karen Sweetzer, and I'm very much alive," she said indignantly. She had one of those raspy, whiskey voices, which only contributed to her hostile tone. Of course, I'd forgotten that it was two hours later where she was, given the different time zone, so maybe I'd woken her up and she had good reason to be hostile.

"You're Karen Sweetzer?" I said.

"Yeah, but the better question is who are you?"

"Oh. Sorry. My name is Stacey Reiser and I'm calling long distance from Los Angeles."

"I don't know anyone named Stacey Reiser, from Los Angeles or anywhere else," she snapped. "Good-bye."

"No! Wait!" I said before she could hang up. "Could you give me just another second?"

"Why? If you're one of those telemarketers, I'll tell you what you can do with your sales pitch at this hour of the night."

"I'm not a telemarketer, I swear," I said. "I'm just trying to get information about a Karen Sweetzer who was married at the Pfister Hotel in Milwaukee a few years ago."

Silence.

"Karen?" I said. "Are you there?"

More silence.

"Please, Karen. This is urgent. Are you by any chance the same Karen Sweetzer who got married at the Pfister four years ago? To a man named Victor Chellus?"

"Okay, honey. Now you're really pissing me off. I'm not discussing my marriage to Victor. Not with you. Not with anybody. Got it? That nightmare is in the past and that's where it's gonna stay."

So she *was* Victor's second wife, but she *hadn't* been murdered. I was relieved. Sort of. Still, my head was starting to pound. I never expected Karen to be alive. I really, truly believed he had killed her, killed both his wives. But perhaps he had simply dumped her, and his sin was one of omission rather than murder.

"Please," I said. "It's very important that I talk to you about Victor. You see, I had no idea you existed. He never told my mother he was married to anyone except Mary Elizabeth."

"Your mother? What does she have to do with all this?"

"My mother is Helen Reiser, Karen. You know, the 'Make No Bones About It' Lady from the Fin's tuna commercials?"

*"Helen Reiser is your mother?"* She nearly broke my eardrum screaming this into the phone. "I *adore* her. She's so *real.* She reminds me of my own mother, may she rest in peace. But what does she have to do with Victor?"

"She's about to marry him, Karen."

"No way. She's too smart to get taken in by a bastard like him."

"A year ago, I would have agreed with you, but ever since she came to Hollywood and became a star, she's lost all common sense when it comes to men, to most things, in fact."

"Well, how can I help?"

"You can tell me why Victor never mentioned you to anyone, including my mother, who's under the impression that he shares everything with her."

She laughed scornfully. "Victor is afraid to mention me, afraid somebody will start asking questions about me."

"What kind of questions?"

"Like what that monster did to me and why."

"I don't understand, Karen. Did you have a disagreement with Victor about how much alimony he was supposed to pay you? Are we talking about a bitter divorce trial or something?"

"Alimony? I wouldn't take a penny from him. I don't want anything to do with him. I wouldn't even be talking to you about him if I didn't think your mother was in danger."

"So you agree that she's in danger? I've been trying to warn her for months and she won't listen. The subject has become such a battleground that she's stopped speaking to me."

"That's Victor for you, coming between family members like that. The same thing happened to me."

"I'm sorry to hear that, but tell me, Karen: how is my mother in danger? Did Victor hurt you when you two were married?"

"Hurt me? He tried to kill me!"

"He *what?*"

"Well, it was that Latin heartthrob who tried to kill me."

"Carlos?"

"Yeah, but he was just following orders and couldn't delegate. I'm only alive today because Victor couldn't get decent help."

"Okay, okay. Let's get more specific here, Karen. Tell me exactly what happened. My mother's life depends on it."

"What happened was that Victor and I had a volatile relationship right from the get-go. I always suspected that he married me for my money, but he was such a flatterer that I bought his act. Still, I was insecure and it didn't take a lot of alcohol to bring out the worst in me. One night I picked a fight with him. I baited him about Mary Elizabeth, the first wife. I accused him of marrying her for her money, too. I backed him into a corner and the next thing I knew he was admitting that he did marry her for the bucks and that he killed her in order to have the bucks for himself and that, if I didn't keep my mouth shut, I would find myself in the same predicament."

"My God, Karen. Why didn't you go straight to the police after he said that?"

"Because I figured it was just the booze talking. And because I loved the jerk."

"Then what happened?"

"Turned out it wasn't the booze talking. Carlos was in charge of supervising the other members of Victor's staff, including Vincent, the chauffeur, who took care of all the cars. I found him working on my Mercedes one day and asked what the problem was. He said

Carlos told him to check the oil or something. I got into the car a few hours later and what do you know? As I was on my way to Saks, the brakes failed, and I ended up wrapped around a tree. I was supposed to die, but I didn't. I survived, and the minute I was out of that hospital, I was on the phone to my lawyer dissolving the marriage."

"But if Victor really tried to kill you, why didn't you go to the police then?"

"With what proof? My car had bad brakes. I couldn't make any-one believe that Victor *caused* the car to have bad brakes. You know what a smooth talker he is. Who's gonna believe a boozy bitch like me over Mr. Hollywood Snake Oil Salesman? And then there was the issue of publicity; I didn't want any. My father was a pillar of the community and the family didn't need a scandal. I'd given them enough headaches over the years, including marrying a man they didn't trust from day one."

"So Victor really tried to kill you."

"You got it."

"And he admitted to killing Mary Elizabeth?"

"He claimed he got Rosa to do it. You've met the señora, I as-sume?"

"Yes, but–"

"But nothing. She was as corrupt as the rest of them. The night of Victor's big confession, he told me she put something in Mary Elizabeth's food–something that killed her. Apparently, Rosa always prepared them a cooler full of treats to take on their sailing trips. Mary Elizabeth had a lot of food allergies, he said, so she liked to bring her own meals whenever possible. The day she supposedly drowned, Rosa must have given her something she wasn't allowed to eat, and that was the end of her."

"And whatever it was didn't show up in the autopsy," I mused. "It's amazing that Victor got away with what he did."

"Not so amazing, honey. That man always gets away with what he does. He'll never get nailed."

"Oh, yes he will. And I'm going to be the one to nail him. Thanks to you, my mother won't end up like Mary Elizabeth."

"Thanks to me? I already told you. I'm not telling my story to the police."

"Forget the police. My mother doesn't need the negative publicity any more than you do. Police lead to reporters and photographers and TV cameras. If they all got hold of the fact that she was about to marry a criminal, her career as the straight-shooting Fin's Premium Tuna Lady would be history. She'd be the butt of jokes, lose her credibility, wonder why her phone has stopped ringing. She'd be devastated to find out what it's like to fail in this town."

"That would be messy, wouldn't it?" said Karen.

"Very. In addition to the professional fiasco, there would be an emotional toll on her if the cops burst in on her love nest and dragged Victor away in handcuffs. She might go into denial. She might view him as a martyr. She might refuse to believe he did anything wrong. She might even think I put the police up to arresting him, just to come between them. That's what she believes about me anyway—that I can't bear for her to be happy."

"So what's the solution? You can't let her go ahead and marry Victor."

"You're right. I can't. So I guess the solution is for her to catch him in the act of being a liar and a cheat, to discover for herself what a creep he is. The revelation will knock her for a loop no matter how I handle this, but I might be able to soften the blow just a little if I arrange it so she sees him for who he really is and then breaks it off with him—herself. That's the only way she'll emerge with a shred of self-respect, with any sense of empowerment."

"Wow. Your mother's a lucky lady to have such a caring and creative daughter," said Karen. "It's cool that you want her to save face like that. But Victor is a cagey guy, honey. How are you going to arrange for her to catch him in the act of being a louse?"

"Yeah, how?" said Jack and Maura, who were listening in on an extension.

"I have an idea," I said to all of them.

# Chapter
# Thirty-one

☆

JACK ACCOMPANIED ME on my trip to Wisconsin. Talk about a good sport. For a guy who'd spent his life avoiding emotional involvement, not to mention fearing exposure about taking Victor's bribe, he demonstrated his commitment to me by telling his producers he had a "family emergency" and would have to skip a taping or two of his show. It's a cliché to say that it's in crisis situations that you find out who your true friends are, but I found out what a true friend he was during my mission to save my mother.

And he wasn't just along for moral support. He had an important job to do. Since he was a professional interviewer and was skilled at getting people to say and do things they might not otherwise say and do, he had the task of helping me convince the former Mrs. Chellus to participate in my scheme.

Was I comfortable leaving my mother in Victor's clutches up in Montecito while the two of us were flying to Milwaukee? Hardly. But I was counting on putting my plan in motion in time to keep her from walking down the aisle with that crackpot.

So there we were, standing on Karen Sweetzer's front porch,

waiting for her to let us in. She lived in a white, Southern colonial in the Fox Point section of the city and, judging by the house's size and setting, she wasn't hurting financially. She was cordial when she finally answered the door, although our presence clearly pained her. She had thought she'd gotten rid of Victor and the memories of their turbulent time together, and now here we were dredging everything up again.

She stood at the door, a cigarette in hand, her shoulder-length platinum blond hair so teased and stiff with spray it had the look and texture of cotton candy. She was in her mid-to-late fifties, I guessed, but seemed older, due to the heaviness around her hips and the deep crevices around her mouth. She wore tight-fitting black Capri pants, black mules with pom-poms on them, and a white button-down blouse that was opened to reveal a great deal of cleavage. She wasn't beautiful–her nose was a little too long for her face and her blue eyes were obscured by too much mascara and her lips had been collagened into miniballoons–but she was striking in a showy sort of way. Obviously, Victor must have found her so, along with her family's financial portfolio.

"Come in," she said, waving us inside, her fingernails painted the same vermilion red as her mouth. "Oh, and don't mind my precious Luther. He'll calm down once he gets to know you."

Precious Luther was a Doberman. He was getting to know us all right, first by baring his teeth and growling at us, then by sniffing our crotches.

We sat in her living room. The sofa and chairs were draped in sheets of plastic, perhaps to prevent Luther from devouring the up-holstery. I've never understood this–why have furniture if you're going to cover it up?–but there we were.

"Karen," Jack began once we were all settled and Luther had left us alone. "Let me begin by thanking you for all the information you gave Stacey on the phone, and, of course, for agreeing to see us now."

"Hey, I'm not wild about this, but I couldn't live with myself if I didn't tell you everything I know about Victor. The fact that you turn out to be the guy on *Good Morning, Hollywood* doesn't hurt, either. I'm as big a star fucker as the next person."

Karen had a bit of a potty mouth, but I hadn't expected a nun.

Jack cleared his throat. "Karen, we came here to ask you a favor."

"What kind of favor? I already told you more than I intended." As her body tensed, so did Luther's, and so, as a result, did mine.

"As Stacey explained on the phone, we don't want to send the police to the hotel in Montecito to arrest Victor. We want Helen to find out what a rat he is on her own."

"And as I also explained, my mother isn't speaking to me," I added. "So it's not as if I'm the one who can persuade her that he's a rat. I can't even show my face there."

"Which leaves you, Karen," said Jack. "You're the one who can reach Helen."

"Me? How?" She gestured wildly with her cigarette, causing the ashes to fall onto the carpet. Perhaps she should have put plastic on the floor, too.

"By flying back to California with us," said Jack. "Our idea is that we'll get you a room at the San Ysidro Ranch, where Helen and Victor are staying, and that you'll confront him—both of them—with the truth. Helen will be able to hear your story for herself, without a clue that Stacey had anything to do with it. What's more, she'll be able to watch Victor reveal his dark side as you accuse him of being a murderer. She'll be so appalled by the horrific nature of the whole affair that she'll leave him so fast, he won't know what hit him *and* she'll realize Stacey was right about him, thereby repairing their relationship."

"Oh, Karen," I said, taking her hand in what I hoped would be a display of sisterhood. Luther thought otherwise and appeared to want to maul me. "Tell us you'll do this. Tell us you'll save my mother's life. It'll only take a day or two out of your schedule and, of course, we'll pick up all your expenses."

"I'm sorry," she said. "I'd like to help—as I told you, I think your mother's a real role model for women—but I can't bring myself to face off with Victor, not after what he tried to do to me. The man wanted me dead. Dead! I can barely spit out his name, let alone be in the same room with him."

With that pronouncement, she broke into big, bronchial sobs that soaked her face with tears blackened by her mascara.

Jack rushed over with a handkerchief. She took it and blew her nose loudly. Then she looked up at us. "Please don't think I'm a bad person," she said, her tough-broad image deserting her. "It's just that I'm afraid."

"I understand," I said. "I'd be afraid, too, if my husband tried to murder me. But Jack and I will be right outside the door while you're having it out with Victor. He won't be able to hurt you. I promise, Karen. Please trust me, trust us."

"I do trust you. It's just that I'm *scared*!" Karen wailed, shredding the tissue into tiny pieces, most of which clung to her black capri pants. "Why do you think I keep Luther around? You don't get over it when someone tries to kill you."

"But imagine how sweet the revenge will be," Jack reminded her. "Just picture Victor's face when you show up and ruin his seduction of Stacey's mother."

"We need you to go to Montecito, Karen," I said, taking both of her hands in mine this time—before she could light another cigarette and make the room even smokier than it was. "Remember what I told you on the phone. In order for my mother to emerge with her self-esteem intact, as well as her career, it's essential that she be the one to catch Victor in his lies and then dump him quietly, rather than watch him be carted off by the police and see herself on the front pages of the tabloids. That's why you have to arrive at the hotel and surprise Victor. He'll go postal, right in front of my mother, and she won't have any recourse but to give him the boot."

"I wish I had a daughter like you," said Karen, drying her tears. "I have nobody but Luther, while you have this tight bond with your mother—when you're speaking to each other, that is."

"You know, only a few months ago I would have *paid* a man to marry her, just so she'd get off my back and focus on someone else for a change. But this mess with Victor has made me realize that I want a relationship with her, even if it means putting up with her harangues. I want her in my life more than I don't want her in my life. I love her more than I want her to change. In a nutshell, I understand now that if I want her to accept me for who I am, I'll have to accept her for who she is. Does any of that make sense to you?"

Karen nodded. "The question is: Does my not wanting to go with you to California make sense to *you*?"

"Of course. I'm sympathetic to the fact that you're afraid of being around Victor. But what if you took Luther with you?"

"Come on. You can't just pick up and go places when you've got a *dog*," she said as if I were an idiot, "especially one with Luther's special needs." Luther was, at that moment, caressing his balls.

"So you won't change your mind?" said Jack, looking defeated.

"I can't. I'm sorry."

I wasn't giving up. Not yet. "But remember, my mother's your role model," I persisted. "You said you adore her, Karen. She's the same woman who wags her finger and scolds the audience about buying the best tuna fish and you're in a position to help her. She's been having a great run, getting parts in sitcoms, dramas, and feature films. She's even appeared on Oprah twice. Her entire image—the very foundation of her success—is based on her credibility, her reputation for being a woman of solid, upright, no-nonsense values. If the media found out she was marrying a murderer, that would be the end of her career in show business. I know from firsthand experience how hard it is to get where she's gotten, and I'm not about to let her blow it all because of some guy with a screw loose."

"What do you mean, you know from firsthand experience?" said Karen.

"Oh," I replied. "I guess I should have said something about my own background. It just didn't seem important in view of what my mother is going through. I'm an actress, too."

"Stacey is a fine actress," said Jack. "Maybe you caught her in the Jim Carrey comedy *Pet Peeve*. The movie was a stinker and she didn't have much to work with in terms of a script, but she rose above the material. I didn't realize how good she was the first time I screened the picture, but I've seen it again since then and I can tell you she's wonderful."

I smiled at him, flattered that he was praising me to a perfect stranger, gratified that he was admitting he'd been wrong about me, comforted that he was in love with me and had proven it by his words and deeds in my hour of need. But the fact remained that even if I did have all the talent in the world, even if I was better than my résumé suggested, even if I were to achieve the level of stardom I'd always dreamed of, it wouldn't prevent my mother's career from crashing and burning, and it was her career I was worried about at that moment, not mine.

Of course, it didn't occur to me until a minute or two later that by finally letting go of my professional disappointments–from the juicy parts I'd never landed to the rave reviews I'd never garnered– and simply trusting my acting ability for once, I might actually be able to salvage Mom's career, not to mention my own. Why did I need Karen to show up in Montecito, I realized, when I could just as easily play her?

# Chapter
# Thirty-two

☆

TELL US EXACTLY what happened the night you and Victor were drinking and arguing and you got him to admit he'd murdered Mary Elizabeth," said Jack. We were still seated in Karen's living room, but now we were taking notes. Jack was writing down the specifics of the scenario during which Victor had been sufficiently provoked to confess his crime. I was writing down the specifics of Karen's appearance, her mannerisms, her gestures, and, most important, her speech patterns. Our plan was for me to show up in Montecito and play the part of Karen Sweetzer Chellus, and for Jack to create the script I would deliver in order to force Victor into revealing his true colors in front of my mother.

"I was standing in the middle of the room," said Karen, "a glass of scotch in my hand—"

"Which hand?" I interrupted.

"My right hand," she said.

"What were you wearing?" I asked.

"Oh, let's see. Probably something like the outfit I've got on. Anyway, I was standing there with a glass of scotch in my right hand

and a cigarette—a Marlboro Light—in my left, and I said something like, 'Go on, you bastard. Be honest for a change. You married me for my money. Didn't you? Didn't you?' I was taunting him, goading him, trying to get him to admit what I knew deep down. Obviously, this was not a relationship based on trust."

"Obviously," said Jack. "But I assume Victor denied your accusation at first."

"Over and over. I didn't get a straight answer out of him until I managed to push the right button."

"Which was?" said Jack.

"Which was to say, 'You've lost money on business venture after business venture, Victor, and now you don't have anything close to resembling a j-o-b. Basically, you're a bum, a deadbeat, a nobody, and yet you live like a king who is somehow able to keep up with your ritzy friends in Beverly Hills. How is that possible? I'll tell you how. You conned me into marrying you and paying the bills for everything, including that over-the-top wardrobe of yours.'"

"Did you really pay all the bills?" asked Jack.

"No, but like I said before, this was partly the booze talking. I'm one of those people who shouldn't go near the stuff."

"How did he respond to being called a deadbeat?" I asked.

"He got all red in the face and started shouting at me. He's a man, and men don't appreciate it when you challenge their ability to earn a living. Macho asshole. He said, 'I'm an entrepreneur! I take risks in business! I win some, I lose some.' Then I said, 'You're a deadbeat, plain and simple. You found yourself in a financial hole and you married me. Admit it, Victor. Admit it!' He still wouldn't bite, so I pushed his other button."

"How many buttons does he have?" I said.

"Plenty, but it's the mother button that's really worth pushing."

"Are you saying he didn't get along with his mother?" I asked, being an authority on the subject.

"He was crazy about her, just crushed when she passed away. If you want to make him mad, all you have to do is say something mean about his mommy."

"That's what you did?" I said.

"You bet. I said, 'Maybe it was your sainted mother who gave you the idea that it's okay to marry women for their money. She probably taught you that if you can't hack it in business, find a woman to bail you out.' He shook his fist at me and said, 'You want the truth? Here it is and it has nothing to do with my mother, so leave her out of it. It has to do with you. Why would anyone in his right mind marry a lush like you if not for that money your family never spends? Cheap. You're all cheap!' So now he was criticizing me and my family, and I wasn't amused. I waltzed over to him and threw my drink in his face."

She threw her drink in his face? Well, I tried not to look at Jack, naturally. I was ashamed that I had behaved toward him the way Karen had toward Victor. On the other hand, playing this scene would be a snap for me, given the practice.

"What did he do after you threw the drink at him?" Jack asked Karen.

"He grabbed me by my hair and said, 'You'd better watch yourself, Mrs. Chellus. I was a widower when I met you, remember? You might want to think about how I got that way.'"

"He was referring to Mary Elizabeth then," said Jack.

"Right. I said, 'Oh, so you needed her money, too, is that it? How'd you get rid of her, Victor? Did you have one of your crackerjack household staff throw her overboard on your sailboat—or, should I say *her* sailboat?' He scowled, as if I had insulted his manhood again. And then he filled me in about Mary Elizabeth and her food allergies, and how Rosa doctored their lunch cooler that day. You know, at first I thought he was kidding or bragging or just trying to pay me back for saying something bad about his precious mother. But then I realized he was telling the truth. I sobered up very quickly and decided to make nice to him. I sat in his lap and said I was sorry for drinking too much and that we should just forget everything and be friends. He said that was fine with him, but I knew I was toast. Two days after our fight, I had my 'accident' in the car, just like Mary Elizabeth had her 'accident' in the boat. A pretty story, huh?"

"Not pretty at all," I said. "To think that my mother's with that lunatic right this minute."

"Then go to her," urged Karen. "You two have a great plan. Just remember to push Victor's button—say something nasty about his mother in your script—and you'll have him right where you want him."

Jack and I thanked her, peeled ourselves off the plastic, and hurried out of there before Luther could lick us good-bye.

I phoned Maura from the Milwaukee airport and told her everything.

"I love this!" she said when I outlined what I would need her to do. "I absolutely love this. And of course I'll help. I've got some sick days coming to me, so I'll take them starting tomorrow and concentrate on you, on your one-woman show!"

"It *will* be the acting job of a lifetime," I said. "I've never been able to fool my mother about anything, so convincing her I'm Victor's ex-wife should be quite a trick. Mostly, I just want to watch him squirm."

"And you will. Your idea is brilliant. It's not only going to save your mother's life, it's going to allow her to walk away from this nightmare feeling lucky to be free of Victor forever."

"That's the plan."

We did get started the very next morning. Maura and I made a shopping list of the supplies we'd need in order to physically transform me into Karen. And then off we went to Burbank, to an L.A. retailing institution called Cinema Secrets, which sells makeup and beauty and hair products, along with specialty items. Maura has a spare bedroom full of such products, but for the big jobs–like the one I was plotting–she relies on Cinema Secrets, where she's a regular client, as are many professional makeup artists.

"Let's start with Karen's hair," she said, guiding me through the aisles and stopping in the wigs department. "You told me she has teased-up platinum hair, right?"

"Right. Think Phyllis Diller on a good day."

Maura scanned the shelves and found a wig she thought would fit the bill–literally. "Since we're on a budget, I'm going with nylon," she said, "unless you want to pay five hundred bucks for the real hair kind."

"As you pointed out, we're on a budget," I said. "The nylon will be perfect."

"Okay, now let's deal with Karen's skin. You said she's in her fifties, which means we've got to age you." We wandered into another area of the store. "Here it is," she said after searching through the rows and rows of bottles and jars. "Balloon latex. It's a thin rubbery liquid that'll give us the lines we'll need. It takes a few applications, but once it's on, you'll look years older."

"Most actresses are having surgery to look younger. I'm having balloon latex to look older. I hope my mother appreciates this."

"How can she not?"

"Right. How long does this stuff stay on once you apply it to my skin?"

"Several hours, unless you start sweating profusely. Then it could flake at the edges and peel off."

"So I either have to remain calm or remember to stand near an air-conditioning vent."

"Don't worry. It'll be fine," said Maura, who moved to a shelf full of tape.

"Now what?" I asked as she sorted through boxes.

"You said Karen is bosomy. We've got to give you cleavage."

"Mickey's been telling me that for years."

"Well, thanks to Karen, you'll have those knockers he always wanted you to have–temporarily." She plucked two kinds of tape off the shelf: surgical and the much heavier electrical. "We're going to pull you and tape you and lift you until you're spilling out of your blouse."

"Excellent."

She headed for another section and took down a tin of wax from the shelf. "What's that for?" I said.

"It's mortician's wax. They use it at funeral homes to fill in parts of the body that have been injured or broken off or whatever. We use it for theatrical makeup if we don't have time to create an actual prosthetic. You said Karen has a long nose. After a little of this wax, you'll have one, too. Now we need to buy stuff that will plump up your lips. You did say Karen has had her share of collagen injections, right?"

I nodded. "I don't know how she eats with those things. They're like inflatable rafts."

"I have the answer right here." She held up a lipstick called Plump & Polish. "It swells your lips within a minute after you apply it and lasts for hours."

"What's in it? Shellfish? My lips swell up if I take even a bite of shrimp."

"I don't know what's in it. I only know it works."

We concluded our shopping spree at Cinema Secrets, then moved on to a store called Western Costume, where we rented foam pads to simulate Karen's wide hips and generous butt.

"Pretty soon it'll be showtime," said Maura as I started to feel jittery, the way I always did before a performance.

# Chapter
# Thirty-three

☆

THE SAN YSIDRO RANCH is one of those resorts that's as luxurious as it is legendary. Laurence Olivier and Vivien Leigh were married there. John and Jackie Kennedy spent their honeymoon there. And now Victor Chellus and Helen Reiser were under the delusion that they were about to do both there.

Set on five hundred acres overlooking the Pacific Ocean and the Santa Ynez mountains, the ranch is definitely the spot for romance, with its cozy cottages and gourmet restaurants and numerous amentities. (Along with the usual stuff like facials, they also offer massages—for your pet. Yes, should you bring Fido along, they not only provide "doggie turndown service" but have a Reiki master on hand to align Fido's energies and target his or her twelve body points. In other words, Luther would have enjoyed himself immensely.)

The three of us—Jack, Maura, and I—drove the ninety miles from L.A. to Montecito in Jack's car, armed with our props, our products, and our sense of purpose. Jack had totally dedicated himself to The Plan, not only extending his "family emergency" in order to put himself at my disposal for the few days I needed him, but insisting on paying for our accommodations. And not just any accommodations. He splurged on a two-bedroom suite at a whopping $1,350 per night. As extravagant and generous as it was, it was also the perfect set-up–Jack and I would stay in one bedroom, Maura in the other, with a large living room in which I could quickly do my makeup, wig, and wardrobe changes.

We checked in at the hotel under a fake name and, within minutes after settling into our suite, Maura sat me down and got to work. She was going to transform me into Karen, and there was no time to waste.

On went the padding around my hips and buttocks. On went the tape pulling my breasts inward and upward. And on went the balloon latex.

"We'll start the aging process by giving you some nice crow's feet," said Maura.

"Nice crow's feet," I said. "That's got to be an oxymoron."

"Sit still," she shushed me, and began to stretch the skin around my eyes with her fingers, tugging it gently toward my ears, and applying a thin layer of the liquid latex onto it with a cosmetic sponge, a process known in the trade as stretch and stipple. While she was still stretching my skin, she dried the latex with a blow-dryer, powdered it, and repeated the application two more times. Before I knew it, I had genuine crow's feet.

"Why would anyone get a face-lift?" I said, admiring Maura's handiwork in the mirror. "These lines give me character."

Jack laughed. "Let's see how you feel about the lines when they're real."

Maura stretched and stippled the skin on my forehead, on both sides of my mouth, along the center of my neck, even on the backs of my hands.

"Now what are you doing?" I said when she squirted a different kind of liquid on the end of my nose.

"It's glue," she said. "I'm attaching the mortician's wax to it to give you a longer shnozzola."

On came the wax, which she sculpted and smoothed until it no longer looked like a tumor. Then she coated it all with a clear sealer, followed by foundation and powder.

"Voilà," she said. "Karen's nose."

"Amazing," I said, marveling at the new me.

"Now pucker up," she said, pulling out the Plush & Plump lipstick, and painting my lips with it, after which she painted on the rest of my makeup, including the heavy black mascara Karen wore. As for my hair, she pinned it back and covered it in the platinum wig we'd bought. Then she dressed me in clingy black pants and a low-cut white shirt and flip-floppy mules, making sure my hip and butt pads were securely tied beneath the clothes.

"And here are your stage props," she said, sticking a glass of scotch in my right hand and a Marlboro Light between the fingers of my left. When I gazed at myself in the mirror and took in the whole picture, I could only shake my temporarily blond head. "I look more like Karen than Karen does," I marveled.

"Not unless you do her voice," Jack reminded me.

"Right," I said, lowering my register a couple of octaves. Karen had that deep, husky, smoker's rasp. I had practiced it and I had it down pretty well. As a matter of fact, I had Karen down pretty well—the sexpot walk, the hurried gesturing with her hands, the boozy, tough-broad attitude. I was more than ready for the curtain to rise.

"Do you want to go over the script one more time?" Jack asked, giving my arm an affectionate squeeze.

"No," I said. "I think we rehearsed it enough in the car. But I do want to go over what happens after I do my scene."

"Well, what we hope will happen is that you'll trap Victor into admitting things he would never have admitted otherwise, and that your mother will be so horrified that she'll throw him out. As soon as he leaves, you'll run back to our cottage, where Maura and I will be waiting, and you'll change into your own identity. Then, after a reasonable amount of time, you'll call your mother in her cottage, pretending you're in L.A., and she'll tell you how terrible Victor turned out to be, how right about him you turned out to be, and how she wishes she'd listened to you in the first place. Then you'll tell her you're so glad she's seen the light, even though you're sorry she's hurt, and you'll offer to drive up and bring her home. She'll be thrilled you're coming to get her—all three of us will be coming to get her, obviously—and that will be that. Once we have her back safe and sound, we'll talk to her about getting in touch with the police."

I took a deep breath. "What if I screw up?"

"You're not going to screw up," he said. "You're a professional actress, Stacey. But if something does go wrong and you're not back at the cottage within, say, a half hour, Maura and I will come and get you."

"What do you think could go wrong?" I said.

"Victor," he said. "He might not appreciate being given the boot by your mother. But the good news is that he's not violent; he hires people to do his dirty work. So I'm sure you and Helen will be fine."

"Famous last words," I said. "The truth is, we won't know what he's going to do unless I get over there and start the show."

I picked up the phone and asked to be connected to Victor's cottage. I needed to find out which building he and my mother were in—and to make sure they were there, right that moment, as opposed to sight-seeing or, God forbid, exchanging wedding vows. Disguising my voice, I pretended to be the hostess in the dining room. I felt my heart clutch when it was my mother's adenoidal honk I heard through the earpiece in the phone.

"Hello?" she said.

"Good evening, Ms. Reiser. This is Rhonda in the Stonehouse restaurant. I'm calling to let you know that the chef has some lovely offerings this evening, and I'm wondering if you and Mr. Chellus will be dining with us. I don't see your reservation here."

"It most certainly should be there," my mother said, sounding huffy, the way she always did when the service she was getting was questionable. "I made the reservation myself. Don't you see it? Chellus for two at seven-thirty? We're in the Willow Tree Suite, aren't we, Victor?" Good. So he was there, too.

"Ah, yes. There you are," I said, pleased that I had gotten the information I needed. "I don't know how I missed it. So sorry for bothering you and Mr. Chellus, and I look forward to seeing you both at seven-thirty."

I was about to hang up when my mother said, "Now just you wait a minute."

I froze, wondering if she had recognized my voice. "Yes?"

"You said the chef had some lovely offerings. Like what?"

"Oh." A reprieve. "For entrées, he's preparing a coriander-crusted Muscovy duck breast tonight," I improvised. "It's served with an apple-potato pancake, fennel ragout, and calvados *jus*."

"Too fatty," said the same woman who'd fed me creamed everything as a child. "What else?"

"Well, if you prefer fish, we're serving sea bass tonight. It comes with roasted shallots, Swiss chard, fingerling potatoes, and apple smoked bacon." I was making myself hungry. All I had in the way of sustenance at that moment was the glass of scotch in my right hand. It was supposed to be a prop, but I figured it couldn't hurt to take a sip, so I did.

"I'm in the mood for pasta," she said, prolonging my agony. "What can you do for me?"

"We have something very special for you, Ms. Reiser," I said. "The chef is preparing truffled potato ravioli with marscapone cheese. It comes with wild mushroom ragout and chervil butter emulsion." Not bad from someone who never cooked, right? Rosa would have been impressed.

"Perfect. I'll have that."

"A beautiful choice," I said. "I'll tell the kitchen to save a serving for you. See you later, Ms. Reiser."

I hung up before she could ask about dessert.

"Okay, you guys," I said to Jack and Maura. "They're in something called the Willow Tree Suite. All I've got to do is find it, and we're off and running."

"Good luck, Stacey," said Jack.

"Yeah, break a leg," said Maura.

Armed with my scotch and my cigarette, I made my way to the Willow Tree Suite. I lit the cigarette, took another swig of scotch, and knocked on the door.

"Who is it?" Victor boomed.

"An old friend," I said in Karen's rasp.

"Who?"

"Open the door and find out."

He swung open the door. I was tempted to shout "Trick or treat! Happy Halloween!" but restrained myself. Instead, I took a drag on the Marlboro and said, "Long time no see, honey," then sashayed into the room before he could get an up-close-and-personal look at me.

"What the hell?" he said, staggering a little but remaining by the still-open door, as if he hoped I might use it to leave as suddenly as I'd arrived.

"This is an impromptu visit from your devoted ex-wife," I said.

"I happened to be staying at the hotel and heard you were here, too. Some coincidence, huh?"

He was too dumbstruck to respond.

"The guy at the front desk told me you were here with your lady friend, Victor. Where is she?" I asked this because my mother was supposed to be there but was nowhere in sight.

"Karen?" he said, his cheeks flushing slightly. "Is...is it really you?"

"Yes, honey. We've established that it's me, so let's move on, okay?" I took another drag on the cigarette and inadvertantly blew the smoke up my own nose. The coughing only lasted a second or two, thank God. "You didn't answer me. Where's the woman who's crazy enough to hook up with you, Victor?"

"She's...she's not...she went to browse in the gift shop," he stammered, clearly thrown by my cameo appearance. "But she'll be back pretty soon, and I'd rather not–"

"Rather not introduce us?" I taunted him, faking a bravado I certainly didn't feel. Why did my mother have to slip out for a quickie shopping spree when I needed her to be right there in the damn cottage? I had planned to perform my act with *both* of them in the audience. That was the whole point. What's more, I wasn't thrilled about being alone with a homicidal maniac. What if my showing up made him snap and kill me? There would be no witnesses, no one to stop him, no one to save me. Maybe this idea wasn't so hot after all.

"I'm not introducing you to anyone," said Victor, recovering, his upper lip in a curl.

"Oh, my. Don't tell me she doesn't know about me? That's it, isn't it? She doesn't have a clue that you and I were married once upon a time. Not that we were the love match of the century."

He ran his eyes over me as I strutted around the room. I was petrified he would recognize me underneath all the makeup and camouflage but he didn't, probably because he maintained his position near the door, far enough away not to see that my nose was the consistency of a candle.

"What do you want, Karen?" he said. "Talk fast and then get out. Is it money?"

I laughed. "Why would I come to you for money? It was the other way around with us, remember?" I realized then that it was incredibly hot in there, not a breath of fresh air in the place. I assumed this was my mother's doing, as she was always "chilly" and, therefore, liked the windows closed and the air conditioner off.

"Then what is it? You prance in here after all these years with your booze and your attitude, and I demand to know why. Are you trying to make trouble for me just for sport? If you are, you'll be sorry."

"Aw, is that any way to talk to me, honey?" I was stalling for time, hoping my mother would come back so I could deliver my lines and be done with it. How long could it take to pick out a couple of souvenirs? I was on her shit list, so she wasn't buying me any San Ysidro Ranch T-shirts. Where was she, for God's sake?

"I'll talk to you any way I feel like it," he said, sounding tougher now.

"Well, you always were the little dictator. Must be your height. The Napoleon thing."

"Karen, if you don't get out I'm calling hotel security and having them throw you out."

"Don't even think about it or I'll have the police here faster than you can spell 'murderer.'"

He flinched. "You're such a bitch, you know that, Karen?"

"How sweet. Okay, you want to know why I came here? To clear something up. You did marry me for my money, isn't that true? The same way you married Mary Elizabeth for hers?"

This was where the script kicked in. My goal was to replicate, as closely as possible, the circumstances of the night Victor admitted he'd killed Mary Elizabeth and then threatened to kill Karen. I couldn't circle the room and make small talk with Victor forever. I had to get started and play the scene I'd been rehearsing and hope that my mother would walk in before I finished my performance or Victor finished me.

"I did no such thing," he said.

"Yes, you did. You lost money on business venture after business venture and now you don't have anything close to resembling a j-o-b. Basically, you've always been a bum, a deadbeat, a nobody, and yet you live like a king down in Beverly Hills. How have you managed that, Victor? I'll tell you how: You con women into marrying you and then you let them pay the bills."

"Shut up, Karen! Just shut up!" yelled Victor, his face turning purple with fury. He had finally closed the door to the cottage and moved closer to where I was standing. Oh, where was my mother? I thought as I tried to keep my distance from him.

"You don't like it when a woman challenges your ability to earn a living, do you?" I said, carrying on with the show.

"I'm an entrepreneur. I've taken risks in business. I've won some and lost some. What's wrong with that?"

"Plenty," I said, dying to wipe my face. The room had to be a hundred degrees, and I was sweating like a pig. But I couldn't think about my perspiration problem. I was about to bring out the heavy artillery. "If you hadn't been such a mama's boy, running and hiding under your mommy's skirts, you would have learned that it's not acceptable to depend on women for money."

Victor slammed his hand against the wall. I had pushed his button all right. "Don't you dare talk about my mother like that, you tramp. Say what you want about me, but leave her out of it."

"Fine. I'll say what I want about you. You married Mary Elizabeth for her money and killed her. Then you married me for my money and tried to kill me, too. But you failed, Victor. I'm alive. I'm so alive that I'm going to make you suffer for what you've done."

With those fighting words, I marched over to him and threw my drink in his face. As anticipated, the gesture provoked an instant replay of the scene Karen had described to Jack and me. Victor became furious, out of control, ballistic. He grabbed me by my hair (fortunately, he didn't pull the wig off entirely; just caused it to slip a little) and said, "I wish I *had* killed you like I killed Mary Elizabeth. You're a lush and a liar and you've brought me nothing but misery."

"Victor!" shouted my mother, who had entered the cottage without our notice, which was not surprising given the decibel level of our voices. I was so relieved to see her that I almost called out "Mom!" but reminded myself to stay in character.

Victor let go of me and rushed over to her. "Cookie, I can explain," he said frantically. "Don't believe a word you heard."

She stared openmouthed, first at him, then at me. She was stunned by his outburst, by his admission—how could she not be?—and must have been trying to figure out who *I* was on top of it.

"Believe every word you heard," I said, drawing on my cigarette. "I'm Karen, Victor's ex-wife, and I assure you it's all true."

"You told me you were only married once, to Mary Elizabeth," Mom said to Vic, her expression a mixture of confusion and hurt and anger.

"I wanted to tell you about Karen, but she wasn't a happy chapter in my life and I didn't want to burden you with our sad story," he had the nerve to reply.

"You burdened me with your sad story about Mary Elizabeth," Mom pointed out.

"That was different, because I—"

"Don't lie to me!" she barked. "I just heard you tell this woman you killed Mary Elizabeth."

"You're damn right he did," I said. "He had Rosa poison her the day they went sailing. Didn't you ever wonder why he didn't get tossed overboard in that storm like she did?"

My mother shook her head. "My daughter wondered. I was too blind to wonder."

"Don't listen to this, Cookie," Victor pleaded. "She's a drunk and doesn't know what she's saying."

"What about you?" she countered. "What about what you were saying? You admitted that you wanted her dead, too!"

"He sure did," I said. "He had his chauffeur tamper with the brakes in my car, and I crashed into a tree. That's his m.o. He marries vulnerable women–vulnerable, wealthy women–and steals their money any way he can, even if it means murder. I hate to break it to you, honey, but you were next. Once he got you to walk down that aisle, you were fair game. It was only a matter of time."

"I don't have to listen to any of this," Victor said as he backed toward the door.

"Oh, yes you do, buster," my mother said, wagging her finger at him. The truth had set her free of him, free of the spell he'd cast on her, and not a moment too soon. "Even if you didn't kill Mary Elizabeth, even if you didn't try to kill Karen, even if you didn't con both of them out of their money, you didn't tell me you were married twice and I'll never forgive you for that. When a man lies about one thing, chances are he'll lie about other things. I've had it with you. I never want to see you again as long as I live–and I intend to live a very long time, now that you're out of the picture."

"Don't say that, Cookie. We can work this out," Victor whimpered.

"Work *this* out," my mother retorted, flipping him the bird, a most un-Helen-like gesture. "My daughter tried to tip me off about you. She said you were out to take advantage of me, that you were dangerous even, but I was too gullible, too caught up in all the flattery to believe her. But this courageous woman went out of her way to save me from the same fate she endured." She approached me then, to shake my hand or hug me or something, but stopped when she got close to me. She pointed at my face. "What's wrong with you, Karen? You're . . . you're flaking."

Oh, crap. Maura had warned me that the balloon latex would start to peel off if I sweated profusely, which, of course, I was doing.

"It's a skin condition," I said quickly. "I think it's caused by my smoking. Cigarettes are bad for the complexion."

Good try, right? Well, in an effort to pat down the flaking latex, my hand made contact with the mortician's wax on my nose and knocked the little lump of it off onto the floor.

"Hey! What is this, anyway?" said Victor.

He and my mother both peered at me. By this time, my wig had slipped a little more and, together with the flaking latex and the vanishing wax, my act was fading fast. But it wasn't until my sweating caused one of the pieces of tape around my breasts to lose its adhesive that I came apart at the seams, literally.

My mother took one look at me and said, "What *is* going on? Who in the world—" She took another look, a closer look, and honked, "Stacey! Is that you in there?"

"Yes, it is," I confessed. I put the glass of scotch down on the table and extinguished the cigarette into it and pulled off the wig. "I didn't know how else to get you to believe me about Victor, so after I went to see his ex-wife in Milwaukee and heard the story of what he did to her, I decided to play her, because she was too afraid to show up and tell you everything herself. Maura did my makeup and Jack wrote the script and the three of us came to save you. I hope you're not angry."

"Angry? Oh, my dear, dear daughter. You went to all that trouble for me and you think I'd be angry?" She threw her arms around me and held me tightly, clung to me as if she never wanted to let go. I could feel her starting to cry, just a little. She wasn't one for sentimental moments, but she'd been shaken to the core by Victor's deceit and the extent to which I'd gone to expose it, and she was moved, clearly.

"Of course I did," I said, tears welling up in my own eyes. "I love you, Mom. I've always loved you. Even when we didn't get along. Even when we stopped speaking altogether. Even when it seemed that we'd never have the kind of mother-daughter relationship both of us wanted, each in our own way. The bottom line is, I'd do anything for you, just as you would do for me."

She was so choked up she couldn't utter a single word at first. But then she held me at arm's length and looked me straight in the eye, and, with her customary honk having been replaced by a soft quiver, she said, "I don't know what I did to deserve such a wonderful daughter, but I'm so proud of you I could burst."

"Oh, Mom," I said, not used to hearing this sort of praise from her. "You're proud of me?"

"More than you can imagine." She wiped a tear from her cheek, tried to swallow her emotion. "I realize I've been difficult over the years—critical, overbearing, insensitive to your needs, especially when they conflicted with mine—and I'm sorry for that. Deeply sorry. It's just that you really are the center of my universe, for better or worse. I love you as much as a mother can possibly love a child. I want you to know that, Stacey. Know it now and know it forever, because I won't always be here to tell you."

"That's for sure!" said Victor, who apparently had viewed our warm and fuzzy rapprochment as an opportunity to locate his gun and point it at us.

Yes, just when it appeared that Mom and I had finally resolved our differences, we had bigger problems.

# Chapter
# Thirty-four

☆

PUT THAT THING DOWN, Victor. You're only making a fool of yourself," my mother ordered her former fiancé. She was not the least bit intimidated by him now, I was relieved to see, not even with a gun in his hand. The revelations about his character really seemed to have transformed her back into her old feisty self.

"I'm not doing anything until I get you two out of this cottage and into my car," he said, waving the pistol at us.

"Then what?" she said. "Are you going to drive us to some remote location and shoot us?"

"Not a bad idea," he said.

"Yes, it is," I countered. "Everyone will know you did it. Jack will know. Maura will know. Karen will know. You won't get away with murder this time, Victor."

"Don't be so sure," he said. "Everyone also knows how you and Helen are always at each other's throats. Maybe I'll set it up so it looks like one of you shot the other. Now. Do as I tell you. You're going to walk out of this cottage and into my car, and you're going to do it without making a peep. Got it?"

"What if we don't?" said my mother. "What if we stay right here and wait for Stacey's friends to come and check on us?"

"Then I'll shoot you now, and they can find you riddled with bullets."

"Victor!" my mother snapped at him. "Listen to me. I want you to give yourself up."

"You might as well," I agreed. "You don't shoot people, Vic. You leave the dirty details to your servants, and they're not around."

"That's enough!" he shouted. "Out of this cottage! Both of you! Right this instant!"

He shoved my mother and me out the door, only to be greeted by Jack and Maura. He was not thrilled.

"Stacey! We got worried when you didn't come back," said Jack. He made a move toward me, only to be waved off by Victor, who nevertheless was beginning to panic at his odds. It was four against one now.

In desperation, he yanked my mother's arm, pulling her closer to him, and pressed the gun against her temple.

"Don't!" I yelled. "Let her go, Victor. Please!"

"My daughter's right, Victor. Be a good boy and let me go." For emphasis, she kicked him in the shins.

"Ouch! Cut it out!" he said. "We're outta here." He turned to us to issue a threat. "If you value Helen's safety, you'll stay put."

With that, he dragged her out of the cottage.

"My God, we've got to call the police now," I said. "To hell with the bad publicity. My mother's career won't mean a thing if she's dead."

*Dead.* There were many times over the years that I had pictured my mother dead, but that had merely been a petulant daughter's wishful thinking. The possibility that she could actually *be* dead–at the hands of a stupid little dork like Victor yet–was too gruesome to contemplate.

Jack used his cell phone to call 911. He told the dispatcher every-thing, including that Victor had already raced to his car to make his getaway and that he had taken the movie and television star Helen Reiser hostage. We were promised that help would be on the way as soon as possible.

"We've got to follow them," I said. "They have a lead on us, but we can catch up."

"How do we know where Victor's going?" said Maura.

"My guess is he's going north, as opposed to back to Beverly Hills," said Jack. "But let's hit the road and take it from there."

The three of us hurried back to our cottage, where Jack's car was parked in the spot out front. We piled into the car, peeled out, and caught a fleeting glimpse of Victor's Cadillac as it was pulling out of the hotel's driveway.

"There they are!" said Maura.

"I'm on them. I'm on them," said Jack. "They're probably headed for the 101 north."

"The police just *have* to rescue Mom," I said, clawing at the dash-board. "I can only imagine how freaked out she must be."

"I gave them a description of Victor's Caddy," said Jack. "For all we know, they're about to arrest him as we speak."

"Maybe, but I'm really worried about her. Look how she's stuck there in the passenger's seat next to him. A sitting duck."

"She's a strong woman," said Jack. "A brave woman. She doesn't scare easily. Remember that, Stacey."

We tailed Victor and my mother onto the 101 freeway, believing somehow that we could overtake them, separate them, be heroes.

"Damn," said Jack, banging his hand on the steering wheel in anger. "I lost them. Victor must have sped up and switched lanes and now he's hiding between other cars and I can't see him."

"I don't believe this," I said. "I just don't believe it."

"Try to relax," Maura said. "It'll all work out in the end."

The end, I thought ominously, visualizing my mother's funeral and all the celebrity mourners who would turn out for it. I would make a speech, I decided. A touching tribute to the woman who traveled all the way from Cleveland to Hollywood and took the town by storm. The woman who stood for morality and honesty and making the world a safer place for tuna fish eaters. Yes, it would be a lovely event that would make her very proud. Poor, poor Mom.

No! I stopped myself from even entertaining the idea of my mother's demise. Instead, I bargained with God. Yes, I made a deal in which I said silently, If you let my mother live, I promise I'll never fight with her again. You heard me. I'll hold my tongue when she nags me. I'll suck it up when she criticizes me. I'll answer her questions politely, even if the questions are intrusive or insensitive or just plain annoying. Thank you, God. Amen.

We kept driving, the dusk making it difficult to differentiate one car from another. "Maybe we should turn around and go back the other way," I said, given that Victor had given us the slip. "He may have decided to beat it back to Beverly Hills after all."

"Look! Up ahead!" said Jack, pointing to the car that was weaving from lane to lane. "That's his Cadillac, isn't it?"

I sat up straight and squinted. "Yes! Oh, yes! There they are! But something's very wrong."

"Victor seems to have lost control of the car," said Jack as we watched the Caddy edge dangerously close to other cars.

"Do you think he's got a bottle of booze with him and taken a few nips too many?" said Maura.

Before I could answer, Victor's Cadillac suddenly and terrifyingly swerved wildly to the right and veered across the freeway, miraculously avoiding the cars in its path, until it crashed into the guardrail.

"Oh, please no!" I said, fearing the worst. "If he killed her, I'll rip his heart out, I swear it."

Traffic on the 101 came to a standstill as some passersby stopped to help at the crash site, others merely to rubberneck. The point is, we were thwarted in our efforts to reach Mom, and it was frustrating to say the least.

"How are we going to–"

"Listen. Do you hear them?" Jack interrupted me. "Sirens."

I looked in the rearview mirror and, sure enough, the police had finally arrived. Several squad cars snaked their way up the shoulder of the 101 and surrounded Victor's Caddy.

"I can't just sit here and wait for the traffic to move," I said, my hysteria growing. "I've got to get to Mom now."

I jumped out of Jack's car and ran toward the action, hoping against all hope that my mother was still alive. When I got close to the Cadillac, an officer prevented me from going further.

"This isn't your run-of-the-mill accident. It's a crime scene," he said. "Nobody's allowed in, especially curiosity seekers." He stared at my peeling latex, my swollen lips, and my disheveled clothes, and muttered, "Wacko."

"You don't understand! I'm the daughter of the woman in there!" I shouted. "I've got to go to her. I don't care what condition she's in. Just let me see her before she lapses into a coma and won't even recognize me!"

"Hey, hey. Take it easy," said the cop. "If your mother is the lady we removed from the Cadillac, she's doing fine. It's the guy who needs medical attention."

"What?"

He led me inside the labyrinth of cars and cops until we came upon the Caddy, its hood wrapped around the guardrail like a pretzel. Victor was sprawled across the driver's seat unconscious, blood spilling out of his forehead. My mother was stretched out in the back of one of the police cars, her eyes closed as if she were . . .

"Mom!" I said as I ran to her. "Don't leave me now. I can't let you go. Not after we had that beautiful talk back at the cottage. Not after we finally mended fences and achieved closure and–"

"What's all the racket?" she said, coming to.

"It's Stacey, Mom. You're okay?"

"Me? You bet I am. I was just dozing."

"Dozing? From the look of that Cadillac, you could have been a candidate for the morgue."

"No question about it," said Jack, who, with Maura in tow, had found his way to us. "Tell us what happened, Helen."

"I took charge of the situation, that's what happened," she said. "I wasn't about to be some passive little ninny. Not again, anyway. Victor may have gotten the better of me once, but he certainly wasn't going to get the better of me twice."

"So what did you do?" I said.

"I stole a page from your script. I saw how nutty he got when Karen–I mean, you, Stacey–taunted him about his mother, so I kept criticizing his mama, over and over, figuring he'd have to take his eyes off the road at some point to shut me up. And I was right. He turned to slap me, and I was ready. I bashed him in the head with the heel of my shoe–several times, in fact. With each blow, he became more and more disoriented and eventually lost complete control of the car. As he was blacking out, I leaned over and grabbed the steering wheel and drove us smack into that guardrail. I figured it was the only way to get the police's attention, and it worked, although I suppose I nearly killed Victor, never mind myself." Her expression darkened.

"What is it, Mom? Don't tell me you're sorry Victor got hurt."

"God, no. I'm sorry I damaged my shoe. The heel broke off the minute it made contact with him. We're talking about two-hundred and-fifty-dollar Bruno Magli pumps that I got for ninety-nine dollars at Loehmann's. Now that I think about it, I wonder if they were defective. I don't see why a heel should break off just because it hits a person's head. Perhaps there's a quality control issue that needs to be looked into. I should write the manufacturer one of my complaint letters."

"Good idea," I said. "But other than the shoe, everything's all right? You're not bruised anywhere?"

She shrugged. "My right shoulder's sore, but it's my ego that's bruised. I thought Victor cared about me. It's going to take a while for the reality to sink in."

"There are plenty of other men in Los Angeles, Mrs. Reiser," said Maura, who, of course, had intimate knowledge of most of them, particularly men Mom's age.

"Other men? Please," she said. "I intend to focus my energies on my daughter and my career—in that order."

I looked at Maura and Jack, and felt my heart go out to my mother. Someone would have to tell her. Someone would have to break the news that once the media got wind of her involvement with a criminal, it was a no-brainer that Fin's would drop her, that her other projects would evaporate, and that her agent and manager and publicist and stylist would all desert her for less controversial clients.

"You know, Mom," I began, "the reason we didn't involve the police in the beginning was because we were trying to shield you from negative publicity. The media people pick things up on police scanners, and once they do, there are no secrets."

"That was sweet of you, but I can take the negative publicity."

"The glare of the spotlight can be pretty harsh, Helen," said Jack. "Your image is based on your credibility. You may find that your association with Victor puts a dent in that credibility."

"You're trying to tell me that I could lose the Fin's account, not to mention my acting jobs?"

"Yes, Mom. It's very possible. I'm so sorry."

She clucked. "Don't you worry about that. The truth is, while I've loved every minute of the visibility and the accolades and, of course, the money, I won't be crushed if it all disappears. There are other opportunities, other ways for me to feel useful. I know that now."

I kissed her cheek. "It sounds as if you have a much healthier attitude toward the entertainment industry than I do."

"Speaking of which," she said, "my loss just might be your gain, Stacey. When the media finds out about how you played the part of Karen well enough to fool your own mother, your acting career will soar. I wouldn't be surprised if the offers come pouring in for you, dear."

"Well, I'd love it if I got more roles, but not at your expense, Mom."

"Let's just be happy that we're all safe and sound," she said. She hugged Maura and Jack. "I have the three of you to thank for that."

"You're very welcome, Mrs. Reiser," said Maura.

"You certainly are," said Jack. "Now, when the police are through questioning you, we'll get you to a doctor so you can have that shoulder examined."

"Nonsense," said my mother. "I'll put a little Ben-Gay on it and it'll be fine. I once wrote them a complaint letter and they sent me a whole case of tubes."

He squelched a laugh. "Then we'll just drive back to the hotel and get your things, and then we'll take you down to L.A. You must be exhausted."

"A decent night's sleep would be nice," Mom conceded.

"You probably don't want to be alone tonight, so feel free to stay with me at my apartment," I offered as Jack and Maura left us to talk to the police officer in charge. "You can have the bedroom and I'll take the sofa. I know you have most of your clothes at Victor's, but we can pick them up once he's in custody."

"That's so thoughtful of you, dear. Especially about letting me stay with you."

"You're my mother. You're welcome to stay as long as you like."

"What a generous, considerate daughter I have. Your bed is one of those mattresses that's practically on the floor, isn't it?"

"It's a platform bed, right. But it's comfortable, you'll see."

"I have seen, and it doesn't look comfortable to me."

"It may not look comfortable, but it is."

"Without a good, solid box spring? How could it be comfortable?"

"Well, because it's great support for your back."

"Yes, but what does it do for the rest of you? There are reasons that people in underdeveloped nations have health problems, dear, and one of them is that they sleep on the floor."

"It's not *on* the floor," I said, feeling myself tense in reaction to her critical assessment of my damn bed. Why did she have to start in? Why couldn't she just accept my invitation and leave it at that? Had she and I slipped back into our roles as the Domineering Mother and the Defensive Daughter so soon after our brush with death?

Well, I hadn't slipped back, no sir. I'd been changed by the Victor crisis. I viewed my mother differently now. I valued her and appreciated her and was grateful for her, having come so close to losing her. *I want a relationship with her even if it means putting up with her harangues.* That's what I'd told Karen Sweetzer. *I love her more than I want her to change,* I'd said. *If I want her to accept me for who I am, I have to accept her for who she is.* Besides, I'd made that bargain with God, remember? In exchange for Mom's safety, I had agreed to keep my mouth shut when she got on my nerves (except when she *really* got on my nerves). So now it was time to hold up my end of the deal by continuing to provide innocuous responses to her exasperating remarks and refrain from telling her to shove it.

"I just wish you'd buy better quality furniture for that apartment of yours," she went on. "A person could get sick sleeping on the floor, Stacey, so listen to your mother and–"

She stopped midsentence and emitted an actual gasp, as if she'd caught herself badgering me, as if she'd recognized that she had reverted to type, as if she'd actually heard her own words and, for the first time in her life, rejected them.

"Listen to your mother and what?" I said, spotting the twinkle in her eye now.

"And remember that she could be wrong."

Well, what do you know? I thought, putting my arm around her shoulders and walking her toward Jack and Maura. I guess she's changed, too. Not completely, but a little. Maybe more than a little.

# Epilogue

☆

Aᴺᴰ ꜰɪɴᴀʟʟʏ, a spokesperson for Rest E-zy recliners confirmed that the company is recalling a hundred thousand of its new Football Guy lounge chairs, due to a defect that just might land *your* football guy on his rear end. For more information, go to Rest E-zy's website at www.restezy.com. Reporting live, this is News Four's Helen Reiser, the eyes and ears of southern California consumers."

I hit the power button on the television and turned to Jack. "Is this the job she was born for or what," I said.

"It's another example of how it can take some people years to figure out what they really want to be when they grow up," he said.

I nodded. We were lying next to each other in bed, our legs intertwined. We'd been watching the eleven o'clock news, the half-hour nightly program on which my mother has been the consumer reporter for three months. As we'd feared, she'd been dumped by Fin's Premium Tuna once her adventures with Victor had become tabloid fodder. Her agent and manager and all the other hangers-on had defected, too. There'd been no more acting jobs, no more commercial endorsements, no more power lunches. The sad fact was, her phone had stopped ringing, but, oddly enough, she hadn't seemed to mind. Not even when my phone had started ringing off the hook.

She'd been right about my career getting a boost from the avalanche of media stories about my portrayal of Karen and my ability to convince my own mother that I was Victor's ex-wife. Producers and directors had bombarded Mickey with calls about me, and it was dizzying how fast I'd gone from nobody to somebody. Right now, for example, I'm starring in a new hour-long drama series for CBS. I play a medical examiner who spends a lot of time sifting through blood and guts to solve crimes. I enjoy the work, am thrilled to be making good money at my chosen profession instead of slaving away at Cornucopia!, and get a big kick out of being considered hot, knowing all too well how quickly I could go back to being cold.

When I'd first been offered the television series, I was reluctant to tell my mother about it, given how our fortunes had reversed themselves yet again. This time I was the one who was up and she was the one who was down, and I wasn't sure how she'd react. But, as I said, she'd handled the situation much better than I would have.

"You're the actress in the family," she'd reassured me. "You always have been. I was a fluke."

And so, with her blessing, I'd become a medical examiner on TV. I'd also become engaged to Jack—more or less with her blessing. He'd popped the question shortly after Victor was taken into custody along with Vincent, the chauffeur, who, it turned out, had not driven Vic and Mom to Montecito so he could stay behind in Beverly Hills and off Rosa and Carlos. He was thwarted when they got wind of his plan and fled the house and the country. Jack heard a rumor that they're Mexican movie stars now—as Carmen and Ramon!

Anyhow, we had decided to have the wedding ceremony and reception at the Bel Air Hotel. Maura was going to be my maid of honor and Tim was going to be his brother's best man, and we were going to say our "I do's" with only our family and close friends in attendance. We wanted to avoid the circus atmosphere that accompanies many celebrity weddings and to simply pledge our love to each other, not broadcast it to all the world.

There had just been the matter of Mom, who, as I said, had more or less given us our blessing: "more" in the sense that she could finally brag to everybody that her spinster daughter was getting married; "less" in the sense that she disagreed with virtually every choice Jack and I made regarding the wedding. Why weren't we having it at her house? Why were we inviting so few people? What about Aunt Minny and Uncle Seymour, never mind poor Cousin Iris, who'd undergone triple bypass surgery and was recently widowed and was depressed enough without having to be excluded from a family function? And how was she supposed to explain to her friends back in Cleveland that they, too, were being deliberately left out of the festivities? How could Jack and I be so insensitive to *her* needs?

There'd come a point during the conversations about the wedding that the guilt she'd inflicted on me nearly forced me to call the whole thing off. Yes, she had changed, but not on the subject of my nuptials.

"It's not worth the aggravation," I'd said to Jack one night. "She's driving me insane."

"She's not even my mother and she's driving *me* insane," he'd said.

We'd been beaten down by Mom's meddling and were on the verge of running off and eloping when Mickey called me one morning to say that he'd been contacted by the news director at our local NBC affiliate about my mother.

"Why did he call you about her?" I'd said.

"I guess he figured I'd know where to find her, since I represent her daughter."

"Logical. What did he want?"

"He read a piece in the paper about how Helen bashed Chellus in the head with her Bruno Magli shoe and how the heel broke off and how she wrote to the company and demanded a new pair. And, of course, he remembered how outrageous she was in those Fin's commercials. He put two and two together and decided she was the perfect person to fill his slot for a consumer reporter, despite the fact that she's not twenty with the tits and ass to match."

"That's fantastic," I'd said. "Do you want me to call her and set up a meeting for you two, since you've never met?"

"Yeah, do that, would you, kid?"

"Would I ever," I'd said, and dialed my mother's number the second I hung up.

I'd told her about the opening at KNBC and she'd relished the prospect of reporting on consumer issues. Within the week, she'd landed the job and begun to channel all the energy she'd been expending on our wedding into badgering companies about the quality of their products. No more nagging us about her friends in Cleveland. No more bitching about Aunt Minny and Uncle Seymour. No more guilt trips about poor Cousin Iris. She'd stumbled into another career–a life that didn't revolve exclusively around me.

"We're so lucky," I said after thinking back on the events of the past few months and leaning over in bed to kiss Jack. "We're in love. We're getting married. My career is going well. Your career is going better than ever. And my mother is too busy to tell us what kind of flowers we should order for the centerpieces."

"Or what kind of food we should serve at the reception."

"Amen. We can plan our wedding without her interference."

"And without her dragging us into some melodrama involving a man."

"Amen to that, too," I said, so grateful that the Victor saga was behind us.

Jack stroked my cheek, and his caress prompted another kiss

from me, and before I knew it, we were in each other's arms, as lusty and adoring as an engaged couple should be.

We were interrupted at an especially intimate moment by the ringing of the telephone.

"It's late. Let the machine get it," said Jack.

We let the machine get it and refocused on each other, only to have the phone ring again.

"I know, I know. Let the machine get it," I said.

We let the machine get it and resumed our lovemaking, only to have the phone ring a third time.

"I'd better get it," I said. "Whoever it is will only keep trying."

*Whoever it is.* Please. There was only one person who called and called and called, whether it was late or not. The question was: What was she calling about?

I rolled over and picked up the phone. "Hello?"

"Stacey, it's your mother."

"Everything okay, Mom? We saw your segment tonight. Good work on that Rest E-zy thing."

"Yes, yes, but I'm calling to talk to you about romance."

I sat up in bed, my blood pressure skyrocketing. "Look, Mom. If this is about my wedding, I just want to say that while Jack and I value your opinion, we're adamant about setting boundaries, about making our own decisions, and we hope you'll respect that." And I'd thought her new job had solved this particular problem.

"This isn't about you and Jack," she said, sounding—what?—sort of breathless. "It's about Mickey and me."

"I'm not following you."

"Mickey Offerman. Our agent."

"What about him, Mom?" I was impatient. Impatient and eager to jump my fiancé's bones.

"We're having an affair."

*"What?"*

"You heard me. Mickey and I are seeing each other."

"That's crazy. Mickey's a complete womanizer."

"Used to be. He says *I'm* the only woman he wants from now on."

"But when did you two even—"

Before I could finish the sentence, Jack had snatched the phone out of my hand.

"It's almost midnight, Helen," he said to my mother. "Stacey will call you tomorrow. Sleep tight." And then he hung up.

I stared at him. "She claims she and Mickey are a couple."

"Good for them," he said as he nuzzled my neck.

"I've never known him to date women her age," I said.

"I love the way your skin feels right here," he said, sucking on my right earlobe.

"I'm telling you, he's totally wrong for her," I said.

"But most of all, I love the way your skin feels right *here*," said Jack, who pressed his lips against mine and put an end to the discussion.